PROTECTING OUR FAMILY

A BLACKTHORNE SECURITY NOVEL

NICOLE VIDAL

COPYRIGHT

TABLE OF CONTENTS

KEEP IN TOUCH WITH NV

Facebook (http://fb.me/NicoleVidalAuthor)

Instagram (http://instagram.com/nicolevidal_author)

Amazon (https://www.amazon.com/Nicole-Vidal/e/B082DJHPXP?ref_=dbs_p_ebk_r00_abau_000000)

My website (www.nicolevidal.com)

Pinterest (http://pinterest.com/NicoleVidal_Author)

Goodreads (https://www.goodreads.com/author/show/19827329.Nicole_Vidal)

CHAPTER ONE

MAIA

THREE YEARS AGO

Crescent Bay is a small town. Main Street is exactly as you would picture it. There's a hardware store owned by the same family for generations, a general store also family owned, a florist, and a candy store. The Blackthorne office, and The Nook is next door. My research of the area indicates it's the newest addition to the quaint street.

Parking across the street from the nondescript brick building, I take a deep breath and hope for the best. Nothing about my background would indicate personal security would suit me, but here I am. The challenge will be worth it to support myself. From a young age, I've been on my own, alternating between retail and food service jobs, usually two at a time to keep a roof over my head. My last food service job was in DC, and the tips were exponentially higher, which enabled me to maintain only one job. Unfortunately, the restaurant was shut down in a sting operation by the FBI. Now I'm scrambling for a way to feed myself and a place to live.

"Good morning. Welcome to Blackthorne Security. How can I help you?" A woman about my age with short pink hair greets me as I step over the threshold.

"Morning. Maia Park. I have an interview."

"Of course. I'm Gemma. Nice to meet you." She extends her hand to me. "Would you like a drink?" Although her hair color makes her stand out, Gemma has a similar build to me.

"No, thank you."

"Right this way." She leads me into a masculine conference room where a fit, built man is waiting.

"Morning, Gemma."

"Morning, Mr. Blackthorne. Miss Park is here for her interview."

"Thank you." He extends his hand to me, and I take it. "Nice to meet you, Miss Park."

"Mr. Blackthorne. Nice to meet you as well."

He motions for me to take a seat. "I'm a bit unorthodox when I interview candidates. Although you've never worked in personal security, you meet the requirements for self-defense training. Our program will hone those skills and teach you the other skills necessary for the position. Why apply here?"

Concerned my chances of being hired are minimal, I decide to be completely honest. "My life before now hasn't been roses. I've been on my own since I was sixteen. Managing two or three jobs is stressful. This position will afford me the opportunity to have one job and build my future."

"I understand. Why have you been on your own?" he asks, direct and to the point.

No reason not to share. I'm confident my background check was deep and extensive. "My parents came here on student visas from Vietnam. They never returned home after their schooling. The system caught up with them when I was in high school."

"They left you here?" Unmistakable disgust laces his response.

"Yes." Their choice was likely a gut-wrenching decision. However, it still pisses me off to know they left me on my own. "I belong here. They don't. Their words, not mine."

"Are you in contact with them?"

"Initially, I was focused on my survival and not drawing a straight line from me to them. I should've become part of the foster system, but I didn't want to become a ward of the government. I stayed with a classmate through high school. My living arrangements weren't official or anything. Once I graduated, I was on my own. I received cards on my birthday until two years ago, but nothing else."

Mr. Blackthorne steeples his fingers. "How did you pull that off?"

"I forwarded my mail from our old apartment to a drop box and checked it periodically."

He nods. "I appreciate your candor and empathize with your position about being in the foster system."

Intriguing statement, but I don't press him on it.

He continues. "As I'm sure you're aware, the position includes paid training and a room in the bunkhouse. Food expenses are shared among the staff. Still interested?"

"Yes."

"Okay." He pulls out his phone and taps out a text. "I sent you the address to the farm. It's a large compound where my home and the bunkhouse are located. Can you meet me there in thirty minutes?"

"Sure. Thank you, Mr. Blackthorne."

"You're welcome. Please call me Jake. I look for my father when I hear 'Mr. Blackthorne.' I've asked Gemma numerous times as well, but it hasn't stuck yet."

"I'll meet you there, Jake." After using the restroom, I hop into my beat-up Honda and regroup a bit. Everything seems to be going fine. He wouldn't invite me to see the provided accommodations without me having a shot at the position. *Right? Right!* I input the address into my phone. A few minutes after I park behind a large steel gate, a tinted SUV pulls beside me. Mr. Black... Jake hops out, inputs a code, and waves me through the gate. I follow along the driveway and park near a small, fenced area.

The property is beautiful. There's a large—but in dire need of updating—colonial with a huge wraparound porch off to the right. Beside it is a barn that has also seen better days. Beyond where I parked, a large building sits parallel to a smaller one that looks like a motel. Further back is the shore along a rolling river.

"Your property is gorgeous," I state when he joins me in the driveway.

"Thanks. I'm working on the house myself."

I follow him into the larger building. Awe strikes me. The interior is a state-of-the-art gym, including a boxing ring. Two guys are sparring in the ring. One is tall, blond, and built similarly to Jake. The other is tall and fit but more like a martial artist rather than a gym rat.

"As an employee, you would have full access to this gym as well as the bunkhouse. When you aren't on assignment, we have weekly meetings on Mondays at nine. If you're on assignment, you're exempt from attending and will receive an email with pertinent information from Gemma, if necessary."

I nod.

Jake waves the two guys over. "Connor and Nolan, please meet Maia." He indicates Connor is the blond.

Both acknowledge me and move to our side of the ring.

"Nice to meet you." Nolan tugs off his boxing glove, leans down, and extends his hand to me.

I shake his hand. "You as well." Then I follow suit with Connor.

"Do you have a few minutes to spar with Maia?" Jake asks Nolan.

"Sure. There are spare gloves in the bin to the right." Nolan directs me.

I flip open the bin and pull out the smallest pair of gloves. After shucking my hoodie and watch, I tug them on. Once in the ring, we tap gloves.

"I won't go easy on you," Nolan warns.

I like him already. No bullshit and doesn't care I'm a woman. Forget the fact he's exactly my type: lean, fit, and deceptively handsome. "Don't expect you to," I reply and strike out with my right hand. "How long have you worked for Blackthorne?"

He blocks me. "A few months. I worked for another company in Florida, but they folded."

We spar for a solid ten minutes, trading jabs and crosses while circling the ring. Jake and Connor watch but don't comment. The door to the gym opens, and I seize the opportunity to knock Nolan on his ass with a swipe of his ankles.

Shock appears on his face. He rises from the floor, offers a fist bump, and says, "Well played. You caught me distracted and used it to your advantage."

"Thank you."

"Ready to move on?" Jake shouts from the floor. Apparently, he's seen enough.

"Sure."

Nolan and I tap gloves before I exit the ring. "If you have any questions, please ask when your tour is over," Nolan offers. "I'll be here."

"I will. Thank you."

I remove the gloves, set them in the bin, and wash my hands and face in the small bathroom. Dutifully, I follow Jake to the motel-style building next door. My description from afar is on point. The upper floor has six semiprivate sleeping areas and two bathrooms similar to the sleeping quarters on *Chicago Fire*. The lower floor has a kitchen, large living room, office, laundry room, and an additional powder room.

"The job comes with a bunk. Currently, there are three other staff members rooming here. You met Nolan. Callen and Christoph are on assignment right now. Connor doesn't live on the property."

"Understood."

"Do you have any questions?"

"No."

Jake continues, "I have two more candidates to interview tomorrow. I'll reach out by the end of the week with my decision."

"Thank you. I look forward to hearing from you." We shake hands, and I walk to my car. Before closing my door, I inhale the fresh air, hoping it won't be the last time I'm here.

CHAPTER TWO

NOLAN

"Last chance to back out. My family thinks you and I are dating," I offer.

"You're my best friend. Well, guy best friend. If you tell Alex, I'll deny I said that. You need a buffer for your sister's engagement party. I'm here for you," Maia replies.

Alex—short for Alejandra—is our coworker. She was assigned protection detail for Reese, the daughter of a top NFL wide receiver. While she was on the job, she and Reese's father, Jordan, fell in love. Alex operates the company gym and training program for new hires instead of taking client assignments to remain closer to Reese.

Extending my hand toward her, I take her luggage and set it in the back of my SUV. "Thanks. I would do the same for you."

"I know."

She dropped me on my ass in our first sparring session during her interview. Her confidence alone was the spark of our immediate friendship. Over the last few years, I've tucked away my growing feelings for her. We can't be a couple and work together. More accurately, we shouldn't be a couple and work together. I refuse to put either of us or our bosses in a bind.

Halfway through our car ride, I pull off the interstate for coffee and snacks. "Want anything?"

"A coffee would be great. I'm going to use the restroom while we're here."

Over the last three years, I've learned many details about Maia, including her coffee order and penchant for Millie's dark chocolate caramel bars. Millie's is the chocolate shop in the center of Crescent Bay.

When I return to the car, Maia is nowhere in sight. If she were my girlfriend and didn't have skills to protect herself, I would be worried. Maia is petite and fit. Her eyes are a unique shade of brown similar to the center of her favorite chocolate bar. She's flat-out gorgeous. Most people would mistake her for a pushover. She's anything but. Her self-defense skills are finely honed to the point she's defeated me in sparring matches more times than I care to admit.

"Everything okay?" I ask.

She waves me off as she approaches the car. "Yeah, there was a line, and I let a little girl go first. It seemed urgent for her." Her actions don't surprise me one bit. Maia puts everyone ahead of herself. It's a great quality to have for this line of work from the client's perspective. I benefit from that particular quality, given our previous conversations about taking our friendship into a romantic relationship.

Each time we end up in the same spot. Losing our friendship isn't worth the risk to our hearts or jobs. Out loud during those conversations, I agree. Deep down, I know we would be amazing together.

"Can you remind me of your family again?" she asks as we enter the last half hour of driving.

"Sure. My parents, Michael and Sharon, have been married for nearly thirty years. Not all those years were happy, but they stuck it out." A tiny white lie, but a necessary one.

Maia nods. "What's Lara's fiancé's name again?"

"Paul." After a few terrible country songs on the radio, I pull into my parents' driveway. A massive mansion looms in front of my SUV.

Her eyes widen, and she twists in my direction. "Did you fail to mention you're rich?"

I laugh. "I'm not rich. My parents are."

An undiscernible look crosses her face. "Only a person raised with money would say that."

"Have I ever given you the impression I have obscene amounts of money in the bank?"

"No, not at all. Could've warned me though."

"Fair. Maia, my parents are uber rich. My father is a partner in an international commodities firm and has hundreds of millions of dollars."

She laughs and moves to get her door.

"I'll get your door. If you were mine, I would always get your door."

Maia's hand slides off the door and into her lap. A sigh echoes in the front of my vehicle.

Did she change her mind about us? I ignore my thoughts and offer her my hand after pulling our luggage from the trunk. "Last chan—"

"Nolan, it's been so long!" My mother is a tall, thin woman with sharp, angular features. She's dressed for dinner at a five-star restaurant. Yet, she's welcoming her son into the family home, his childhood home.

"Times up," Maia replies with a wink and a smile on her face.

I thread our fingers and lead her to the door. It's the first time I've held her hand, and it feels spectacular. Her hand fits as if it were molded for mine. If the goose bumps on her skin are any indication, her reaction is similar.

"Aren't you stunning," my mother states as we approach.

"Thank you," I reply.

"Nolan, I was speaking to your lovely girlfriend," Mother scowls at me.

I shake my head inwardly. Without a doubt, I know my mother wasn't speaking about me. It appears my attempt at levity missed the mark, at least from her perspective.

"Thank you, Mrs. Dalton. It's a pleasure to meet you."

"Please call me Sharon. Let's get inside so you can show her off to everyone, son."

I tighten my fingers in Maia's, and she squeezes back, a silent show of support, and I'm grateful.

"Who is everyone? The party is tomorrow."

She waves her hand to cast away my statement. "Your father invited his business partners for dinner tonight as they aren't able to attend tomorrow."

I lean into Maia and whisper, "I'm sorry."

A shiver cascades through her. She turns her head and catches my gaze. Her lips are a hairsbreadth away from mine before she replies, "We've got this."

I'm glad one of us is confident about this weekend. Our proximity is already messing with my head. Her nearness messed with me daily when she was in the next bunk. However, now she lives in Connor's condo alone. When Connor met Callie and became a partner in the business, he built a house at the compound. He decided to keep his condo, mostly due to the amazing rooftop patio, and offer it to long-term staff members. I declined to keep distance between me and Maia. Sharing a home, only the two of us, would have broken my resolve much sooner. She accepted and lived alone for a little while until Alex joined the team. Now she's alone again.

After an exhausting round of introductions, small talk, and a four-course meal, Carl, my parents' house manager, leads us to the guest suite.

"Thank you, Carl. Where will I be staying?" I ask, assuming he brought us to Maia's room first.

"Master Nolan, I'm afraid there's only one available suite for your visit. Your mother indicated you and Miss Park are a couple and didn't see the need to adhere to antiquated norms."

Maia sets her hand on my forearm and grips lightly. I look into her eyes and know she's in to figure out a suite with one bed for this trip.

"I see. Surprised, but I understand."

"As was I. Will there be anything else this evening?"

"No, thank you. Good night, Carl."

When the door snicks closed, I survey the suite before offering, "I can sleep on the love seat."

Maia shakes her head. "Don't be silly. It would make more sense for me to sleep there."

"No, you're my guest. You take the bed."

She steps into my space and sets her hand on my chest. The heat of her seeping through my dress shirt scrambles my thoughts. Her hands on me feel… right. Inwardly, I shake my head. No, this is fake. Pretend. Not real. Yet we're behind closed doors. "I think we can manage to share a king-size bed for a few nights."

Wordlessly and in shock, I nod. Perhaps she can keep her thoughts in the friend zone, but slipping into a bed next to her isn't going to be an easy feat. Her hand drifts off my chest, and she retreats toward her bag.

"Do you want the bathroom first?" she asks.

"Sure." I rifle through my bag and grab a change of clothes and my toiletries. Closing the door behind me, I exhale sharply. *Get it together!* We can pull this off. We've been here for a few hours, and I'm doubting whether we can do exactly that. Leading others to believe we're in a relationship is one thing. Acting as if it were true is something else. Holding her hand and the feel of her tucked against me is amazing. Forgetting through the rest of the weekend without breaking our stated rules will be difficult.

Our rules included separate rooms, limited touching, and absolutely no intimate contact. I may not have broken the last one, but I was dangerously close to kissing her when I whispered my apology earlier today. I remind myself of the ground rules before stepping back into the bedroom.

Maia clad in silky shorts and a camisole beneath a matching robe steals my breath when she turns in my direction.

Damn! She's tempting. Always has been. "Since when do you wear silk pajamas to bed instead of shorts and a tee?" When we lived in the bunkhouse at the same time, boring shorts and a shirt were her sleepwear of choice.

She tugs the robe closed and ties the sash, eliminating my view of her fit, tight body. "Since I started living in the condo. I planned on having my own room. It's either this or bra and panties. Your choice."

I scrub my hand down my face. "I'm sorry. I wasn't expecting… never mind. Bathroom is free."

She whooshes past me, and a faint trace of her orchid perfume teases me. After putting my dirty clothes away, I move toward the bed. With an alarm set for the morning, I take the side closer to the door and slide beneath the sheets. Minutes later, Maia emerges from the bathroom and joins me.

"Good night, Maia."

"Night." She flicks off the light and rolls away from me.

Only after her breathing shallows do I allow sleep to overtake me.

Streams of light trickle in between the slightly open damask drapery in the suite. I'm disoriented at first. After staring at the ceiling, I recall where I am. Then I realize precisely how screwed I am as well. At some point during the night, we cuddled together. Maia is snug in my arms, her leg thrown over mine and her delicate hand flat against my chest. She belongs tucked against me.

Before I can parse out my emotions and how to move without disturbing her, Maia wakes and notices she's draped over me despite the huge bed. "Sorry," she murmurs and moves away.

Hollow and bereft feelings replace the lust coursing through me the instant her warm body draws away from mine. "Nothing to be sorry for." My alarm sounds beside me. I silence it and say, "Why don't you shower first? Breakfast starts at seven, but no one will be there until closer to eight."

"Okay. We'll be able to change before the party, right?"

"Yes."

She pushes off the edge of the bed. When she pulls on her robe, the short silky bottoms ride up, revealing the curve of her ass. My eyes clamp closed. The last thing I need is visual evidence for my attraction to Maia. The list is long and expansive enough.

Within the hour, we head to the dining room for breakfast.

"Good morning, Master Nolan. Miss Park."

"Hi, Carl. How are you this morning?" Maia asks immediately.

"I'm well, Miss Park. Would you like coffee?"

"Yes, please!"

Carl chuckles and serves us both our first cup of coffee. I haven't lived here in many years, but Carl is a steel trap of details, right down to the perfectly prepared cup of coffee. Soon after we get our food, my parents and Mr. Mixton take seats at the table. He's my father's partner at his commodities firm.

"Morning, son. Maia," my father greets us.

I cringe internally at him calling me "son." It's accurate as far as the title, but I've never felt like more than a nuisance. I'm here for Lara and no one else.

"Morning," Maia and I reply in unison.

"How did you and Maia meet, Nolan?" he asks and accepts his coffee from Carl.

The details of our relationship have been carefully planned and set forth to answer these questions. Additionally, I have shared them numerous times with my parents. It's why they insisted Maia join me this weekend. "Maia works at the same security firm I do."

"You're a bodyguard?" Mother asks.

"Yes." Maia's answer emerges proud and unwavering.

"But you're so tiny. How can you protect someone when their attacker is larger than you?" she asks.

Maia replies, "Self-defense or defending another isn't usually about size. It's about leverage and seizing opportunities when your opponent is distracted."

I squeeze her hand under the table.

"She's smart too, Sharon," my father offers.

Mother continues, "How long have you been dating my son? He didn't see fit to share about your relationship until Lara pressed him at our behest."

I cut Maia off. "We met three years ago but started dating in the last six months."

Mr. Mixton captures my father's attention, and my mother's questioning ends there. It appears she was only making small talk and not truly interested in my answers. I'm not surprised.

"I see. Lara and Paul will be here around three to dress for the party. Cocktail hour will be on the covered veranda before dinner is served in the tents outside."

"The schedule changed?" I ask.

"Yes. Paul's parents and sister couldn't get here last night, so we pushed everything back."

The lack of respect I receive from my parents is mind-blowing. Sensing my anger, Maia leans closer and whispers, "It's fine. We can go for a walk or something." Before pulling away, she places a light kiss on my cheek.

Turning slightly to catch her gaze more fully, I mumble, "Okay." After breakfast, we return to our suite before heading outside.

"We can hang out in here instead, if you want," I offer.

She shakes her head. "You need to get out of this house."

I'm not surprised. Maia knows me better than anyone else. "I do. I would've preferred to come this morning if I had known about the schedule change." However, waking up with Maia plastered against me was heavenly. I wouldn't want to give that moment up for anything.

"I know. Why don't you give me a tour?"

I offer her my arm, and she loops hers around mine. We slip out the side door and walk away from my parents' massive home.

When we're far enough away, Maia stops near a bench. "Sit with me for a minute?"

I shrug and do what she asks.

She's right beside me, our hands linked atop my thigh. "Are there any cameras out here?"

I frown but answer her anyway. "No. Why?"

"Take a deep breath. It's only you and me here. No watchful eyes or prying questions."

I comply with her request. "I'm so grateful you're here. Without you beside me, this trip would be unbearable."

"No place I would rather be." Her hold tightens on my hand, and she rests her head against my shoulder.

I exhale and lean into her. "Can I ask you something?"

"Anything."

I shift slightly to view her reaction to my question more fully. "Why did you kiss me at breakfast?"

A soft sigh falls from her lips. It's a sexy sound, one I never cared for much unless it's her. "Honestly?"

"Always. You're honest to a fault."

"I would like to say I kissed your cheek because I'm playing your other half here. Truth is… I wanted to."

Fear and a dash of hope flutter through me. *She has feelings for me too?* I swallow hard before asking, "Do we need to talk about us?"

"No. There can't be an us."

"Why not?"

She lifts her legs and crosses them over mine, one arm around my shoulder while our others stay linked. "We decided there can't be."

"Doesn't mean we can't change our minds. Did you change your mind?"

"Maybe. All the reasons against an us remain valid. I can't lose you as my guy best friend, sounding board, or sparring and dominoes partner. Plus, what about our jobs?"

"It can only get better between us, not worse. Right?" Leaning forward, I kiss her near the shell of her ear. Goose bumps erupt on her smooth skin.

"What are you saying?" Her voice is soft and nearly inaudible.

"We should explore us, what an us would be, while we're here."

She pulls back to look at me fully. She's silent for what seems like a long, torturous hour but is more likely a minute. At least she didn't shut me down instantly. "What happens on Monday afternoon when we get home?"

"Before I drop you off at your condo, we'll make a decision whether we're going to be together or never speak of this weekend ever again."

"Really?" Her question comes out more like a squeal.

"Yes."

"I need you to pinky promise me we'll still be friends if this dating experiment doesn't work out."

"I promise. Same goes for you." I raise my hooked pinky in her direction.

"I promise," she replies before locking her pinky around mine.

I press a kiss to her temple. Time slows as our eyes lock. Her hand slides up my chest to cup my jaw, and her tongue darts out between her lips, wetting them. The touch of her mouth to mine is heavenly, and it takes restraint to stay in this moment and not second-guess waiting until now. Each twist of our tongues pushes me deeper into my head.

Adding a slight space between us, I stare into her eyes, our breath mixing.

"What?" Her question is laced with concern.

"Verifying it's you. I dreamt of this moment more times than I care to admit."

"Was it worth it?"

"Kissing you is beyond what I ever imagined."

"Then we need to hurry back to our suite."

"Why?"

A sultry look I've never seen on Maia's gorgeous face appears before she whispers, "It'll offer us more privacy."

The instant her words register in my mind, I set her on her feet, link our hands, and take off running toward the house. Briefly, we're held up by event staff shuttling chairs through the house for the party.

CHAPTER THREE

MAIA

Without overthinking my actions, I grip the zipper of Nolan's coat and start to draw it down once we're in our locked suite. His hands cover mine, and I freeze. "Changing your mind?" I question.

"No, definitely not. Slowing you down a little."

He releases my hands, And I finish unzipping his coat while he pushes mine off my shoulders to the floor. We move with precision over to the edge of the bed. On assignment in the field, we are cogs in the same wheel. Here we're approaching each other with caution and intrigue. Nolan grips the hem of my sweater and lifts, revealing the sexiest bra I own. Did I know we would end up here? No, but when I dress up, I dress up, down to my lingerie. Pink lace with a ribbon tied between my breasts stops him cold for a moment. He unsnaps my jeans and pushes them over my hips.

"Holy hell, you're gorgeous."

My cheeks heat, and my body warms. No man has blatantly shared their feelings or opinions about me physically. "Nolan." My eyes drop to the floor.

"What? Absolutely a true statement. I've known since the moment we met but have never been able to verbalize it until now." He sets his fingers under my chin and lifts my gaze to his. "Don't get shy on me now. We haven't done anything scandalous… yet."

I smirk at him and take off his clothes, admiring each inch of exposed skin with my mouth as I remove it. Each touch of my lips raises goose bumps on his body. Nolan shirtless isn't a new sight, but completely naked with the decadent V-cut at his hips is noteworthy.

"My turn," he whispers, tugging at the satin ribbon. The fabric slides apart, and the cups of my bra gape but don't fully expose my chest to him. Hands softer than I expect, given his propensity for martial arts, slide north between my breasts and skim the swells. Sneaking beneath the straps, he pushes the bra down my arms. "I was wrong. You're incredible."

"We aren't done yet," I murmur with a boldness that isn't like me at all.

He lowers himself to sitting onto the bed. "I may pass out when we get closer to done."

I giggle until he draws me between his strong thighs, and his tongue darts out, circling one taut nipple while his hand rolls the other between his fingers. Different sensations melt my senses. Hot and wet on my left, in contrast to hard tingles on the right. Reaching down, I surround his length with both hands and glide along him in even strokes.

"Maia." My name sounds like a prayer and a demand at the same time. Without discontinuing his masterful sucking of my breast, his hands slide down my skin and peel my panties to the floor.

I try to ignore the fact Nolan is drawing these fantastic sensations from my body and set my thighs outside his. I can't forget it's him though. Our underlying friendship matters and impacts how this—us—feels. His gaze meets mine before he twists, caging me beneath him in the middle of the bed. The duvet under me is luxurious against my skin, but not more than the heat of him hovering over me.

"Still with me?"

"I have been since the moment we met." My reply comes out raspy and unintentionally sultry.

"Me too." Without another word, he sits back on his heels and painstakingly explores each inch of my body with his eyes. I've never been the subject of such adoration before. Next, featherlike touches bring tempting tingles to the surface. The sensation of his hands traveling up my inner thighs is enough for my core to clench and wetness to pool.

The tease of his thumbs from bottom to top has me arching off the bed. No man has made me feel this spectacular with the touch of his hand.

"You good?" A hint of concern is clear in his tone.

His attention to me is off the charts. "Good is nowhere near an accurate description of how I feel right now."

Without another word, he slips two fingers into my center and drags his thumb along my swollen nub left to right. *Damn!* Need skyrockets through me, and I plunge down as he pushes deliberately deeper into me. Waves of pleasure meet the mounting pressure in my low belly.

"Let go, Maia."

His words are all it takes. The tension explodes, and unmatched bliss ripples through my entire body. As the aftershocks decrease, I push up and slide a pillow beneath me. Taking him in my hand, I tease the head along my core. The corded muscle of his chest and abdomen contract at once. Scooting forward, the bare tip of his length pushes inside.

A strong knock on the door freezes us both. "Master Nolan."

He takes a settling breath to hide our activities behind the heavy wooden door. "Yes, Carl."

"Your sister and Paul are set to arrive within the hour—earlier than expected. Your mother requests your presence."

"Thank you, Carl. We'll be there."

"You're welcome." I hear his retreating footsteps and attempt to wiggle away from Nolan.

He stills me by gripping my hip before whispering, "Make me come with your hands while I make you come again. Later, we're going to finish this properly, and more than once."

Anticipation, for now and after the party, cascades through me. We haven't been together fully, and I'm in trouble. Opening the door to a relationship with him surpasses my expectations. I shift enough to take him in my hands and stroke him in time with his curled fingers inside me. My inner muscles pulse around his fingers as he throbs in mine.

"Faster, Maia."

"You too," I demand and increase my pace. Before long, I'm careening off the edge into heaven. In time with the ripples of bliss, I stroke him until he collapses on top of me, exploding between us onto my belly. Our breathing regulates, and he shifts to his forearms.

"I'll grab a towel for you." With a sweet kiss to the tip of my nose, he peels himself up and hops off the bed.

Although I shouldn't move much, I turn slightly to watch him walk to the en suite bathroom.

"How did I miss the perfection of your ass until now?"

He grins at me. "Did you really, or were you pretending not to notice?"

I giggle softly. "Most likely the latter." He offers me a warm, wet towel and I clean up. "Will I be able to shower before dressing for the party?"

"Yeah. I'll stay downstairs while you do, so we'll be ready on time."

I finish cleaning up and tug on my lingerie and clothes again. "I don't think that will be necessary, do you?"

"Absolutely. I want to keep you naked and be with you now, but—"

"Your sister is arriving early."

We redress and join Sharon in the drawing room to wait for Lara and Paul to arrive. Nolan's father is conveniently missing.

"Miss Lara Dalton and Mr. Paul Goldman," Carl announces their arrival. So formal. I mean, it's her mother and brother.

Lara passes Sharon and hugs Nolan first. She whispers something I can't make out. Then I hear, "You didn't share she's beautiful."

When she pulls away and turns to me, I say, "Nice to meet you, Lara. Nolan talks about you constantly."

She draws me into a hug as well. "I could say the same about you." Releasing me, she turns and adds, "Where are my manners? Paul, please meet my brother, Nolan, and his girlfriend, Maia."

We greet one another, and Sharon overtakes the conversation with a discussion of details about the party. Not only do Paul's eyes glaze over, but Nolan's too. Honestly, mine as well. I would prefer to be in our suite still naked rather than suffer through this. The little voice in my head reminds me I'm here to make this easier for Nolan. Naked time is a wrinkle we added. I lean into him and thread my fingers through his. Lifting our joined hands, he kisses the back of mine before we take a seat beside Paul.

One mind-numbing hour later, Carl ushers us into the dining room for lunch. We make quick work of our meal, then excuse ourselves back to our suite. Do I need two hours? No, but I'll fuss with my hair to allow Nolan to decompress. Noticeably out of sorts, Nolan rifles through his bag, pulling out shorts and a tee.

"What's wrong?"

"I need to go for a run or hit a heavy bag. I'll be back in plenty of time to get ready for the party. You should take a shower first."

"Did I miss something?" I rapidly scan through my memory of the time with his sister and lunch.

"No. I'm not surprised my father didn't show up to greet Lara and Paul, especially since he set them up. Yet it irks me anyway. I'll be fine after I run off some of this aggression."

"I can think of a better way to release the tension." My voice emerges unintentionally sultry and seductive, sounding foreign falling from my lips and being directed at Nolan, but I'm owning it.

Nolan steps closer, slides his arm around my waist, and presses a kiss to my lips. "I agree. However, when we're together for the first time, I don't want to be rushed. I need to do this right for Lara. At a minimum, I'll be there for her whenever she needs me. Today is one of those days."

"What about your needs?"

"Once their engagement is out in the press, Lara will be thrust into high society, and she won't have time to see her lowly bodyguard brother anymore."

The pain laced in his words is hard to hear. "Are those your words or hers?"

"Neither. They're my father's. I can't hash this out right now." He kisses me hard with an edge of possession, which is new. Then again, kissing him is as well. "I'll be back."

More than ninety minutes later, Nolan saunters back into our suite, dripping in sweat while chugging a sports drink.

He looks relaxed and hot as hell! "Feeling better?"

Nolan shrugs. "Are you ready?"

"Except for my dress."

"Good, because you in a silk robe isn't happening anywhere outside of a bedroom."

"A tad possessive?"

"Until we make a decision, yes. One hundred percent."

"Get moving or we'll be late."

With a wink, Nolan steps into the bathroom and is ready to leave within fifteen minutes of his return. "You look sexy in this dress," he states. While he showered, I slipped into my dress.

"Thank you." My dress is emerald silk with spaghetti straps and a tapered drape skirt with a midthigh slit.

Thankfully, Lara and Paul are the center of attention—as they should be—and dinner passes uneventfully, at least for us. Toast after toast mark the courses. Once dinner is complete, Sharon invites the guests to the dance floor.

"Will you dance with me?" Nolan asks.

I lean closer and murmur, "I'm in for anything appropriate, which includes physical proximity and your hands on me."

Nolan clears this throat and extends his hand to me. With an elegance and grace I noticed from the first time I saw him working through his Tae Kwan Do positions in our gym, he leads me to the edge of the parquet floor.

"How are you doing?" My heels make me tall enough to murmur near his ear.

"I wouldn't be able to do this without you here."

"I appreciate that, and I'm happy to be here, but what do you mean?"

"As picture-perfect as my family looks, it's a façade. Completely and utterly fake. My father doesn't approve of my job, and despite his polite greeting of you, he won't accept any woman as my girlfriend or wife unless he chooses her for me."

"Is that why he didn't greet Lara and Paul when they arrived?"

"Because of you? Possibly. I'm sure he decided whatever he was doing was more productive and lucrative than small talk with his family."

I'm stunned silent for a moment. The music changes, and he eliminates the little space between our bodies. The heat between us increases the longer we're pressed together from chest to hip. "I would like to say I know how you feel, but I don't. I'll be here for you until you say otherwise."

He presses a sweet kiss to my head, and we sway to the music. Most of the older guests left immediately after dinner. It appears the only people left in the room are the guests of honor, Sharon, and Paul's parents and sister. A few songs later, we offer our well-wishes to Lara and Paul.

"We'll see you at breakfast," Lara offers as we leave the tent and make our way to the house.

Each step brings us closer to finishing what we started earlier today.

"We don't have to…," Nolan whispers.

I stop on the top step of the patio. It makes us the same height. "Yes, we do. I've wanted to be with you for nearly three years. I understand it may be only for this weekend, but I need to know."

Under the twinkling starlight, Nolan kisses me breathless before leading me to our suite. With the door locked behind him, Nolan unzips my dress with painstaking precision. He kisses his way up each knob of my spine and then across my shoulders from right to left before shimmying the dress over my hips into a silky heap at my feet.

"Is hot-as-hell lingerie a Maia fact I learned for the first time today?" His voice comes out strangled with lust.

My lingerie for dinner is sexier than normal. My dress didn't allow for a normal bra. My undergarments are a nude, cropped lacy corset and matching thong. "Yes, it has evolved like my pajamas since I moved."

"I approve."

"You're a guy. Not surprised."

"Your guy."

My gut twists in knots, and fear trickles in. Is he truly, or will we be done in seventy-two hours?

"Beautiful, where did you mind go? You aren't here with me anymore."

Damn him for knowing me so well. "We're going to be okay after this"—I motion between us—"right?"

"Do you want to stop?"

"No, hell no, but I'm terrified we're going to ruin our friendship."

"Adding another layer can only increase what we share."

"Promise?"

"Pinky promise." He raises his hand in front of me, and I link our pinkies. With our fingers still connected, he wastes no time before dragging the flat of his tongue along the nape of my neck.

Unimaginable tingles streak down my arm. As if we've done this before, he unclasps my bra and drops it to the floor. After twisting me in his hold, we dance toward the edge of the bed.

He freezes, and a look I can't discern crosses his gorgeous face. Nolan is sexy—strong and lean with a deep sense of himself beneath the surface, a place only one other person has access to… me.

"Any chance you're prepared for our change of mind?" he whispers, his eyes caressing my body. The heat in his gaze increases the likelihood of potential heartbreak, if we fall apart.

"No. Any chance Carl would anticipate such a need? I get the birth control shot but would prefer extra protection."

Nolan chuckles and kisses me quickly before rushing into the en suite bathroom.

Chills cascade over my entire body the moment he walks away.

"Success!" he shouts from the bathroom.

"Carl is the best!"

"That's the last time you say another man's name in the bedroom." A serious look overtakes his face until he laughs and deposits the strip of condoms on the bed.

Raising an eyebrow at him, I ask, "Do we need the whole strip?"

"Yes, if we're exploring us this weekend, we're doing it thoroughly, completely, and numerous times." He eliminates some space between us. The warmth of him surrounds me, but he hasn't touched me. "Maia, are you sure?"

"Absolutely."

With reverence, Nolan skims his thumb across my lips. Greedily, I work the buttons of his shirt and strip him bare rather than take my time. Once we're both sans clothes, our pace becomes frantic.

"I don't think slow is an option right now," he states.

"Fast now, slow exploration later."

He reaches for me, tears a foil packet off the strip, and rolls it down his length. Nolan positions himself between my creamy thighs and drags the head along my core.

"Nolan, please... we've waited long enough."

Slowly, he pushes forward inch by inch. Once he's fully seated, his gaze meets mine.

"I need you to move," I murmur.

Without a second thought, he pulls out and buries himself to the hilt. My inner walls grip tighter as he meets me thrust for thrust.

"You feel...."

"Yes. Harder, Nolan."

My request seems to cause Nolan to cast his inner gentleman aside. Bruising my hip with his hand, we ride the intensifying energy between us. My skin heats up, and I tremble around him in unconditional surrender.

Never before has being with a man felt as phenomenal as being with Nolan. After catching our breath, Nolan rolls off the bed and disposes of the condom. I follow him into the en suite but don't say anything.

After we finish cleaning up, he leads me back to the bed and cocoons me against his rock-hard chest.

"You okay?"

I nod but say nothing.

A solid five minutes of silence passes before he turns me in his arms and asks again, "You okay?"

I'm paralyzed by the emotions swirling in my heart. Pure unfiltered love gazes back at me. Honestly, fear creeps in. Then I recall it's Nolan. He's my best friend and confidant. We can handle anything together.

"Maia, sweetheart, you're making me nervous."

My hand slithers between us and rests over his heart. "It never.... I never...."

"It's me. Say what you need to say."

I exhale sharply and purse my lips. "While my experience is limited, we are mind-blowing."

"How limited?" Sex was one topic we didn't discuss.

"I wasn't a virgin, if that's your concern."

"A little bit. Like you, my sexual experience doesn't qualify me for player status. I'm a choirboy considering I've been with three women, including you. We're exceptional."

I press a row of kisses across his chest and snuggle against him. A few hours later, I wake and travel down his flank with my mouth. "Time for me to explore," I murmur against his skin.

I'm waiting for him to stop me, but he doesn't. Rolling my tongue around the head makes his muscle string tight. I take him to the back of my throat and continue to stroke him.

"Maia, if you don't want me to…."

I hum with him deep in my throat, and he explodes in my mouth. I wash up in the bathroom before returning to bed.

We exhaust the strip of condoms over the course of the weekend, each time reaching unimaginable peaks of ravenous pleasure. Flipping the switch from best friends to more is incredible.

CHAPTER FOUR

MAIA

Test one—two pink lines.

I look at test number two—a plus sign.

Test three reads "pregnant" in all caps. Instant judgment.

Three tests lined up in a row with the same result.

We took every conceivable precaution. *Conceivable. Hilarious.* There's only one person I can call right now.

Me: Are you free right now?

Alex: Where are you?

Me: Home.

Alex: I'll be there in twenty. Do you need anything?

I reply with a shrug and crying emoji. Less than twenty minutes later, I hear her call my name from downstairs.

I can assume Alex is in the entryway. She's my bestie and soon-to-be former roommate. I knew the moment she met Jordan she wasn't moving back in here. She's gorgeous, fit, and has curves I would kill for.

It won't take her long to find me. I go one of two places when I'm upset, my room or the rooftop.

Alex appears at the top of the steps and sets pastries and coffee in front of me. She takes one solid look at me and asks, "How badly do I need to hurt Nolan?"

I'm curled up in an oversized chair with my arms crossed over my chest with the tests clutched in my hand. My face is without a doubt puffy from crying, and Alex will notice. "I don't want to hurt him. I want to stop hurting." I wave my hand dismissively. "He's gone anyway."

"Where?"

"Australia."

"He took the assignment with Miss Swisher."

It's a statement, but I answer anyway. "More like she requested him."

"It isn't unusual. What did he say before he left?"

"Nothing other than a simple goodbye." I shift and pull my legs up into my chest and close my arms around them. Alex knows most of the details of our weekend away for the engagement party.

The instant she notices the tests, Alex kneels on the floor and hugs me tight.

"How long have you suspected?"

"My periods are erratic. I missed two in a row though and considered it as a potential reason."

She tilts her head to the side, urging me to continue. When I don't, she asks, "How are you feeling, otherwise?"

"I'm a little tired is all."

"Does he know?"

"No. He won't grant me the courtesy of answering my calls. This isn't something I intend to put in an email or text."

"What is your plan?"

"Still working one out."

Her arms tighten around me. "Whatever you need, I've got you."

"Thanks, Alex. Let's talk about you instead."

"Or we could sit here and savagely attack these pastries," Alex recommends.

"Did you get my favorite?"

"I got one of everything, just in case."

"You're the bestest bestie eva!"

"I love you too, Maia."

I lean forward and pluck a bear claw from the pink box. "Spill, sister."

"Nothing really to spill. I haven't hidden anything from you. Things are going well. I'm happy, truly happy. I'm sorry to say that when you aren't in a good place."

I shake my head because my mouth is overfull with the delicious sugary confection. "You deserve it, Alex. Frankly, so do I. Maybe I was wrong, Nolan isn't my person. I'm not upset about the baby. We made a choice, and despite our best efforts, consequences occurred. His actions are upsetting me more than I thought he ever could."

"I'm squarely on team Maia and baby."

After a second pastry, we chat until it's time for Alex to leave.

"I need to pick up Reese. Want us to come back here afterward?"

"No, thanks. I'll be fine. The pregnancy tests are merely confirmation. I need a plan, actually two, and then to act accordingly."

"Two?"

"One where Nolan decides to step up and one where he doesn't."

We hug, and she bounds down the stairs to get Reese, her daughter. Without a doubt, she's squashing her instinct to reach out to Nolan to slap some sense into him. He needs to figure it out on his own. Hopefully, he'll snap out of his stupidity soon. If not for me, for our baby.

No reason to put it off any longer, I clean up the pastry remnants and settle behind the massive desk in the office. With two fresh sheets of paper, I get to work on making plans. I don't make it far. More like nowhere, considering I've only written "with" and "without" at the top of the pages. Resigned and upset, but still hopeful, I pluck my phone from my pocket and text Nolan again.

Me: I know you're working, but we need to talk.

Me: I wouldn't continue to text you if it wasn't important.

Those three infamous dots appear on the screen, then disappear and reappear twice before stopping. Hurt sinks deeper into my heart. He chose to remain only friends after our weekend together for his sister's engagement party—a weekend where I felt like we could have it all as a couple.

Being with my best friend, completely and unhindered by fear, was the single most exquisite experience of my life. When the earth-shattering, blissful sex and deep conversations ended and it was time to return home,

Nolan asked for time before deciding. Now, we're in a weird state of limbo. I hate it despite my acquiescence to his request. Our little bean changes things, at least he or she does for me.

Since we weren't a true couple, we've never discussed our families outside of the basic information. Hell, I didn't know Nolan's parents are multimillionaires until we parked in front of their home. His choice to wait longer makes me more curious about his family, not less.

Nolan: I won't be free to talk for a few days. Just tell me.

I shake my head despite the fact he can't see me.

Me: It's not a conversation to have over text. Please call me when you can.

Nolan: Fine.

I grip my phone tightly, and my knuckles turn white. After a few settling breaths, I crumple the papers and setup a meeting with my bosses. The only thing I know for sure is I need some time off and a plane ticket to Australia. If he won't call me, I'll go to him.

A week later and no call from Nolan, I park in front of the office and organize my thoughts. After greeting Gemma, she informs me the guys are waiting in the conference room.

Jake, Connor, and Christoph are amazing bosses and exemplary men. I would prefer not to share the news of my pregnancy with them before telling Nolan, but… I've given him ample opportunities to learn about our child as soon as I knew.

"How can we help you, Maia?" Connor asks.

Before I can answer, Alex rushes into the conference room and grabs the seat beside me.

The guys nod, and Connor urges me to continue.

"I need to use the balance of my personal time immediately and the details of Nolan's itinerary."

The three men who are like older, protective brothers look at one another. Nolan and I have had two pointed conversations with our bosses since our friendship started. The first was after I was abducted instead of Jake's wife, Norah, by an assassin named Iris. She drugged me and in the course of my rescue and the days immediately following, our feelings beyond friendship became evident to our bosses. The bottom line was our relationship status, whatever it may be, could not interfere with our work. They requested a heads-up if our friendship evolved into something more. I was hoping the more would be a relationship, not coparenting.

"Does he know?" Connor asks in a low voice.

"No. I don't want to share via text and requested a call, but he hasn't done it."

Jake steeples his fingers like he does when he's working logistics out in his head. "Your request is granted. You can travel with Sawyer, who is relieving Nolan for a week of rest. You have two days to prepare. I'll email you the travel itinerary and accommodations." Sawyer Huntington is a marine veteran and expert in close-quarter combat. He joined the team when Connor became a partner. He's a nice guy and great coworker, but he's quiet and reserved.

"Thank you."

Christoph replies, "You're welcome. We can discuss your future assignments in more detail when you return."

The tears I was holding back trickle down my face. "Really?"

"Absolutely," Connor replies.

"I can't thank you enough."

"None are necessary," Jake offers before the guys leave the conference room.

Alex leans forward and throws her arms around me. "That wasn't so bad."

"No, not at all. I can only hope sharing the news with my baby daddy goes so well."

She attempts to stifle a laugh.

"Go ahead, laugh. It was funny, and I kind of meant it to be." We laugh together and make our way next door for coffee. Well, decaf for me. I've already had my single caffeinated cup of the day.

Norah Blackthorne's store, The Nook, is a unique bookstore. Not only does she sell books, but there's a lending library as well.

"Hey, ladies," Jessa, the store manager, greets us.

"Hi," we reply at once. Alex and I round the corner and serve ourselves coffee. It's a sweet perk of working for Jake—free coffee at his wife's store. At least no one will notice the decaf for now. I'm not ready to share my news with too many more people—although I'm sure Norah, Callie, and Madeleine will know by the end of the day. I shared about their pregnancies with Nolan, despite the sworn secrecy of girls' night.

"Have you ever been to Australia?" she asks.

"No, you?"

Alex shakes her head. "Regardless of the reason, you're going to Australia in two days!"

"True."

"After pickup, Reese and I can come help you pack for your trip."

"Sounds good. We can have Chinese on the roof too."

"Perfect! It's a girls' date." She hugs me and slips out the front door with a bag of books for Reese. Reese is a book fiend, and Norah refills her shelves regularly. After savoring the remainder of my coffee, I cross the street and buy chocolates at Millie's before heading home.

CHAPTER FIVE

NOLAN

This assignment is my second international one and first in Australia. Angelica Swisher is an A-list movie star who became Hollywood's "It Girl" after starring in the smash hit thriller "The Devil you Know" as Ellis Barnett's daughter. Ellis Barnett is one of the most sought-after actors of our time. Whether he's in front of the camera or directing, his name atop the credits affords instant notoriety to those around him.

Her sudden rise to fame has required security during filming of her current movie. After the premiere of the thriller, the jaded and disgusting letters began being delivered. One crazed fan broke into her apartment in New York City. He slashed the contents of her closet and wrote a disturbing missive on her white sofa in barbeque sauce. She hasn't been back since the intrusion was discovered by her assistant.

Angelica is her stage name. Her real name is Rachel. She's a blonde bombshell with a slight British accent. She's been described physically as a young Marilyn Monroe with the acting chops of Helen Mirren.

I adjust my shirt and knock on the door adjoining our suites. "Rachel, time to go."

"Come in, Nolan. It's open," she calls from the opposite side of the door.

When I enter her suite, she's tying her sneakers. Over the last few weeks, we've figured out a system for timely arrival and the best route to avoid paparazzi. The key to avoid the photogs is early call times.

"All set?"

"Yes, let's get today started. It's going to be a long one." She pulls the ball cap on and follows me out the door of her suite.

Jake arranged an override key for the elevator and private parking on the staff level of the garage. Every employee of the Oakley, our hotel accommodations for the entirety of filming, has been screened and through a thorough background check.

She settles into the back seat of the blacked-out SUV, and we exit the parking garage.

"Are you looking forward to your time off next week?" she asks.

"Yes and no."

"I'm not that bad, Nolan." She emphasizes the word "bad" when she answers.

I laugh. "No, you're refreshing and mostly compliant as far as security measures are concerned."

"You mean my agent and my mother overreacted."

With a shake of my head, I glance at her in the rearview mirror. "No. Another set of eyes watching out for you is never a bad idea. When I'm working, I'm on and keyed up, constantly surveying the surroundings for threats. I'll be able to relax, at least regarding vigilance." I exhale, considering whether to share the simmering drama at home with her. "No, because the downtime will allow me to ponder some personal stuff going on at home."

"Want to talk about her?"

I raise my gaze back to Rachel in the rearview mirror. "How do you know it's about a woman?"

"Problems boil down to one of three things: money, family, or love. I know money isn't an issue since you have a well-paying job. I write the checks for the invoices myself—abnormal for someone in my position, but I don't trust people with my money. Too many child actors and actresses were screwed over by their parents. Mine are steady, but nonetheless I handle my business affairs. I suppose it could be a family issue, but those usually work themselves out when the parent realizes their child is grown and can make their own decisions."

"Speaking from experience?"

"No, but we're talking about you right now. That leaves love. What's her name?"

Sharing with someone other than my best friend and blazing-hot weekend lover couldn't hurt. *Right?* "It's a combination of family and love. Maia. Her name is Maia."

"Pretty name. What happened?"

Lucky for me, we arrive on set before I can answer her question. Rachel is all business during work hours and has been from the moment we met. Her Angelica façade switches on, and she becomes her character.

In this case, a fierce young woman trying to save her family business, a wildlife refuge.

"We'll continue this conversation on the way back to the hotel tonight."

"Maybe." I round the car, open her door, and escort her to the makeup trailer. Once she's safely ensconced inside, I grab a coffee and check my messages.

Maia: We need to talk. It's important.

I scrub my hand down my face. She has been reaching out since a week after I left for this assignment. Whatever she needs to share isn't something she wants to say over text. Frankly, I don't have the bandwidth to add an in-depth conversation about our relationship now.

Me: I'm off next week. I'll call you then.

It's the first reply I've sent in the last few weeks. I know, I'm a terrible best friend. Our weekend together as a couple messed with my head. Hurting her was and never will be my intention. Until I sort out how I feel about a romantic relationship with her, I need space. The problem is I know we're magical together. I know her flawless skin is soft and smooth. I've buried myself to the hilt into her petite body, and it felt like nothing could come between us, but the idea of a future with her terrifies me. Not because she isn't worthy or I don't love her. I do. At least I think I do. I don't have many exemplary examples of a stable marriage to use as a guide.

Maia: Thank you.

I pocket my phone and sweep the set while Angelica is in makeup. I wander past the set for the office of the refuge and a few of the enclosures for the animals. Out of the corner of my eye, I see movement outside the gated area. Instead of investigating further, which is my instinct, I run back to the trailer where my client should be.

I bust through the door and shock materializes on Angelica and Carrie's faces.

"Do not leave this trailer," I shout at Angelica.

She acknowledges my words. Closing the door behind me, I hurry to the set security area and notify the team. Set security is better than decent, and they investigate after I share my observation of two uncredentialed males outside the gate. With nothing else to do, I head back to the makeup trailer and wait outside. While I wait, I check my email.

Only the weekly email from Gemma requires my attention. I skim the details and note Sawyer will be here to relieve me by the time filming is over on Friday afternoon. Then I'll be free for nine days of rest and relaxation. Angelica finishes in the trailer over an hour later and emerges ready to film. Nearly fourteen hours and two meals later, we're heading back to the hotel.

"Do you need anything?" I ask her while pulling out of the gated parking.

"Nothing other than sleep. You?"

"Same. What is your call time for tomorrow?"

"Noon. Tomorrow is a short day."

I shrug. "Makes up for the crazy long one today."

"True."

We follow the same procedure in reverse back up to our rooms. I key into her room and check it before leaving for the night. "Good night."

"Still want to talk about Maia?"

"Not tonight, but thanks. I'm exhausted."

"Same, but my offer stands."

I nod and slip through the adjoining door into my room, closing it behind me. Stripping off my clothes, I leave a trail toward the bathroom. Steamy water flows as I step inside the glass enclosure. As far as hotels go, this one is better than most. I'm not an overly picky guy; I don't need opulence. After the length of my workday, I'm grateful for the rainfall showerhead, high-end tile, and above-average water temperature. Talking to the client about Maia, or not in this case, doesn't remove her from my mind. Flashes of our time together haunt me.

My number of sexual partners is remarkably low—not a huge deal in a guy's life. The profession I chose lends itself to a string of one-night stands. I've never been a single-night type of guy. Sharing two and a half days with Maia was beyond what I imagined, and I can't fathom sex and friendship being better with anyone else. By the time I finish showering, I'm no closer to figuring out how to get from the disaster we are right now to the best choice for us: together or apart. Asking for more time wasn't ideal, but it's what I needed.

CHAPTER SIX

MAIA

Bright and early, two days later, a car service picks me up after Sawyer. He hops out of the car and loads my luggage into the trunk. "Morning."

I grumble, "Morning," in response.

"Not a fan?"

"Normally, I'm fine with mornings, but sleep has been elusive lately."

"Fair enough." The first flight is to the west coast of the United States. While we wait for our connecting flight, Sawyer and I chat over tacos at LAX.

"Have you ever been to Australia?" I ask.

"No. You?" Sawyer is quite tall and fit with light brown hair and striking hazel eyes. He's a quiet, gentle giant. Then again, everyone is taller than me.

I shake my head.

"Can I pry bit?"

"You can ask."

He drops his head in acknowledgment. "How long have you and Nolan been a couple?"

I inhale sharply. "It's complicated."

"I've got an insanely long international flight to be a sounding board for you."

"Thanks." After we board, I share about my relationship with Nolan.

"Let me get this straight, you both have been harboring feelings for one another for the past three years and have discussed becoming a couple more than once but decided not to risk your friendship and your jobs."

"Correct, until a few months ago—"

"When fake dating became real, and you have an unexpected consequence."

"Unexpected only considering we were abundantly cautious."

Sawyer turns to face me more fully. "I know Nolan as a coworker and not much more. However, I am a guy."

I chuckle. "No? Really?"

"Nolan freezing you out isn't about you at all, and I would bet my truck on it. It's a more deeply rooted concern. Putting up a wall to avoid you adding to the positives on your side of the equation is his way of hashing out the issue, whatever it may be."

"I understand. However, we're best friends, and if he hasn't or can't share with me, then we have a larger issue than our little bean."

"Fair point."

I glance at him again and look away before replying, "Thanks, Sawyer."

"You're welcome."

"What about you?"

"Me? Not talking about me right now, Maia."

"Well, I'm a fantastic listener as well and happen to be a girl if you need some perspective."

He laughs and huffs, "Maybe later." Then he closes his eyes and promptly falls asleep.

The ability to fall asleep at the drop of a dime is a skill I yearn to possess. Almost every coworker who was in the military can do it. Frankly, I'm envious.

We touch down too many hours later and retrieve our luggage. A car service whisks us to the hotel, and we check in. It's late afternoon on Friday. According to Miss Swisher's itinerary, she should be returning to her hotel within the hour. It gives us—me and Sawyer, not me and Nolan—time to drop off our things and settle in a little. Well, I do anyway. Sawyer will be using the adjoining suite to our client's.

When it's time to head to her room, Sawyer knocks on my door. "Ready?"

I shake my head. "Not even a little. My stomach is in knots because I have no idea how he's going to react to my presence here, never mind what I need to share with him."

"I hope it works out for you, Maia."

Me too. I may talk a tough game, but I want it all with him and the little bean. "Thanks."

Sawyer knocks on the door, and Nolan whips it open. "Sawy... Maia, what are you doing here?"

"I came to see you. Why don't you handle your work, and then we can talk?"

Shock evident on his face, he waves us into Miss Swisher's suite. Nolan introduces Sawyer to our client. Then she steps away to allow them to talk. While Nolan and Sawyer discuss the client information and best practices Nolan has gleaned, I glance around her suite. Nosy, sure. Do I care? Not a bit.

A streak of jealousy grips me when I notice the pizza, two plates, and paused rom-com on the television screen. Is he...? I can't even fathom. Angelica Swisher is stunning, rich, and successful. Competing with her would be impossible. She is a shining example of a woman Mr. Dalton would seek out for his son. She's my antithesis in every way imaginable. Perhaps coming here was a mistake.

No. He needs to know sooner rather than later.

While the guys talk about logistics, she approaches in what I assume is casual clothes for her. Her curvy body in tight, shiny leggings and an off-the-shoulder dolman top with the strap of a camisole visible is impossible to ignore. "Maia, right?"

"Yes. Miss Swisher. Pleasure to meet you."

"You as well. Please call me Rachel. Nolan mentioned you."

Interesting. "How is filming going?"

"We're making progress. Working with the animals is great though. I forgot how much I missed having a dog. Would you like a drink?"

"No, thank you. The guys shouldn't be long."

Uncomfortable silence descends between us until she adds, "I hope you and Nolan can work out whatever is going on between you."

He certainly isn't talking to me. I resist the urge to throttle her and politely thank her. Jealousy is a funny thing. Mine appears to be unfounded. She moves back to the table and continues eating her now presumably cold pizza. Less than thirty minutes later, Nolan ushers me through the connecting door and scoops up his bag.

"Where are you staying?" His tone is gruff and unhappy.

"On the fourth floor."

Without another word, he guides me to the elevator with his bag slung over his shoulder and feverishly pushes the button for my floor.

"Which way?"

I point right and mumble, "Room 420." Keying us inside, he steps in first and sweeps the room. Necessary, no. Protective and sweet, yes. I can take care of myself and do the same sweeps for clients. He's probably still in work mode despite handing Miss Swisher off to Sawyer.

"What are you doing here?" he asks, pacing the floor.

"I don't want to argue with you. You haven't been returning my calls. It isn't like you. I need to know why."

He sits on the edge of the bed with his head in his hands and his gaze toward the Berber carpet. "I'm not ready to discuss our relationship or whatever we are."

"Why?"

"My family life is more twisted and complex than I let on. I can't involve you any deeper."

"I'm in it deep enough already, and that isn't solely your choice to make, not anymore. Truthfully, it stopped being solely your choice the moment we kissed and the entire world but you and I ceased to exist."

He lifts his head and stares directly at me. "What do you mean?"

"I want to be with you, but you don't want a relationship with me."

"Not true." I frown at him and wait for him to continue. "It isn't as simple as me wanting to be with you or not."

"I need more, Nolan. More details. Until we went to the party and opened the relationship box, I was fine. No, that's a lie. My desire to be more than friends with you has never wavered. I merely pushed it aside. Now, not so much. Our actions have consequences, intended or otherwise. I don't want to stay in limbo with you. However, life is ironic." I kneel on the floor in front of him and take his hands in mine. No doubt a flash of our time at his parents' raced through his mind. "I'm pregnant."

Silence blankets the room. The longer it takes for him to acknowledge my words, the more my concern ratchets up. I can only imagine the thoughts in his head. When I pictured this moment, none of the scenarios played out like this.

"Nolan, please look at me." I slide my hands around his face and tilt upward. I'm floored by what I see.

A single tear streams over his cheek. A mixture of joy and anguish clash on his face. Fear leads me to believe anguish will win out.

"Please say something." My voice comes out desperate and pleading.

"I… you're… a baby? We were over-the-top careful."

My eyes close briefly. "I know. Look, I came here to share with you in person because it's the right thing to do. I thought… it doesn't matter what I thought. I'm having a baby, our baby. Take some time to process and let me know what you want."

"What does that mean?" The sound of his voice is harsher than I expect.

Rocking back onto my heels, I push to standing. "To be crystal clear, I want you. You are my crane. I want a life with you and our child. Whether or not you feel the same is for you to determine. How much or how little you want to be involved is up to you. Figure out what you want, Nolan." Stepping back, I reach into my carry-on, pluck an envelope from the zippered pocket, and hand it to him. "I'm going for a walk. Here are the baby's first pictures. Open it, don't open it. The choice is yours."

"What do you mean your crane?"

I lean forward and press a kiss to his forehead. "Cranes, specifically the Sandhill variety, mate for life." Before I can overthink it, I grab my room key and phone. Torn between wanting to force him to talk and running away from the inevitable pain I'm certain is coming, I take the stairs rather than wait for the elevator.

I exit the lobby and turn right. Walking without a plan in the early evening in a foreign country, probably not my smartest choice. The hotel is near the Barangaroo. Before we left home, I did some basic research about the area. I follow the signs for the Wulugul walk. It isn't long before my phone chimes in my hand.

I answer the call. "What are you doing up, Alex?" I consider the time difference. The only reasonable explanation is she was getting dirty with Jordan. "Don't answer that."

She laughs. "I wanted to check in. Have you seen Nolan?"

"Yes. He knows, and I left him in my room."

"What did he say?"

"Enough and not enough at the same time. I'm sure that doesn't make sense. I told him what I want and left to give him time to decide. I fully anticipate raising the peanut on my own. I'll figure it out."

"I'm proud of you for owning your feelings and your choices."

"Despite how much my heart is breaking, I am too."

"Are you staying the whole week or coming home straightaway?"

I take a seat on one of the benches along the shoreline. "Not sure yet. It's beautiful here. I have the time. I may use it."

"I'll see you when you get home, and we can figure out your next move."

"Thanks, Alex. Love you."

"Love you too, Mai."

I sigh and fall deeper into my thoughts. Sharing with Nolan in person was the right thing to do. Not having any solid parental role models should add fear to this adventure. Honestly, seeing my family—found family, but family nonetheless—have kids and how they interact with their better halves makes me believe we could pull this off.

Well, our village will help me if I'm on my own. I wonder what Nolan meant when he said his family is twisted and complex. Deep down, it doesn't matter to me. I wasn't a fan of his father, and Sharon had a steady flow of alcohol in her system the entire weekend. Although, those details barely registered during the incredible time I had with Nolan on our visit.

I push the decadent memory of our twisted, tangled sexy time out of my mind and set my hands on my lower abdomen. "I promise to be there for you always, little one. It may be difficult, but I've handled difficult before. I'll do it again."

As the sun dips beneath the horizon, I start my trek back to the hotel. I don't expect to find Nolan in my room, and he isn't. I order room service for a late dinner and turn in for the night.

CHAPTER SEVEN

NOLAN

A dad? Maia is pregnant with our child. Although unplanned, I'm ecstatic. The irony is I've always wanted to be a dad. Perhaps not to the level Cruz does, but fatherhood was always something I wanted for myself. A way to do things right. Right the wrongs inflicted upon me as a child and continue into the present.

I drag my fingers over the seam of the envelope she left me. Instead of tearing into the paper, I force my feet to move to my new room a few floors away. Despite how well I know Maia, I don't know if she expects me to leave her room or wait for her to return. Fighting her to stay and talk would've been the appropriate choice. I failed her there, myself as well.

A strange sense of increased protectiveness washed over me the moment the words "I'm pregnant" left her lips. Lips that… make me feel maybe I could get past my childhood and… well, all obstacles life could throw at me. Maia can take care of herself and won't take kindly to me hovering or making her feel as if she's incapable. Although the protection I yearn to offer now isn't in contrast to her protecting herself; it's to supplement or back up.

I haven't purposely lied to Maia, but I've certainly omitted details. My parents were married before my sister, Lara, was born and stayed married until I was fifteen. They separated for a few years. The break was precisely what they needed to rebuild from mistrust and infidelity. Infidelity occurred on both sides, but the extent of the betrayal affected me as well. My parents had a vow renewal ceremony five years ago. Before the ceremony, I learned the true reason my father treats me in the manner he does. I'm not his son.

Michael and my mother took steps to prevent me from determining the identity of my biological father, but at my request, Blaine located him. More accurately, my deep and thorough background check when I started at Blackthorne informed Jake of my parental discord. However, I haven't had the gumption or courage to open the file or make the connection. The file is locked away in the office safe—a safe only my bosses have access to.

The reality of my parentage is the sole reason I chose my first job in security. A bodyguard is not deemed acceptable in Michael's eyes. Additionally, Maia would never be an appropriate choice in their opinion either. If he were my biological father, I would be forced to locate a station-appropriate wife, just as Lara is being forced to endure with her future husband. Paul is a nice enough guy, but their marriage is, by the strictest definition, arranged. Meaning my purpose after working for his commodities firm would be to find a debutante, marry her, and have a few children to carry on his name—a name that isn't truly mine.

I strip out of my clothes and redress in shorts and a tee. Within fifteen minutes, I key myself into the gym and try to clear my head with some miles. Clear my head isn't accurate. I need to sort out the changes before me, draft, and execute a flawless plan. Five hard and fast miles later, I slow my pace without progress toward a plan to manage the changes in my life. I have six months at most to navigate my family issues and my relationship with Maia before our child is born.

After a shower, I pick up the phone and call Jake. It doesn't surprise me he answers despite the hour at home.

"How can I help, Nolan?"

"Can you have Blaine update the information about my father?" Blaine is a white hat hacker, purveyor of information, and our private investigator. He's one of the best in the world.

"Yes. Do you want the file I have in the office?" Jakes asks.

"No." I scrub my hand down my face. "Yes, when you get the update."

"Anything else?"

"Not at this time."

"Do you plan to use the information or are you simply updating?"

I pinch the bridge of my nose. His question makes me wonder if he read the file. "I likely need to act on it now. I assume you know Maia is here."

"Yes, she informed us of her travels. If you're asking if she shared what she needed to discuss with you, no, not specifically. However, it isn't a far leap considering our previous conversations about your personal relationship with one another and the requirements we set forth."

"I understand. When I utilize the information from Blaine, things in my life may need to change significantly."

"We're family. A plan for you and your family will be well thought out and agreed upon."

"Thank you, Jake."

"You're welcome. Do I need to replace you on Miss Swisher's detail?"

"Undetermined. I'll give you as much notice as possible."

"We're here for you, Nolan. I'll send the update when I have it."

"Much appreciated." Ending the call, I exhale slowly.

Without a second thought, I sit and write a letter to Maia with our unborn child's first image front and center on the desk.

Maia,

I have so many things to share with you. Some I know for certain, like my feelings for you and our child. Others I need to organize and sort through first. Before I can share or commit to raising our child, I need time. More time. I know it's been months since I asked for time. The family issues need to be handled because they could affect our future. Time to make choices for our child.

I realize it may be difficult to understand, but I need to deal with these issues alone. Please know I'm not asking for this time lightly, but I need to do it for us.

I promise to share every detail with you when I can. I would appreciate updates about you and our baby while I deal with my issues.

With love, Nolan

Before I overthink my words or this monumental choice I'm making, I seal the envelope. My instinct is to deliver the letter immediately. However, considering more fully, I decide to wait until before Maia is set to return home. While we may not enjoy her time here together, she should be able to enjoy Australia as she wishes before I crush her expectations.

There isn't anything I can do but wait for the update from Blaine at this point. My plan was to travel during this respite from my assignment. However, given the new, amazing, and slightly terrifying news about my impending fatherhood, I plan to stay closer to the hotel. An unfair and selfish part of me would love to spend this time exploring the area with Maia while she's here.

I pick up my phone and text her.

Me: Please let me know when you get back to the hotel.

Me: I know you can handle yourself in my head, but… I need to know.

Truthfully, I was hoping for an immediate response. When one doesn't come, I raid the mini fridge and flick on a movie. In the wee hours of the morning, I wake to an infomercial on the screen and crumbs strewn over my chest and the bed. Shifting, I clean off the crumbs and check my phone.

Maia: I'm back at the hotel.

Me: Thank you.

Almost instantly, I get a second response.

Maia: You're welcome.

Me: Did I wake you?

Maia: No, sleep is elusive right now. I never wanted to share about our child here and like that.

Me: I know and I'm sorry. The visit to my parents' unearthed lots of buried stuff for me. Family issues that have nothing to do with you.

Maia: When you're ready to share, I'm here.

Me: Thanks. Try to sleep.

Maia: You too.

I throw myself back onto the pillows to sleep. Instead, my choice not to chase down my father five years ago haunts my thoughts. I didn't want to upset Lara or my mother. My impending fatherhood changes everything. At first, I thought it was a mistake going to the party and more so bringing Maia. Now I realize it may have been the smartest decision I've ever made. The pull of dreamland tugs me under, and when I wake again, it's nearly lunchtime.

I decide leaving my room is necessary. I dress, pocket my phone and the letter to Maia, and go in search of coffee and food. Why am I carrying the letter to Maia? Not sure, other than I feel better having it with me. The Barangaroo area has dozens of different restaurant options. I choose a sandwich from the closest spot and meander to the Paddington Reservoir Gardens. It's a sunken garden with brick arches and stone pathways. It's serene and settling.

Nearly halfway through my meal, I spot Maia walking in awe of this hidden oasis. She's my other half, but I need to clean up my issues before I can fully commit to her and our baby.

I tug my phone out and text her.

Me: To your left, eight o'clock.

After she checks the message, her gaze meets mine, and she walks in my direction. "Hey, fancy seeing you here," Maia says once she's in earshot.

"I'm not surprised we're drawn to the same out-of-the-way tourist attraction."

She shrugs. "Me either. How are you?"

"I should be asking you the same thing. Despite my reaction, I'm ecstatic about being a dad. We never discussed it before, but it's something I've always wanted. As far as dealing with the other stuff, Blaine is working on it for me."

She gasps. "How much trouble are you in?" Right to the point as usual.

"Not in trouble. He's trying to unbury some family truths for me. You didn't answer my question."

"The morning sickness is more like evening sickness for me. Ironic it doesn't only happen in the morning. Manageable, if I eat frequently."

"Good."

"You know I'm a vault, right?"

"Yes, and I appreciate the offer. Right now, I only have a sparse outline of…." I might as well share what I know regardless of how little it is. "I'll tell you what I know, and then I'll be done talking about it until I know more. Fair?"

"Yes."

Over the next twenty minutes, I explain the history of my family as I know it.

"Their demeanor and treatment of you makes so much more sense now, specifically your father's—Michael's—absence when you were in the room."

I acknowledge her observation and then shut down this topic of conversation. "That is what I know. Blaine is filling in the rest. Have you come up with a plan for yourself yet?"

"No. My first instinct was to share with you, and it took longer than I anticipated."

"Completely my fault." I tug her closer and press a kiss to her temple.

"It is, but I understand better now." She inhales sharply. "I decided to leave tomorrow. My flight is at five in the morning. Using all my personal time for this trip isn't wise."

"Will you be taking assignments?"

"Yes, I need to work. I'll talk to the guys and request low-risk assignments."

I shake my head. "I wasn't suggesting—"

"Relax. I know. It's still a conversation I need to have with them. Maybe I can work with Alex at the gym when I can't travel anymore or handle Reese's detail."

My head drops back, and my eyes look skyward. "I'm working on navigating through our baby in my head and heart. I know you can take care of yourself, but… I want to mummify you with bubble wrap and lock you in your condo."

She laughs quietly. "I've had a little more time to adjust. Please look at me."

We turn to face one another.

"Nolan, I promise to be cautious and not take extra risks going forward. You need to do the same."

"I will." Reaching into my pocket, I pull out the letter I wrote and hand it to her. "I wrote this last night. Some of the words are out of date, but my request still remains. I need time. Please take care of yourself and our child while I clear up my past. It needs to be done before we can have a future."

"Is this family issue what you've been working out since the party?"

"Yes." I consider my next question before asking, "Why did I ask you to come to the party with me?"

"You wanted a buffer."

"True, but I haven't seen my parents since I learned about the affairs and the fact Michael isn't my father."

"Why did you go?" she asks. Then she answers her own question. "For Lara."

"I may not agree with her acquiescence to Michael's demands, but she's my sister, and I'll always be there for her."

"I understand. Don't take too long to figure things out, Nolan. We need you now too."

My chest tightens at her words. She's willing to give me time, and I'm grateful. "I won't. I promise." I lean forward and contemplate whether I have the right to kiss her and decide to do it anyway. After a sweet kiss to her lips, I push to my feet. "You staying or coming?"

"Coming, if you don't mind."

"The last thing I want is to be away from you, but...."

She takes my hand, and we walk to our hotel in comfortable silence. When we arrive at her door, I'm not sure what to expect. "Will you stay with me until I need to leave?"

I don't deserve her. Them. "Of course."

We hang out for a little while before she packs her things and prepares to head home. Our huge dinner consists of burgers, fries, and four chocolate desserts from the menu. Afterward we curl up to *Harry Potter and the Deathly Hallows*. Maia is out cold beside me only fifteen minutes into the movie. I set two alarms on my phone and draw her closer. I revel in how perfectly she fits in my arms and fall asleep. It isn't a new feeling, but one I want to experience daily. First, I need to sort out my familial issues.

Four hours before her flight, my alarms blare. I silence them. She slips out of my arms and into the shower. With a newfound desire to memorize her, I watch her dress when she emerges from the bathroom. I would like to say her body is different, and I'm sure to her it is. To me, other than a slight roundness to her lower abdomen, she looks the same. Maia doesn't blanch at me watching her, and I appreciate it.

"You need to leave before eleven," she says while rechecking her luggage.

I twist my legs over the side of the bed and stand. Drawing her into my arms, I hold her flush against me. She's tense at first, but then she melts into me like she did after our first kiss.

"Figure out what you need to. We'll be waiting," she whispers against my neck.

"There are no words for me to thank you for your understanding and—"

"None are necessary. I've got your back, literally and figuratively."

"Please let me know when you're safely home."

She nods against me, and I feel a warm wetness against my skin. Drawing back, I swipe her tears with my thumb and kiss her forehead. Wordlessly, she backs away, grabs her luggage, and steps through the door. After a quick look back, she's gone.

CHAPTER EIGHT

MAIA

Alex and Reese are waiting for me at baggage claim when my plane lands. I'm not surprised at all.

"Hey!" I wave.

Reese gets to me first. "Hi, Aunt Maia! How are you feeling?"

I cast a look over her head at Alex.

"Don't be mad at Mom. I was using her phone and saw some texts between you."

"Not mad. I'm tired but feeling okay considering how long the flight home was. How about you? How's school?" I take a few steps closer to the conveyor belt and grab my rolling luggage.

"Good. School is awesome but easy. I like having kids with athlete dads like me." Her dad, Jordan, and Alex's other half is the top wide receiver in the NFL. Some of her classmates are his teammates' children, unlike her school in New England.

When Reese releases me, Alex takes her place. After a snug hug, she hands me a coat. "It's snowing, and I imagine it's going to feel frigid given the temperature difference between there and here." December through February are typically the hottest months in Australia.

"You're my rock!"

Alex smiles and loops her arm through mine after I pull on the coat. "Where to?"

"Home, please."

Alex looks over at me in the passenger seat—a look that means she wants more details.

"Nothing new to share. Nolan knows, and he asked for time to sort out some family stuff. He doesn't know all the nuances of the family stuff yet, so he didn't share with me."

"Blaine?"

"Yeah." My answer tells Alex more than enough. If Blaine is involved, it's serious.

"Are you together or…?"

"Not sure. We're undefined for now. The determination on his face regarding interpersonal issues was new, and I didn't think pushing him to define our relationship was necessary or wise at this point."

"Understandable."

"Uncle Nolan will figure it out, Auntie. Don't worry," Reese chimes in from the back seat.

"Thanks, sweetie. I'm worried about how he'll handle whatever he learns, not about him as a father."

Reese smiles and looks out her window. The rest of the ride to the condo is largely silent. They escort me inside and leave almost immediately.

"I'll see you on Monday at the staff meeting," Alex states. Reese hugs me close before bounding down the stairs after her.

I drag my luggage to the laundry room and throw in my clothes. While I sort through the mail for nearly a week, I text Nolan.

Me: I'm home.

Nolan: How are you feeling?

Me: Drained but otherwise okay. Don't worry about me.

Nolan: I always worry about you. More so now.

My heart flutters, but I squash the sensation as fast as it arose. I can't allow myself to succumb to the idea we'll end up together. *Right?* As much as I want a nuclear family with Nolan, we aren't there yet.

Me: Thank you. Same for me.

Nolan: I'll handle it.

Me: I know. I'm here if you need me.

Nolan: I need you, but I don't want to burden you with this.

I shake away the tears ready to fall and push the video chat. Without giving him a chance to greet me, I say, "You aren't burdening me. I'm pregnant, not fragile. What aren't you telling me?"

"Nothing," he answers forcefully.

"I know you as well as you know me. Hell, I know you better than anyone else, and you aren't being truthful."

He scrubs his hand down his face and considers his words carefully. "During the party... Michael didn't stay away because of me. He has no issues being in the same room as me if I don't flaunt my choices that don't adhere to his prescribed requirements. Also, I'm confident my mother reminded him to play nice for Lara's benefit."

I process his words. Michael didn't want to be near me. *Why?* "I don't fit the appropriate mold, do I?"

"Not in his opinion, no."

"Because?" The options are numerous. First, I'm not rich or college educated. The other option is I'm not Caucasian. The thought makes my blood boil. Though considering he isn't his biological father, I'm not sure I care one iota.

Anguish mars his gorgeous face. "That's the thing, sweetheart. I don't care what he thinks. Setting him straight is part of what I need to handle alone."

I raise a hand in front of the screen. "Okay."

"You aren't going to push?"

"No."

He arches an eyebrow at me, urging me to continue.

"Figure out what you want, Nolan. If that's a relationship with me and our child, I'm completely on board, as previously mentioned. If it's a coparenting relationship where we're only friends, I'll handle it."

"There were two topics we never discussed before the party: sex and marriage. Well, sex with each other, and we explored it excellently. We've never discussed marriage," he states.

I laugh softly. "No, we haven't. I want to be part of one though, someday. I want the promises, the commitment, the vows—all of it. Look, being left alone at sixteen was an eye-opening experience, as you already know. Blackthorne has given me a sense of family, and I'm grateful. However, I want a nuclear family of my own."

"I don't… only one person in my life has a stable, long-term marriage."

"Who?"

"Carl and Donna were married for forty years before she passed away. Both lived on the property when I was a child."

"I think you're missing a few examples."

"Like?" Skepticism is clear in his tone.

"The Blackthornes and the Michelsons."

Recognition crosses his face. "True."

"While not decades, the boss men have solid marriages. Christoph and Madeleine will be married soon."

"Point taken," he replies, then silence echoes between us.

"Will you…? Are you still willing to be my date, or does your need for time change that?" The wedding is in a few months. *He needs that much more time?*

"I hope it doesn't take until the wedding to speak with Michael and my biological father."

Inwardly, I shudder. The longer it takes for him to figure this out, the less involved he'll be in this pregnancy. *I need to end this call before I lose the fraying grip I have on my emotions.* "I should get some sleep. Don't forget what I said; I'm here for you. Bye, Nolan."

"Good night, Maia."

Despite my exhaustion, my inclination is to beat the heavy bag in my basement. I tug on my running shoes instead and take a moderate jog on the treadmill. As I run, a memory from two years ago floods my brain.

"Are you going to open it?" Nolan asked. We were in the bunkhouse, and Christoph was watching a movie in the common room.

"I'm terrified to read what it says." The letter clutched was in my hands.

He threw his arm around me and guided me outside. We walked along the crunchy ground to the farthest point at the farm. It was a spot Jake set up to reflect.

Nolan spread the blanket on the cold ground, took a seat, and coaxed me into his arms. It was one of the first times I let myself consider we could be more than friends. It was about six months after I was abducted as bait for Norah. Those moments on the plane back to the farm and while Nolan was beside me was the first time I felt cared for. I didn't know then, but those feelings were the beginning of us.

My hands were shaking uncontrollably as I opened the letter from an attorney's office in Hanoi. There's absolutely no chance the news contained inside was good news.

"Whatever it says, I'm here for you. I'll always be here for you. You're becoming everything to me." His words were whispered against the back of my neck. Tingles ran down my spine, and I thought perhaps we could be a couple.

"How can you say that? We've never held hands or kissed."

"No one has made me feel like you do."

I swiped the single tear that rolled over my cheek. "We can't be a couple, Nolan."

"Why not?"

I turned in his arms and bent my legs over his. "Did you forget what Jake said?"

"No."

I canted my head in disbelief.

"He said if we pursue a relationship beyond friendship and coworkers, we need to give him a heads-up."

"Can't you read between the lines?" I scoffed at him. Exasperated, he didn't see the underlying meaning.

"Please enlighten me."

"If we get into a relationship, we won't be able to be on the same assignments anymore. It wouldn't surprise me if he forces one of us to move out of the bunkhouse."

"Jake treats us like family. He would never do that."

"Maybe you're right, but it isn't a risk I'm willing to take if it means losing this job."

"You don't want to pursue a relationship with me because of your job?" The tone and angst in his voice shook me to my core. He had feelings for me too, but the potential losses for chasing a relationship were high.

"Do you want to lose this job?" I countered.

He hesitated long enough for me to determine the risk was high for him as well. His words left the possibility on the table though. "No, but I want to pursue more with you."

"We can't have both... at least not now."

"I'll wait, Maia. You embody each quality a man would want in a partner. You're smart, funny, can flatten me with a well-placed kick, and you're beautiful fresh from sleep. Any man who tells you they need more is lying."

I recall shaking my head and mumbling, "No man has ever looked at me or treated me like you do. I never gave anyone the opportunity."

He replied, "When you're ready, I'll seize the chance with both hands and my heart." Nolan dries my tears with the pad of his thumb and tugged the letter out. He takes a minute to read the contents.

As expected, the look on his face assured me the news wasn't good.

"They're gone?" I whispered.

He leaned within a hairsbreadth of my forehead, presumably to kiss me, but he pulled back at my sharp inhale. "Yes. Your mother died soon after they returned home, and your father a month ago. I'm sorry, Maia."

I shook my head and attempted to move away. His arms circled around me and tugged me closer. The comfort he provided in that terrible moment was unimaginable. The rush of emotion brings me back to the present or at least a few days ago, sharing about our child.

I decrease my speed to a slow jog, then drop down to a walk before pulling the safety switch on the treadmill. After the exhausting run both for my body and mind, I shower and collapse onto my bed until morning. I spend the entire day around the condo cleaning and relaxing.

Bright and early the next day, I park behind the office and walk around the building before the staff meeting.

"Morning, Gemma."

"Hi, Maia. Jake and Christoph will be back in a few. Lane and Barrett are already here." Lane was attached to Jake and Connor's unit for their second tour. He was working at his family farm in Texas until he joined the team. Barrett is a marine veteran and former Dallas police officer. Like most marines, he would say there's no such thing as former. He's a mammoth of a man who recently regained the ability to take assignments after an issue with Cruz and Jill.

"Thanks." I grab a water from the kitchenette on my way by and enter the conference room. "Hey, guys!"

"Hi, Maia," both reply.

As I take a seat, Jake, Connor, and Christoph enter immediately following Alex. She plops into the seat beside me and gives me a quick side hug. "How are you?" she whispers.

Jake calls the meeting to order before I can answer. "I'll keep this short. Lane and Barrett, I have your schedules here." Jake slides them across the table. "If you don't have any questions, you're free to go. As a reminder, your expense reports are due to Gemma by the end of the week."

Both leave without another word.

"Alex, any issues we need to be aware of with the gym or the training schedule?" Alex fell in love with Jordan and Reese and was going to resign from Blackthorne as a team member. When Christoph learned he was becoming a father, he planned to resign and open a gym to allow Madeleine the ability to continue kicking ass and taking names as a sought-after sports agent. Instead, they made Christoph a partner, and the gym plan fell away for a little while. Within the last few months, the guys decided to buy the gym and use it for self-defense classes for clients as well as training for new hires. They asked Alex to run it, which allows her to be available for Reese and continue her work with domestic violence survivors like herself.

"No, issues. The self-defense classes are going well. I have the training manual for the new hires updated and ready for your review. Are we still on track for four new hires after the wedding?"

"Yes. I'll get you the names and arrival dates beforehand," Connor answers.

"Good. Then, I'm set."

Christoph looks in my direction. "Are you okay with Alex being present for our conversation?"

"Yeah. She knows everything anyway," I reply.

Jake nods and says, "Your situation—"

I laugh. "I'm pregnant. You can say it out loud."

The room falls into silence briefly, and then the guys burst into laughter.

Jake continues, "I was going to say, your situation is new for us considering you're a teammate, not one of our wives. Either way, we have an assignment for you. A last-minute, two-day press event with Demi Goldberg in New York City Wednesday evening and Thursday evening."

"No problem." An assignment will be good for me.

"As you near the third trimester of your pregnancy, we'll make adjustments and then take you off the schedule until you're ready to return to work," Connor adds.

"Thank you."

"You're welcome."

I hesitate to ask but decide to give the choice to Jake. "Have you received the report back from Blaine yet?"

Connor looks to Jake before answering, "No, we haven't. Anything further will have to come from Nolan."

I close my eyes and drop my head. The line has been clearly drawn. Either Nolan drew it or our bosses did. Either way, I'll only get information about Nolan from him. "I understand."

"Is there anything else?" Christoph asks.

"No, I'm set."

"Have a nice day, ladies," Jake dismisses us.

Alex throws her arm around me. "Have time for coffee?"

I frown. "I can have decaf."

Alex laughs and leads me next door to Norah's store.

"I'm sure you will be in my boat soon enough, my sweet friend."

"Eventually. I want to get married first." With our drinks in hand, we take seats near the front window. "Spill the details."

"Nothing to share. We've texted since I got back, but that's all. I'm in a holding pattern. The assignment will be good for me. Time away from my four walls and worrying about Nolan."

"You're concerned who his father is, aren't you?"

"Yeah. There must be a solid reason Michael and Sharon kept his biological dad's identity from him. His parents—and I use the term loosely at this point—threw roadblock after roadblock in his way."

"How do you know?"

"Nolan shared his limited knowledge with me. His relationship is a mess, and he won't allow me to help him."

"When did you change your mind about putting Nolan ahead of your job?" Alex knows the extent of my feelings for Nolan and my stalwart desire to keep this job.

"The instant his kiss felt like I was home."

Alex smiles—the radiant smile she has when she thinks about Jordan and Reese. "Same." She pauses a beat. "To clarify, with Jordan not Nolan."

I laugh. "I know."

We finish our coffees and go our separate ways. I head home and prepare for my assignment, while Alex heads to the school to wait for Reese.

CHAPTER NINE

NOLAN

My relaxation has come to a rapid end. After Maia left, I took in some of the touristy sights. I'm not a mainstream attraction kind of guy, but I traipsed through the Sydney Opera House, the Taronga Zoo, and swam the Bondi Icebergs, nonetheless. All three were amazing. Intriguingly... no, not really, I wanted to share it with her.

Over the last few years, I've fallen head over heels for her. However, our timing hasn't been right. The bigger question... is now the right time considering she's carrying my child?

We spend all our downtime together despite not pursuing a romantic relationship with one another. Within six months of working together, my resolve was tested. Norah, who at the time was Jake's friend with benefits, was being sought by the Moretti family. During the investigation, the FBI wanted to speak with Norah. The plan was to use Maia as a decoy. It worked and Maia was drugged and captured. Despite the short time we knew one another then, my heart plummeted to my toes, and we've been joined at the hip ever since. Maia captured me and never let go. Vaulting over our line between friends and more at the engagement party was the best decision I've ever made. Having a best friend of the opposite sex is amazing and adds fun in everyday mundane chores. However, sex with your best friend surpasses the same with a random person without question. Yet asking for time to sort out my life before bringing her fully into it—completely into it—was excruciating... is excruciating.

My phone ringing pulls me out of my thoughts.

"Hey, Jake."

"Ready to resume your duties?" Jake asks over the phone.

"Yes, but I gather this isn't a social call."

"No, I received the report from Blaine about your father."

I grip the back of my neck with my free hand. "Did you read it?"

"No. Do you want me to?"

Pacing the length of my hotel room, I consider his offer. "No, I can handle it myself. Thank you, though."

"Okay. I'll send it to you via an encrypted link. Do you recall your password?"

"Yes." *Maia515*. Romantic or stalkerish—probably both. Maia is the one for me, and I knew when I created this password two years ago.

"If, after you read this, you need me to extend Sawyer with Miss Swisher, please reach out immediately," Jake requests.

"I will. Thank you, Jake." I end the call and boot up my laptop. The two files—the old one and the updated one—are glaring at me in the filing system.

I need to do this for Maia and our child. I need to do this for me. I push the trickles of fear away and input the password for the new file. Blaine is thorough; I'm sure he added to the old one rather than start over.

My biological father is the same age as Sharon and from Delaware. His name is Edward Phillips. *The senator? The senator considering a run for president of the United States?* Nolan Edward Dalton. She gave me his name but led Michael to believe he was my father. He graduated from Brown undergrad and Georgetown Law. That must be where he met my mother. Despite never sitting for the bar exam or practicing law a day in her life, Sharon Dalton graduated from law school summa cum laude. There's a gap in time though. Michael and Sharon got married within days of her graduation from law school, and Lara was born early, seven months later.

Each sentence of this report rocks the foundation I thought my life was built on. Well, it makes me wonder what else is a lie. I snatch my phone from my pocket and dial without thinking.

"Nolan, are you all right?" Maia answers on the first ring. I knew she would regardless of the fissure between us right now.

"No. Jake sent me the file, and I started reading, and I... I assure you I'm not trying to... Ugh!"

"Take a breath." Her voice soothes my soul. It always has.

"Asking for space was me trying not to have you on this roller-coaster ride with me. To allow me to handle my disastrous family before—" A video call request comes through. I accept instantly, without a second thought.

"I know, but it feels a little bit like we are."

"I'm sorry. I'll handle this myself."

Fire flashes in her eyes. "Don't you dare hang up! I want to be here for you, and I'm glad you called. Please back up and share what you learned." I've seen Maia truly angry perhaps twice. It's hot as hell, despite the fact her ire is aimed at me.

I tell her what I know so far.

"You think Lara might not be Michael's as well." A statement, not a question.

"Unfortunately, yes. What do I do with this information?" If Lara is only marrying Paul for the status, she needs to know sooner rather than later.

"Finish reading first. Then we create a plan."

"Not we, me," I assert forcefully.

"We, the three of us, are in this together."

"Precisely why I shouldn't have called. My need to protect you skyrocketed the instant you told me about our child. It was off the charts before I knew."

"I know, you've mentioned it before. Not buying it. What else does the report say?" Maia pushes.

I drop my head and continue reading aloud. "Edward is married to Serafina Visage Phillips. Also a Georgetown Law alumna. She joined one of the largest firms in the country after graduation before opening her own lucrative practice five years later. They have no children."

"You said he's running for president?"

"Yes. Well, he's formed an exploratory committee and has scheduled a press conference with all the major news outlets in Florida early next week."

"It adds another wrinkle to establishing a relationship with him, doesn't it? It's one thing to step away from Michael, which I understand and support completely if it's what you want to do. However, it's something else to seek Senator Phillips out and drop this in his lap."

"You don't think he knows about me?"

She shrugs. "It could go either way. It seems Sharon lied to Michael and Senator Phillips from the start. When you learned the truth, do you believe she told your biological father?"

"No, I'm sure she didn't. It was enough for me to handle being a product of adultery. I didn't consider it much deeper."

"Fair, but if Senator Phillips didn't know Sharon was married, or she didn't tell him about you, it's on your mother."

"True. You know this means I have to go back there, right? Is going to see her before seeking out my biological father smart?"

"You need to speak to or see at least your mother, yes. Does it need to be first? Hmmm." She sets her index finger on her pouty lips and taps lightly. The mannerism drives me to distraction. "Will she try to stop you? Will she reach out to him before you can and thwart your efforts somehow?"

"Before I knew about my true parentage, they were attempting to stop me from finding out. When I found their antenuptial agreement hashing out the changes to be made for their remarriage, the terms pertaining to me were stunningly clear. Michael was to hold himself out as my father and treat me the same as he does Lara."

"That didn't happen because you read the agreement and confronted your mother."

"Correct."

"Did you agree to stay silent?"

My chest tightens, and it grows hard to breathe. "No, not explicitly. Mother likely believes I will because I haven't pursued the issue yet."

Her expression softens. "I would give a lot to be beside you right now."

"Me too. I can't seem to stay away from you."

"I don't want you to stay away. I would prefer to be attached at the hip."

I heard the words she didn't say in my mind. *For the rest of my life.* "I know, but I thought I should to protect you."

"Understandable but unnecessary."

"I don't—" *I don't deserve her.*

"What about your father?" she asks, her words barely audible.

"I may need Jake's help, especially given he's campaigning or about to be campaigning. Hopefully, he has some contacts allowing me to schedule a private meeting with the senator."

"Are you coming home early?" Her question sounds hopeful.

I thread my fingers into the hair at the nape of my neck, which has grown long during this assignment. "Considering it. I need to decide right now, though."

"Why?"

"Jake asked for an immediate heads-up so he can move people around and keep Sawyer here instead of me."

"Makes sense. Will you call me back after you talk to him?"

"Not tonight. You need rest, and I need to talk to Sawyer. Before we hang up, how are you feeling?"

A small smile curls up at the edge of her lips. "Better. I was able to sleep in this morning before I packed for my assignment."

My stomach clenches into a knot. "Where and for who?"

"Easy, Nolan. The guys won't risk our child for an assignment. It's a presser for Demi Goldberg in New York. It's a short one, two nights and then back home."

"In here"—I point to my head—"I hear what you're saying. However"—I point to my chest—"here isn't getting the message."

"I'll be extra vigilant."

"Much appreciated. Rest up. Please call me after you arrive tomorrow," I request.

"I will. Have a good day."

"Rest well, Maia." I swipe to end the call.

A few deep breaths later, I call Jake.

"How bad, Nolan?" Jake asks.

"Sorry to bother you this late."

"No bother." Jake has a rule ever since his relationship with Norah started: No work calls after six in the evening unless it's an emergency. Technically, I'm not sure this qualifies, but given I'm halfway around the world, it seemed prudent to call now.

"I need some assistance setting up a meeting with my biological father." I share what I've learned and authorize Jake to read the file, as he needs to set up the meeting.

"I have some contacts within the Secret Service. A member of my unit for my first tour shifted there after his contract ended. I'll see what I can do."

"Thanks. How do you want to handle Miss Swisher? I can stay until the assignment is over."

"Are you sure?"

I appreciate his willingness to get me home sooner rather than later. "There are four more weeks on the assignment. I'm sure it makes sense to schedule a meeting when the senator is in DC rather than on the campaign trail."

"Okay and—"

I interrupt, "I'll also be back in time for Maia's next ultrasound."

"I wasn't going to pry," Jake admits.

"I know. I plan to be part of my child's life." *And hers.* "Maia and I haven't made any concrete decisions outside of me settling the issues with my family. However, I can't seem to stick to it."

"Meaning?"

"After she agreed to give me time to figure this out, I broke down and called her the second I read my father's name in the file."

"It's understandable. Your bond with Maia was forged the moment she dropped you to the mat the day you met. Your relationship makes you both exceptional and vulnerable in this business."

Laughter bubbles in my chest. "True." Since that moment, we've grown as friends and much more. I share everything with her, and she shares with me. Well, perhaps a bit with Alex too, but… I'll go to the ends of the earth for her and our child.

"What about your mother?"

"I'm open to suggestions. I can reach out to her from here. Being in her presence again, though I asked Maia to join me if I choose to, probably isn't wise. My concern, as I mentioned earlier, is her thwarting my efforts."

"Blaine is thorough and careful. No one will trace his steps. If they did, I would already know about it."

He has a point. "Understood."

"I'll get on this right away."

"Thanks, Jake. I'll connect with Sawyer and take over for him."

"Roger. If you or Maia need anything else, reach out."

I end the call, pack my things, and make my way to Rachel's suite.

Sawyer answers the door wearing only a pair of boxer briefs. "It's not what it looks like."

"Okay." Skepticism laces my response.

"We got back later than normal, and I wanted to shower before my flight. It doesn't matter, nothing happened."

"Honestly, I have a lot going on in my life right now. I can't add more."

Rachel chooses this moment to emerge from the bathroom wrapped in a silky robe. The fabric clings to her curves in spectacular fashion. I love Maia, but Rachel is hot.

"How was your time off, Nolan?" she asks.

"Fine. Thank you." I look behind me and verify the locks of her door. "Please excuse us."

Sawyer drops his head and shuffles back to the adjoining room. I set my bag on the bed and note his story may check out. There's a fresh outfit on the dressing bench and the shower is running.

"I've got Rachel. Do what you need to."

Sawyer hustles into the bathroom. Fifteen minutes later, Sawyer briefs me on the last week and the call time for tomorrow. We swap keys, and he bids farewell to Rachel, who is now fully dressed.

"Did you fix things with Maia?" she asks, leaning against the doorframe between our rooms.

I grin at her. "Nothing to fix. She needed to share information with me in person."

"She's pregnant?"

I tilt my head in her direction. "How?"

"Anything else could be handled by text. Flying to another country to talk is huge, like having a baby huge."

Shaking my head at her correct deduction of the situation, I admit, "She is."

"How do you feel about it?"

I consider if sharing with Rachel is breaking some unwritten rules of dating and decide it's fine. Am I dating Maia? "I've always wanted to be a dad. I would've preferred to properly date her, then marry her first."

"She's your best friend, right?"

"Yeah."

"And you've known her for…?"

"Three years."

"You know more about her than anyone you've ever dated, don't you?"

Yes. "You sound like you're speaking from experience."

"I am. Julian and I were best friends since middle school in rural Montana. We had the same classes, participated in the same after-school activities, sort of. He was a band geek, and I was in every dramatic production the school put on. We were always together."

Motioning for her to take a seat beside me, I ask, "Were?"

"He proposed at a high school graduation party. I said no."

"Why?"

"I knew Juilliard would take the entirety of my focus, and I didn't want to string him along. He would've been miserable in the city. No one has come close to knowing me as well as he does… did."

"Where is he now?"

"He married his college girlfriend two years ago."

"I'm sorry."

She sets her head against my arm. "I am too." After a moment, she realizes where she set her head and bolts straight up to sitting.

"It's fine."

"Thanks. All I'm saying is you may not have said the words, but having a best friend of the opposite sex is awesome. Without trying, you learn everything important about them. There's no stress of what to wear or what to say or angst of the first kiss. Clearly, you got that out of the way."

I smirk at her. "Absolutely."

"It was mind-blowing, right?"

"Without question."

"You?"

She shrugs. "No partner has ever come close to making me feel how he did, and we were teenagers. Looking back on it now, I made a mistake in choosing my career. Maybe we would've made it, maybe not. I'll never know. I won't interfere with his marriage."

"Are you dating anyone?"

"Yes and no. When you date someone who is also in this business, the schedules are hard. Is he my boyfriend? Not really. More like a likeminded booty call."

"I understand. We should get some sleep. Your call time is early tomorrow. Thanks for the advice, Rachel."

"You're welcome. Thanks for listening as well."

I nod as she leaves for her suite, closing the door but not latching it behind her.

CHAPTER TEN

MAIA

The presser for Miss Goldberg is in New York City. The flight was short, and the accommodations are excellent. When the production company is picking up the tab, the hotels are posh and luxurious. This one has a spa and boutique in the heart of the city. After retrieving my room key and settling in, I verify the schedule and change into a black suit for the event.

After a quick snack, I ride upstairs to her suite and knock on the door.

A rail thin woman with striking raven hair answers the door. "Good evening, can I help you?"

"Good evening. I'm Maia from Blackthorne."

"Hello. We've been expecting you. Miss Goldberg will be ready in the next ten minutes. Would you like a drink?"

"No, thank you." I step off to the side and wait for my client to be ready for her event.

Miss Goldberg is an adult now, and her security needs have changed since she took over. Before attaining adulthood, her father was borderline obsessive about her security. She previously had round-the-clock security. Now, Blackthorne handles her pressers and occasionally on-set security, if necessary.

"Maia, right?" The young actress is tall and curvy with wavy strawberry blonde hair. In short, she's stunning.

"Yes. Good evening, Miss Goldberg."

She waves me off. "Please call me Demi. I'm not as formal as my father."

"I understand. You have about ten minutes until we must be in the elevator to meet Mr. Barnett." Ellis Barnett is the director of this film, and his wife, Kelly, the costumer.

She nods and fixes the strap around her ankle. "I'm set."

The ride to the green room is smooth. When we arrive, Mr. Barnett and his wife are present. Miss Goldberg talks with Ellis first.

"Maia, it's good to see you again," Kelly greets me instantly.

"Hi, Kelly. You as well. How are you?"

"I'm well. You?"

She smiles. "When I met Nicholas, I never could've imagined how my life would change. It's amazing being able to capture my dreams with him beside me." Nicholas is Mr. Barnett's given name. Ellis is his stage name.

Exactly what I want with Nolan. The bigger question is what does my dream life look like? I never planned for a future other than surviving. *I can't take assignments after having a child, can I? Do I want to? What about Nolan? The two of us can't…. Ugh!* I push my thoughts away for a later time and refocus on my assignment for tonight. "I'm happy for you."

"Thank you."

"Maia, nice to see you again." Mr. Barnett joins us, his arm sliding around Kelly's waist possessively.

"Hi, Ellis. Pleasure to see you again as well."

We chat for another ten minutes until the moderator indicates the press is ready. The cast advances toward the ballroom for the press conference.

I walk beside Demi as she makes her way along the carpeted walkway. I see the guy move from behind the barrier before she does. He's tall and moderately overweight. Expeditiously, I step between her and the approaching fan.

"Demi! Demi! How could you treat him so poorly?" he shouts.

Who is he talking about? Nothing in her file indicates a recent breakup. I extend my arm and push Demi further away from me and this disgruntled fan. "Sir, go back," I direct and point with my other hand.

"What are you going to do about it? You're a tiny little thing," he goads me.

Good, his ire is now directed on me instead of the client. Except... our baby. No, I'm fine. "Sir, go back behind the rope, please. You don't want to do this in front of these cameras. If you touch me or her, you will be arrested."

"Demi! He did everything you asked, and you dumped him!"

"Sir, go back."

"What are you doing here?" Demi asks over my shoulder.

"Don't engage him," I instruct her.

While I'm momentarily distracted talking to the client, he grabs my wrist tightly. Without another thought, I clasp my hands together and escape his grip. The crowd cheers, and the fan freezes. Hotel security, as well as private security assisting other cast members, approach from all sides.

"Sir—" a deep, masculine voice from my right calls out.

"My name is Aidan," he mutters.

The voice continues. "Aidan, hotel security is going to take you for questioning."

Two members of hotel security flank Aidan and escort him out the door and into the lobby. I assume they're taking him to the security office a few floors down.

"Well done," a striking man from another security company states. He's tall and built like a mountain with intense green eyes and sandy hair.

"Thank you…?"

He extends his hand to me. "Max from Brothers Security."

"Pleasure to meet you. Please excuse me."

"Of course."

I turn to face my client. She hasn't moved since the fan was escorted away. "Demi." It isn't until I set my hand on her forearm does she move or acknowledge me in any way.

"Maia." Her voice is shaky, and her normally serene demeanor is anything but calm.

"Back to the green room?" I suggest.

"Yes, thank you."

I retrace our steps and return to the green room despite the call time for the presser being in five minutes. Wordlessly, I guide her to a chair, grab a water bottle, and hand it to her. I wait a solid ten minutes before speaking again. "Who was that fan?"

"Not important right now. Are you okay?" she asks.

Working with athletes and celebrities never ceases to amaze me. For the most part, they're people who make insane money chasing their next big role. "I'm fine. Thank you." *Nolan is going to freak out though.*

"To answer your question, he's my ex's older brother."

"Which ex?"

"Kellen Oaks."

"The football player for DC?"

She raises an eyebrow in my direction. There's no way for her to know about my personal friendship with Jordan. "Demi, it's my job to know who is in your life and where you have concerns. Kellen nor his brother were mentioned in your known associates."

"Kellen and I were very private. We had to be, given our age difference." If I had to guess, Kellen is five to seven years older than her. Normally not a big deal, but if she was a minor when they met, it would be.

"Okay. Why is Kellen's brother upset with you?"

"It's complicated. In this business, the time away from home for long periods is a lot to handle. I asked for space, and he took it as I wanted to be with someone else. I simply needed a break to refocus some parts of my life that have nothing to do with him. Handling all my affairs on my own was more of a transition than I anticipated."

"Guys don't understand a woman would choose to be alone to figure things out."

"No, they don't."

"After the presser, I'm sure hotel security will want to speak with me. When you're ready, I'll take you to the press conference. Do you need me to call your assistant for a touch up?"

"No. Thank you, Maia."

I nod, then text Jake and request a status update.

Me: I need a status update on the presser. Is it still going forward?

Jake: Problem?

Me: A minor one. It's handled. Just need to know how to proceed.

Jake: Roger. Give me ten.

I grab a water and a packet of crackers while I await Jake's reply and for Demi to regain her composure. Soon thereafter, Jake replies, indicating the presser is proceeding and we can take the tunnel route to avoid the remaining fans.

"All set?"

Demi inhales sharply and replies, "Yes."

We arrive at the conference nearly forty minutes late. I position myself closer than I normally would as I scan the crowd, although another incident is unlikely.

Max, from earlier, approaches from my left. "Surprised to see you here."

"Not the first time I've had a scuffle with the fan and needed to continue on."

"That much was obvious. Would you be interested in grabbing a drink with me later?"

Admittedly, Max is attractive, and most women would be jumping for joy right now. Despite my unnoticeable pregnancy to a stranger, I only want Nolan. "Thank you for the invitation, but I'm not single." Not completely a lie, but not accurate either.

He acknowledges me and steps away. The remainder of the event is smooth. With their hands threaded together, Ellis and Kelly walk closely behind Demi and me. As we near the beginning of the tunnel, the head of hotel security halts our progress.

"Miss Park, we would like to thank you for your handling of the situation with Mr. Oaks. We would appreciate a statement from you before you leave this evening."

"Thank you. I'll come to the office once my client is secure."

"Much appreciated," he replies and allows us to pass.

We ride to their floor in the service elevator.

"I appreciate your presence, Demi. I'm sure it wasn't easy," Ellis offers.

Demi shakes her head. "I was more worried about Maia."

"Understandable. Either way, attending shows grit and will assist you in your career."

"Thank you, Ellis." We walk as a group down the hall, as their room is a few doors away from Demi's.

Once Demi is safely ensconced in her suite, I retreat to the security office and give my statement. I send a summary text to Jake, indicating I gave a statement and would fill him in through my assignment report. Finally, an extra two hours later, I collapse on the bed after kicking off my shoes and promptly fall asleep.

I sleep through normal breakfast hours and numerous texts. I answer Nolan to avoid him worrying.

Nolan: Morning. How are you?

Me: I'm sure you're sound asleep now.

Nolan: Nope, our shoot is in the evening.

Me: Oh. Hi. Can you talk now?

A video request comes through, and I accept it. "Please know, as you can readily see, I'm fine, but there was a scuffle last night before the press conference. A fan grabbed my arm."

Sheer panic washes over his face. "Did you talk to Jake about being replaced?"

"Nolan, I'm fine."

He grips the back of his neck with one hand before looking directly at me again. "I worry about you more now than I did before."

"I'm not going to break."

"Your words make sense, but it doesn't change my level of concern. I was serious when I said I wanted to mummify you and lock you in your condo."

"I didn't doubt you, but I need to work, or I'll lose my mind. Did you decide how to handle your mother?" My subject change is abrupt, but hopefully he'll answer me instead of focusing on last night's incident.

"I called earlier and got her voice mail. I'll try until she responds. Hopefully, she will, or I'll show up. She won't like that at all."

"No, she won't. What about Lara? Are you keeping your hunch to yourself for now?"

"Until I can talk to my mother, yes. Lara and Paul haven't set a date yet. I have a little time."

"Makes sense. I should order some food and get ready for the premiere tonight. Please don't worry. Once she's inside, only VIPs and select press will be present, no fans."

"I'll try."

"Thank you. Please call me when you can," I ask.

"I will."

Reluctantly, I press the end button and order brunch. With a full stomach, I shower, dress for the premiere, and check in with Jake.

"Hey, Jake."

"Morning. The head of security called this morning singing your praises. They were impressed by your handling of the situation."

I shake my head, even though he can't see me. "I did my job, that's all."

"Either way, glad it turned out fine. The premiere should be easier. You're scheduled on the first flight out tomorrow morning."

"Thanks. I'll see you on Monday."

A few hours later, I meet Demi and escort her to the car service waiting to take her to the premiere. The ride is remarkably devoid of traffic. Her walk down the red carpet is issue free. The moment she steps into the theater, her posture relaxes and she smiles widely.

"Thank you, Maia."

"You're welcome."

She takes a seat amongst her other castmates, including Ellis, who offers a nod in acknowledgement. I take a seat along the rear wall and watch the film. At the conclusion, I return Miss Goldberg to her suite before curling up in the luxurious bed in my room until morning.

CHAPTER ELEVEN

NOLAN

Working on the other side of the world from Maia isn't ideal, but we've been talking at least twice a day with a few texts sprinkled in. Filming for today is wrapping up, and I'm anxious to get back to the hotel and chat with her. This assignment is the longest I've ever taken. Frankly, I miss her. We haven't been apart for more than a week since she started at Blackthorne. If we're both unassigned, we train in the morning and spend our days together doing mundane stuff. When we took our relationship a step further, a rush of emotions we kept under tight control erupted. While our child is an unexpected gift, there was always going to be an us. The question was when. Now, it'll be sooner than before.

"All set, Miss Swisher?" I ask as she leaves the costuming trailer.

She casts a death stare in my direction. "Yes." Her tone and demeanor would indicate she isn't happy right now.

Silently, I escort her to the SUV and pull away from the set. "How can I help?"

"You can't. You're a guy."

I can't help but laugh.

She smirks. "Really, Nolan?"

"Sorry, but you can't take your anger out on every male of the species because one pissed you off."

"Says who?"

I chuckle. "Honestly, do you need me to pick up a milkshake or candy for you?"

She shakes her head. "Maia is a lucky woman. No, the room service dessert menu will work fine."

"I'm the lucky one. If you want to share, I'm all ears."

"Thanks." She slumps deeper into the buttery-smooth leather seat and closes her eyes. "Why are guys so stupid?"

"Not all of us are stupid. We make dumb choices occasionally, but... What did he-whom-you-haven't-named do?"

"He wants to see me like... now. He doesn't want to wait until filming ends in a few weeks."

"Is he willing to come here? Given his status, if you will, he can afford to come to you, right?"

"Yeah, but I don't want to start a tabloid gossip storm. I mean, we've been friends with benefits for nearly two years at this point. We've been discreet and careful. No one knows."

"He wants to tell the world, huh?"

"Yeah, Cole wants to claim me as his."

Cole Foster? He has been dubbed Hollywood's next George Clooney. "You don't want that?"

She shrugs and stops talking. I'm sure she realized she shared his name.

I pull into the parking garage and escort her wordlessly to her suite. "Why don't you take a shower, order too much dessert, and we can talk more?"

"Perfect. Thanks, Nolan."

"Anytime dessert is involved, I'm in, even if it includes deep conversations."

"I'm going to say it again because it warrants repeating, Maia is a lucky woman."

I smile. "Thanks." I step into my room and immediately wash off the day. After a scalding shower, I check my messages, finding a text from Maia and a voice mail from Jake.

Maia: Just checking in. Our baby is the size of a pomegranate.

Maia: Or a sugar glider.

Me: Hey, is it from an app?

Maia: Yeah, I'll send you the link. How was filming?

Me: Filming was fine. How are you?

Maia: Honestly, I miss you.

Me: I miss you. I'll be home soon.

Maia: We'll be waiting. Sleep well.

Me: Have a great day.

With a grin on my face because of Maia, I call my mother again. Hopefully, she'll answer this time. The phone rings once and then instantly goes to voice mail. Interesting, she ignored my call. Shaking it off, I move to Jake's voice mail.

"Hey, Nolan. I connected with my friend at the Secret Service. He put me in touch with Senator Phillip's campaign manager, Weston Wentworth. Mr. Wentworth will be reaching out to you in the coming days."

I save the message and send a text to Jake.

Me: Thanks for the update. I look forward to his call.

Jake: No problem.

Me: Can you have Blaine run a background on Cole Foster?

Jake: Yes, why?

Me: He's our client's hush-hush booty call.

Jake: Roger. I'll forward the report when I get it.

Me: Thanks.

A personal step forward. Despite my nervousness surrounding reaching out and the firestorm it could cause for the senator, it needs to be done. Questions ping back and forth in my mind about whether it's the right move. The truth is, it matters if he knew about me and didn't care. If he didn't know, then I have a huge issue with my mother—an insurmountable issue that may not be overcome any time in the near future. I could spin this and say I'm doing it for the senator's own good. I'm allowing his campaign to get out in front of the situation before it becomes a story. I don't doubt Blaine's intel, and I'll do whatever is necessary to prove its accuracy. I consider calling Maia back, but there truly isn't anything to share. I tug on some shorts and a tee soon before Rachel knocks on the door.

"Dessert should be here in fifteen," she states. The concern about going public hasn't changed, but she's relaxed some.

"Cool. I'll be over soon."

My timing is perfect. When I step through the adjoining door, her order arrives. I push the table over to the foot of the bed and take a seat beside Rachel.

"Come to mama!"

I literally laugh out loud. "Did you order one of each dessert on the menu?"

"Yes, I did." Her words are filled with unflinching pride.

"Okay, pick your poison and spill," I direct her.

"Do you have a brother?"

"No, sorry." I don't plan on sharing my issues with her.

She pulls the chocolate crème brûlée closer and scoops out a heaping mouthful. She picks up our conversation where we left off. "Cole feels we should stop hiding. Two years is a long time, but…."

"You don't?"

"It isn't that simple."

"It could be. Are you willing to make the sacrifices necessary to be his partner?"

"No, not with what I know about him."

I dip my fork in the creamy blueberry cheesecake and savor a bite. Jill's is much better. "What do you mean?"

"If I asked you to list Maia's favorite color, candy bar, type of music, or book, could you do it? Not that those things are it in a relationship, but it's a place to start."

"Absolutely. Her favorite color is teal. Candy bar is the caramel dark chocolate from Millie's downtown where we live. She listens to an eclectic array of music, but dislikes techno and club music with a passion. Maia is an avid reader. She reads thrillers, suspense, and romance novels, but dislikes historical fiction. I wouldn't say she has a favorite book, but I could list her favorite authors."

Rachel waves me off. "Not necessary. You proved my point, though. I can't name those things about Cole, and I highly doubt he can for me. We don't know each other well at all, at least outside of the bedroom."

"Do you want to know those things?"

She groans and sets the spoon on the white linen tablecloth. "No. I want the glow you have when you talk about Maia despite the bumpiness between you at the moment."

Happiness tugs at my heart, and my entire body warms. "Cole's not the guy?"

"No, he's not. Thanks, Nolan."

"Happy to help. Are we really going to eat all these desserts?"

"We're sure as hell going to try."

We laugh and dig into the tower of chocolate cake waiting to be sampled. A few hours later, I push the table into the hallway and leave Rachel curled up in her bed.

As the days wear on, Maia and I continue to talk frequently. She feels well, and the morning sickness—evening sickness—has dissipated. Her assignments since she worked with Miss Goldberg in New York have been smooth with no issues. Before I'm set to get Rachel for filming, my phone rings. It's a DC number.

"Hello," I answer.

"I'm looking for Nolan Dalton."

"Speaking."

"My name is Weston Wentworth."

"Thank you for reaching out. I realize it's unorthodox, but this information was brought to my attention recently."

"I understand. I've spoken with the senator, and he requests a DNA test and agreement with a complete background check."

Reasonable. "Fine. I'm on assignment in Australia and can take the test when I return home in about ten days. Does that work?"

"Yes. I'll send you the lab information and make sure the senator's sample is available at the same time."

"Thank you. Mr. Wentworth, my intention isn't to destroy his life. I won't make waves, but I need answers."

"I understand. Pending the results, we'll make time for a face-to-face meeting."

"Thank you." I take a settling breath and consider calling Maia. Realizing I don't have time, I call out before entering Rachel's room. "Rachel."

"Come in." She's threading her ponytail through the back of the baseball cap. "I'm ready to get this day started and over with."

"You're almost done."

"I know. The Cole situation hasn't gotten any better. He continues to reach out, despite me asking him to wait until I return home."

"The easy answer is to block him, which you already know. Why haven't you?"

"I may not want to be with him long term, but I care about him as a person."

"Tell him when we get back from filming tonight."

She rolls her eyes, grabs her sunglasses, and we head to the parking garage. It seems the entire cast and crew have similar sentiments to Rachel. The day has been packed from end to end with limited breaks. Despite feeling as if we arrived mere minutes ago, we're on our way back to the hotel fourteen hours later. My only wish is a scalding shower and comfy bed.

Instead, Rachel has a visitor, an unwelcome one. Cole Foster is leaning against a stone column in the parking garage, waiting for her.

"What are you doing here? How did you know where I was staying?" she asks him.

I wrap my arm around her waist, and then instruct them into the elevator. "Rachel, let's go."

She allows me to guide her inside.

"Who are you?" Cole asks. He's average height, moderate build, and good-looking. I can see why he's a movie star and on everyone's "It" list. Although his listening skills are abysmal.

"Her security detail. Get in the elevator, Mr. Foster." The file I received on him from Blaine indicated he isn't a security threat to Rachel, not physically anyway.

"Him? Are you sleeping with him? He calls you Rachel?" Cole accuses.

I shift Rachel behind me and push her into the corner of the elevator.

"He has nothing to do with my choice not to see you anymore. I can make my own decisions." She shouts over my shoulder as best she can.

"Clearly not," Cole fires back.

"What's that supposed to mean?"

"Not here," I state forcefully, and thankfully, both stop talking. Before I press the button to her floor, I turn to face her. "Do you want him in your suite?"

"No." I can see him cringe in the mirrored wall.

I turn in his direction. "What floor, Mr. Foster?"

"I didn't book a room. I planned to stay...."

Anger is rolling off Rachel in waves; I can feel it despite having my back to her. She holds her tongue though. I press the button for the top floor of the hotel, which has a VIP lounge. I key into the room and do a quick sweep. Unnecessary, probably, but I do it anyway.

"How did you find out where I'm staying?" she calmly asks him.

"Your agent told me."

"I see."

"Don't be like that, Rach. He's my agent now too."

"Since when?"

"I told him I would switch agents if he told me where you were." Cole takes a step forward.

"Well, he's fired as soon as you leave." Rachel retreats deeper into the room away from him. I step between them to halt his progress.

She continues, "You don't listen. Not only did I ask you for time, but I asked to see you when I returned. I want to be crystal clear, and thankfully, this time I have a witness to my words. Cole, we're done. I don't want to be with you anymore. Please leave."

"Where am I supposed to go?"

"Not my problem. I didn't invite you here, nor do I plan to bail you out by allowing you to stay in my suite. Go book a room and stay the hell away from me."

"But… I love you, Rachel."

"No. I'm done. Please leave." She turns and gazes out the window.

My phone rings in my hand, Jake's ringtone.

"Yeah, Jake."

"Where are you and Miss Swisher?"

"In the VIP lounge."

"Has Mr. Foster arrived?"

"Yes, why?"

"Turn on the television." I grab the remote on the nearby table. The screen has breaking news. A banner flashes along the bottom of the screen: *Cole Foster engaged to Angelica Swisher.*

"I'll call you back, Jake." I scurry to the window and gaze downward. Unfortunately, my view of the entrance is obscured, although I'm confident a throng of reporters are camped outside the hotel now.

Fire rises in her eyes after she sees the headline. "Please tell me you didn't. Lie, if you must. I've been here for months, and no one knew. In one stupid move, you messed it up!"

"I didn't, not exactly," Cole replies. "I didn't tell the reporters your whereabouts. Someone must have leaked my purchase, followed me from the airport, or both. As far as the engagement rumor, it's why I'm here." He pulls a velvet box from his pocket and starts to kneel before her.

"Don't," she warns.

Shocked, he pauses halfway down and rises back to his full height.

"How could you? We aren't dating. You're a booty call." Rachel charges toward him.

I surround her waist with my arm and haul her tightly against me. "Relax. I'll handle him and figure out how to get you out of here safely in the morning." My words are low and only for her to hear.

She drops her head. I twist and set her on the floor, keeping my body between them. "Rachel, please sit." I face Cole and point. "You, go take a seat over there, away from the window." I pull out my phone and dial Jake.

"Yeah, Nolan."

"I need Madeleine's media relations guru."

"What's your plan?" Jake asks.

"First, I'm going to get Mr. Foster out of this room. Then, I'm going to contact the PR lady and get a statement started."

"Solid plan. I sent some backup. He'll arrive in the next twenty minutes."

"Who?"

"Ian owns and operates Outback Security. Our units were attached when I was deployed. Use him to get Mr. Foster out of the building. I sent a headshot so you know who to expect."

"Okay."

"What else can I do?"

"Determine if she needs a new hotel for the next week or so."

"On it. I'll text you the number as soon as I have it."

Ending the call, I turn toward Rachel. She hasn't moved, other than to bring her toned legs up to her chest and clasp her arms around them.

"I never meant for any of this to happen. What do you suggest?" Cole asks me.

One glance at the television confirms my suspicion about the press.

"Now you care," she states, disdain dripping from her words.

"You need to leave and preferably take the reporters outside the hotel with you. My boss called in a favor. Ian from Outback Security will be arriving within twenty minutes. He'll escort you from the building. I suggest you find somewhere to stay this evening while we wait."

Cole scowls and drops onto the couch. "What do you plan on saying in this statement?" His question is for Rachel.

"The truth, Cole. Whoever this public relations woman is will release a statement indicating you and I were dating but we aren't any longer."

"That's all?"

"I may not want to be with you anymore, but I have class, Cole. I won't hash out the details of our failed engagement and this grand gesture you created for publicity."

Cole is stunned speechless for a few minutes before he mutters, "Thank you."

My phone vibrates with a text containing a number for Celeste Bronstein. I click the link and reach out. Within ten minutes of her answering, I share the situation and the parameters of the statement Rachel requests.

Celeste replies, "I'll send you a draft within the hour."

When I end the call, Rachel turns her gaze to me. "Nolan, can I have your phone?"

"Why?"

"I need to fire my agent."

I hand over my phone and wait for backup to arrive. Ian arrives, and I thank him for the assist. He escorts Cole out of the room without as much as a look back at Rachel. I take a seat and wait for the latest draft of Celeste's statement. Rachel releases her statement, nearly an exact replica of her words to Cole earlier. We exit the lounge and go directly to her suite.

"Need anything else?" I ask at the adjoining threshold.

"No. Maybe. You don't happen to know an amazing talent agent, do you?"

I smile. "In fact, I do. I can get you her number. Then you can decide for yourself."

"Great. How do you know her?"

"She's marrying one of my bosses soon."

"Perfect. If she's anything like Celeste, she's hired."

I laugh and jot down Madeleine's phone number. "You'll get her assistant, Simon. He's an amazing gatekeeper. Be sure to tell him I referred you to get past him."

"Thanks, Nolan... for everything."

"You're welcome. Let's get some sleep before filming tomorrow."

Luckily, Cole's exit was filmed, and we aren't forced to change hotels. The movie wraps up a few days later, earlier than expected. Now we're on our way home.

CHAPTER TWELVE

MAIA

I should be sleeping, but instead I'm anxiously awaiting a text from Nolan. He's scheduled to be home sometime late this evening. What that means, I'm not sure.

Near one, I drag myself into my bedroom and plug in my phone. Over seven hours later, my backup alarm startles me awake. Crap, I'm going to be late. *Ugh!* I was never late until the bean. I rush out the front door toward the office for our weekly meeting. Halfway to the office, I realize Nolan hasn't texted yet.

With a few deep breaths, I park in the lot, step into the office, and quietly slip into the conference room. Aside from a sideways glance from Connor, no one mentions my tardiness. I lean against the wall until Jake shifts topics before taking the empty seat beside Alex, and she squeezes my forearm briefly. Alex and I listen for any pertinent information.

When the guys end the meeting, Alex drags me next door for coffee. She orders a massive triple-caffeinated vanilla latte, and I grab a boring cup of decaf.

"How are you feeling?" she asks.

"I'm good. We talked two days ago."

She shrugs. "I know. Are you free for girls' night this weekend?"

"Absolutely. It's been too long since the last one."

"What's wrong?"

"I haven't heard from Nolan. He was supposed to be back sometime last night."

"Delays happen, Mai."

"I know in my head, but my ultrasound appointment is this afternoon. We're looking forward to learning the gender of our baby... together. I also know filming wrapped early. This delay is long."

"He'll get there in time."

I sigh and take a sip of my coffee. "How are Jordan and Reese?"

Alex's smile widens. "They're amazing." Her eyes shift to her gorgeous engagement ring.

"How is the adoption coming along?" Alex insisted on adopting Reese officially.

"We're waiting for the papers to be approved by the court."

"I'm crazy happy for you, all of you."

"Thanks. What time is your appointment?"

"Three."

"Please let me know what color I need to buy as soon as you know, 'kay?"

I smile at her. "I will. Don't you need to get to the gym?"

"Yeah. I do. Love you, Mai."

"Love you too, Alex." She hurries out the main door, and I clear our nearly empty cups. Before leaving, I browse the kid's section and grab a few classics for our baby's library, including *Goodnight Moon* and *Corduroy*. I checkout and cross the street to Millie's to pick up my order.

I return home and tug on some workout gear. With the nugget measuring close to the size of a bell pepper, my belly has rounded. An easy jog will help pass some time and maybe clear my head. With the pace set at five, I pound my feet on the belt. I finish a few miles before slowing down to a walk. When I'm finished, I climb the stairs, sipping from a bottle of water, and take a shower.

Freshly dressed, I prepare a light lunch. I resist the urge to text Nolan. He said he would be here, and I'm sure he's doing his best. The bigger issue is I miss him. I miss my best friend and can't wait for him to be home. A few months is a long time for an assignment. Also, the distance between here and there hasn't truly allowed for conversations about our future together or our child and how it'll work.

Resigned Nolan won't make it here before my appointment, I lock up and drive to Dr. Flagstone's office. Pushing away my brewing anger, I park and head inside.

"Hi, beautiful." His voice surrounds me like a warm blanket. Nolan is leaning against the wall near the office.

Beautiful. I'm surprisingly cool with the endearment coming from him. "You're here!" I throw my arms around him and kiss him without thinking.

He kisses me back before adding some space and replying, "Wouldn't miss this for anything. You were nervous I wasn't going to make it?"

"Yeah. You didn't show for the meeting or call."

"There were delays and issues with the client. I'll share later." He opens the office door and then takes my hand in his.

Approaching the receptionist, I give her my name, "Maia Park." She passes a urine sample cup through the window.

Nolan frowns but takes a seat. The questions in his eyes are priceless.

I mouth, "I'll explain later," and disappear into the restroom. I leave the sample and sit beside Nolan. Without hesitation, he threads his fingers through mine. I catch his gaze and smile but don't say anything. Emotions are swirling through me. They make sense. However, the weirdness of them twisting and weaving around Nolan doesn't.

"Maia," a young nurse calls.

We rise and follow her into the room. She instructs me to disrobe from the waist down and informs us the doctor will join us in a few minutes.

Dr. Flagstone arrives not long after. "Maia, lovely to see you. You must be Dad." She extends her hand to Nolan. "Pleasure to meet you. We're going to take some information and get some new photos of the baby. Are you interested in learning the gender?"

I hear her speaking, but my focus is on Nolan. He pulls the chair closer beside the bed and threads our fingers before kissing the back of my hand. I'm so enraptured in his gaze, I don't notice she's waiting for a response to her final question.

"Would you like to know the gender of your baby?" she asks again.

"Yes," we reply in unison.

She squeezes the gel onto my abdomen and directs us to the screen. "There's baby."

I have no idea what I'm actually looking at, except to say our baby is perfect. Nolan kisses me lightly. The doctor pushes buttons on the machine and makes notes in my chart. I'm staring at the screen, mesmerized. I won't say it didn't feel real before, but now....

Dr. Flagstone hands Nolan a strip of images she took from the ultrasound.

"To end the suspense, you're having a boy," she shares.

Nolan squeezes my hand.

"On your way out, you'll make your next few appointments, and Sammie will provide you with a schedule of lab work and a bunch of information. Please continue with the prenatal vitamins. As stated before, you can continue your normal exercise for the most part. The basic rule is, if you're comfortable, your baby is too."

"Thank you."

"Please don't hesitate to call with questions. Congratulations!" she states as she leaves the room.

Sheer elation is coursing through me. I sit up, slide off the table to the floor, and redress. Nolan is staring at the strip of images in his hands. I have only seen that look on his face twice before. Once when I agreed to be with him at the party, and when I shared about our child in Australia. I'm confident in the depths of my soul no other woman has seen that look aimed at them. I set my hand on his forearm and squeeze.

"Ready?"

He nods. When he finally looks at me, I see the tears welled up in his eyes as he fights to hold them back. One escapes down his cheek, and I wipe it away with my fingertips. "I wouldn't want to do this with anyone else."

A few minutes later, he's composed and ready to leave. I make my next few appointments and stop at the restroom on the way out.

When I return, he asks, "Are you busy right now?"

"No, why?"

"I haven't been to the lab for the DNA test yet."

"Will we make it in time?"

He wrinkles his brow. "In the medical building down the street? Yeah, we'll make it."

A chuckle bubbles up. "Of course." Hand in hand, he walks me back to my car. As I get into the driver's seat, I see Norah exiting her car and heading into Dr. Flagstone's office. I smile, start my car, and follow him to the medical building. Repeating the same rough procedure, he gives his name, and we wait for an available room.

"How are you feeling about this?" I ask.

"This? The test… not worried about the test."

"Worried if it's the right decision?"

He shakes his head. "I know it's the right decision. The repercussions could be heavy though."

Leaning closer, I whisper, "We can handle anything that comes our way." I press a kiss to his cheek and lower back into my chair.

His hand hovers over my small bump as if he doesn't have the right to touch me. I suppose we haven't set any boundaries since this is the first time we've been in the same zip code. Covering his hand with mine, I lower it to my belly.

"Have you felt him kick yet?"

I shrug. "Maybe. Sometimes I feel a rolling sensation, but nothing hard like a kick yet. You will be the second person to know… well, third."

A nondescript white door opens to the left. "Nolan," a worker calls his name.

He offers me his hand and escorts me to the room. Nolan guiding me through a door isn't new, yet this time feels different.

The staff member verifies his information and explains the test. Once she swabs his cheek and packages the sample, she asks if he has any questions.

"Yes. Does the order indicate if the other sample has been received?"

She taps a few commands into the computer system and answers, "Yes, it has been received."

"Thanks. How long for the results?"

She looks between us. "Three to five business days."

"Thank you." We exit the room and walk to our cars. "Takeout and a movie?"

"Sure," I answer.

"Any preference or place to avoid?"

Awww. He's so sweet to me. "No, no weird cravings or aversions yet. Whatever you want is fine."

Forty minutes later, we're curled up in front of the television with our huge order from a local Italian place with *A Few Good Men* playing on the screen. A strange sense of awkwardness settles in the narrow space between us on my couch. Ignoring it isn't the right choice.

"Why is this weird?" I ask, setting down my fork.

"You feel it too?"

I turn, bending my knee between us on the cushion. "Yes."

"I can only answer from my perspective. There's a bunch of layers to us now. There were before, but we haven't truly had time face-to-face to talk." He drags his hands through his hair, which is longer than usual, like he does when he is frustrated. "I'm not explaining myself well."

"Start with one layer, whichever one you prefer."

He shifts into the corner of the couch and hauls me into his lap. Despite our little nugget, being in his lap is a new experience. It feels fantastic to have his arms around me while we navigate this tough conversation. He takes a settling breath and presses a kiss to my temple. Stifling the goose bumps is impossible, and I'm sure he doesn't miss them. He never has before.

"There isn't a right order, Nolan."

He closes his eyes and then meets mine. "Okay, in no particular order, my mother still hasn't returned my attempts to speak with her. It pisses me off. I was fine not knowing the truth until we were together. The fact we're having a child now increases my need to have closure, sort of. I don't want closure as far as not having a relationship with the senator. I need to confront my mother and Michael to some extent and make choices about how much or how little I want them in my life. Blaine's file doesn't shed any light on my mother's culpability. I need to line everything up to move forward with you properly."

"I understand. If I were in your position, I would want the same thing."

He shakes his head and buries it into my shoulder. "I don't deserve you. Either of you."

I twist to look at him more fully before replying, "You're completely wrong. You deserve to be happy and have a family. Would you think yourself undeserving if you didn't know about your parents' affairs?"

He pulls back and looks at me. "How do you always know what I need to hear?"

A smile tugs at the corner of my lips. "I know you as well as I know myself."

"You do. No, I probably wouldn't think I'm undeserving."

"Don't let their shortcomings and choices dictate your feelings or decisions. What are you afraid of?"

"You make me feel invincible. It's one of the things Michael mentioned as a reason he cheated on my mother. I refuse to disrespect you in that way."

"So don't."

"I'm terrified about how I feel about you."

"You think I'm not? I'm carrying our child, Nolan. One who was created when we decided to give our love a chance. A child who deserves both of us."

He sets his fingers under my chin and draws me closer. The heaviness of his stare is impossible to miss. His lips skim across mine softly. Despite how light his kiss is, the depth of the words he isn't speaking is unfathomable. The speed ramps up slowly. Our tongues tangle before he nips along my jaw and down the curve of my neck. He continues down, tugging my shirt as low as it will go.

"Are these bigger?"

I giggle. "Of course you would notice."

"I notice every tiny detail about you, always have."

"Like?"

He wrinkles his nose and mumbles, "Bigger breasts."

I shake my head. "Not now, I mean overall."

"Well, they are bigger."

"Not sure I get to keep them. Seriously, though. What details?"

He smiles at me, the kind of smile that settles to the bottom of my heart, and all the jokes fall away. "You have a group of freckles behind your left ear shaped like a heart. You always make sure the kids are safe. I'm not sure you know you're doing it. Whenever Ben, Amara, or Liz get close to danger, you redirect them. You're the most determined woman I've ever had the pleasure to call my best friend."

"Nolan…." Unintentionally, his name sounds like a plea.

He hears it as one and lifts my shirt overhead. His mouth travels over the swell of my larger and more sensitive breasts. The caress of his lips sends prickles of pleasure skittering to my core. With each tender touch, nip, or sweet kiss to my hot skin, pressure builds.

"Can we?" He lifts his eyes to mine.

I giggle softly. "Didn't research thoroughly?"

Surprise then realization crosses his face. Realization that I know his penchant for researching each topic completely, knowing he would worry, and knowing he's always prepared.

I answer him. "Yes. Bare."

Nolan's stare intensifies. "I never… never—"

"Me either."

We peel the layers of clothes between us off without further hesitation. He guides me to my back on the couch and worships each inch of exposed skin with his mouth and hands. My fingers are threaded into his soft hair while he worships my body. Each nip he moves lower, pausing when he's over my belly.

He doesn't say anything, but a wash of emotions plays on his face when he meets my stare again. After a brief pause, he continues kissing over the top of my leg and then up my inner thigh. Lifting my hips, he shoves a pillow beneath me and drags the flat of his tongue from bottom to top.

"Holy hell!"

He laughs softly. "I haven't done anything yet."

"Lies!"

Rather than reply with words, Nolan rests on the cushions and lavishes attention on my core. He alternates between slow, languid strokes to furious teases of my clit until stars explode behind my eyes.

Panting and reveling in the aftershocks, I reach down to drag him up. "I want you. I need you buried inside me."

The gravity of my words has him hesitating momentarily. Sitting back on his heels, he repositions me in his lap with my legs hooked around his waist. I hover over him as he aligns himself with my center. In excruciatingly slow increments, I sheath him with my body.

Speechless. The angle and depth are more than ever before.

"Holy fuck! We feel…. I need you to move, sweetheart."

As I plunge downward, he meets with a thrust from underneath. The rhythm sets scintillating spikes of bliss cascading through me.

"Nolan." His name falls from my lips as my climax spirals downward from the base of my spine.

His body tightens as his release bears down on him. Overwhelmed with throbbing pleasure, my inner walls convulse around him as I careen over the edge. The corded muscle of his chest stretches as he explodes inside me.

When our breathing regulates, we stumble to the guest bathroom to clean up. Returning to the living room, I tug the blanket from the back of the couch over us and face him. "What else do you want to talk about?"

"Well, we've covered two layers already."

"Two?"

"Yeah, my family and what our relationship looks like."

"Having sex answers that question for you?"

"Absolutely."

"Hardly."

Shock appears on his face. "You do want to raise our son together, right?"

"Yes. How does that automatically include sex?"

"Incredible sex. You forgot the word 'incredible.'"

I scowl at him only because he's right. It is incredible. Bare is exponentially better.

"Let me be perfectly clear. I want a relationship with you. I want to raise our son and any future children together. In short, you're stuck with me forever."

"When did you change your mind?" I murmur softly.

"I didn't. Asking for additional time was never about me not wanting you or our son. It was about making sure I'm ready to be the man you deserve and capable of being an amazing dad. I tried to use the space and time I requested, but I failed miserably to stay away, which you already know. Honestly, Rachel helped a bit too."

I raise an eyebrow at him. "Knowing you were with her drove me crazy with jealousy."

"I was never with her, not like that. A friendly ear and occasional meal companion so we weren't eating alone. As you know, she was having issues with her booty call."

"Cole Foster?"

"Yup. I asked her if she wanted to be more than that with him, and her answer was a flat, harsh 'no.' Cole was a booty call. You and I are miles beyond that. We're best friends who know nearly every detail about one another. We need to put the pieces together and move forward."

"How do we get there?" I whisper. I'm terrified we aren't equipped for the long haul—a notion I've never shared with Nolan.

"The answer is up to us, isn't it?" Nolan tugs me closer.

"Yes. Where do we start?"

He looks at me and then away for a moment. He's contemplating. "Do you want to stay here or look for a house? I mean, this condo is great, and the rooftop patio is exceptional, but it isn't a yard. There also isn't a park nearby."

"I'm open to looking for a house. That would lead to talking about work."

His face turns serious. "Other than asking not to be on assignment at the same time, what do you mean?"

"While true, we would need the bosses to buy in and ensure one of us is home to care for our child. Or do I need to find another job? What though? When my parents left, I did what I needed to do to survive. Did I have dreams when I was a child? Of course."

Nolan draws me as close as possible and presses a kiss to my forehead before asking, "What did you want to be?"

I suppose my aspirations were one thing we never discussed. We discussed my previous jobs but not a potential profession. "A preschool teacher."

"Do you want to go back to school? Do you need to?"

"Yes. No. Maybe. I don't know."

"Breathe, beautiful."

As I inhale deeply, my belly rolls and I feel butterflies. Then my stomach flip-flops.

"Did he kick?"

A single tear rolls down my cheek. "Yeah, I think so."

Nolan snakes his hand between us and sets it on my belly. It doesn't take long for us to feel our son move again. It's magical. We silently enjoy the moment in silence before turning in with a promise to continue our conversation and planning tomorrow.

CHAPTER THIRTEEN

NOLAN

Slipping out of bed is easier than I anticipated. While I would prefer to stay wrapped around Maia in bed all day, she needs to eat. I'm not surprised at the scarce choices in her fridge. Rather than do a large order of groceries each week or every other week, Maia picks up items for one or two days. With the limited options in her fridge, I prepare a frittata with ham and loaded with veggies with a side of toast. As I finish, she's padding toward the kitchen. Her hair is mussed, and she's wearing my shirt, which lands midthigh. I'm overprotective considering she's carrying my son, but my shirts amp up the possessiveness.

"Morning." While this isn't the first time I've woken up with Maia, it's the first time at home in the course of our everyday life.

"Morning. You cooked?"

"You know I can cook and cook well."

"True, but I don't have appropriate ingredients for you."

I kiss her cheek and set a cup of decaf coffee beside her, perfectly prepared. It dawns on me in this moment, Rachel was right. I know a lot about Maia from being friends first. It'll help me woo her properly. She may not realize it, but it's going to happen, soon and properly. "You're right, you didn't. I think breakfast is still edible."

She smiles at the plate I place in front of her. With her fork poised to dig in, she asks, "Are you joining me?"

"Definitely." I set a second plate out and round the island.

We eat in silence for a few moments.

"Do you want to talk more?" she asks.

"About?"

"Everything."

"What's the first topic for today?"

"Although it feels backward because we're already going to have a baby—"

I set down my fork, swivel on the stool, and set my hand on her thigh. "Maia."

Her gaze meets mine, and she continues, "Can we start dating?"

I smile at her and try not to laugh. I fail miserably.

She frowns—a rare sight, especially aimed at me. "I'm serious, Nolan."

"We may not have called hanging out 'dates,' but we have done all the things couples do without a label for the past three years. For example, Friday movie night, football Sundays, and our weekly trips to Millie's can be considered dates."

She shrugs, then says, "I guess you're right," and quickly returns to her plate.

"Maia."

"Hmmm?" She doesn't turn her head. The pain in her eyes is evident.

"Please look at me."

Her body doesn't move, only her head twists in my direction. "It's fine." She waves me off and returns her gaze to her food.

I grab her fork, set it down, and then grip her hips. Digging my fingers into her, I swivel the stool, making her face me. "Do you know why I started calling you 'beautiful'?"

Her head moves incrementally left and right, once.

"Your name Maia Linh means 'beautiful soul' in Vietnamese."

Her voice sounds strangled as she manages, "You googled the meaning of my name?"

"Yes… on the day we met. Well, your first name the day we met. I checked your middle name later. I knew then you were going to be special to me. Although, it took me too long to confess to you. To answer your question, I will plan one—" Jake's ringtone breaks our conversations. I mouth, "Sorry," to her. "Yeah, Jake?"

"I know you returned yesterday, but are you willing to take a short assignment this weekend?"

"Where, how long, and for who?"

"Atlanta. The album launch event is Saturday evening. The client is Estelle. She signed with Scala Talent last week and needs a new security team."

"Yes, I'll take it. Please send me the itinerary."

"Will do. Thanks, Nolan."

I end the call and continue where I left off. "I'll plan our first official date for next weekend."

Giddiness like I've never seen before passes over her. "Really?"

"I meant what I said, beautiful. I'll give you and our son everything you need as long as you'll allow me to."

Maia leans forward and presses her lips to mine. It's a light and sweet kiss, but it doesn't diminish the fire coursing through me.

As I pull her closer, the doorbell chimes. "To be continued." I bound down the stairs, expecting Alex on the other side of the door. Instead, I'm faced with… "Mother, what are you doing here?" I hope Maia hears me and scurries into the bedroom. Although, I don't plan on inviting her inside.

"Well, you've been calling, and here I am."

"A return call would've been sufficient."

She points her crooked, manicured finger at me. "Stop digging."

I frown at her. "How did you know I was here?"

"You live here."

Not yet, I don't. Shivers run down my spine. Is she watching Maia? For what reason? "Mother, what do you mean 'stop digging'?"

"You think you're the only person with access to a private investigator because of your job and who your boss is. Not only do I have connections but money as well, lots of it. Stop searching for answers. You're never going to find them."

"Who are you protecting? Me, Lara, or yourself? You forget I read the agreement. I'm your deepest, darkest secret. One of them at least. Are there more? It's the only reason Michael isn't forcing me to fall in line like

Lara. Sharing the truth will set me free but handcuff you to your husband. You might even need to come clean to Lara."

"Don't you dare tell her the truth." Venom laces her words.

"Which part?"

"Any of it."

Is my hunch correct? Is Lara Michael's daughter? "What I choose to share with my sister is between me and her."

"You wouldn't dare divulge this information to your sister." Her words are cold and calculating but seething with anger as well.

"Nothing to stop me."

"I'll stop you."

I literally laugh. "You can't do anything worse to me than you've already done. You kept my true parentage from me and convinced me to stay silent. The only thing you haven't done is throw money at me to buy my silence. Don't bother trying. I've been on my own for the last seven years. I don't need or want money from you. Prepare yourself, Mother. I have no reason to stay quiet. Nor do I plan to. I never did other than some misplaced sense of loyalty to you."

"You'll ruin me." She steps closer to me.

"You and your marriage are not my concern. I need to live my life for me and my future. Please leave and don't come back." Slowly, I start to close the door.

She grips the doorframe with her hand. "Don't do this! Leave it alone. He doesn't know about you."

"You missed your window to be honest years ago."

"What about you? When did you plan to share that I'm going to be a grandmother?"

"Goodbye, Mother."

Her hand slides away, and I latch the door. How does she know about my son? I take the stairs in two steps, grab my phone from the island, and hustle upstairs to find Maia. After drawing her into my arms, I call Jake.

He answers immediately. "Yeah, Nolan?"

"I might have a problem. My mother showed up at Maia's condo." Not hers exactly, but that isn't important right now. "She said sharing the information would ruin her. Honestly, I don't care about the threat. She knows where Maia lives. How? She knows Maia is pregnant. How? I certainly didn't tell her. Only you, Connor, Christoph, and Alex know, besides the doctor."

"I'll put Blaine on it. Come to the office tomorrow. I'll have new phones for both of you. In the meantime, change your email passwords, both personal and work. Maia, too."

"Will do," I reply and end the call.

"Want to talk or sit?" she asks.

"Sit." I gather her against me and lower us to the rattan couch.

She wraps one arm around my back and curls into me deeper. The only aspect of this that is abnormal or new, I suppose, is I want to strip off her clothes and explore her body. Before our weekend together, my raging hard-on would've gone unnoticed or at least unmentioned. We sit in the quiet for almost twenty minutes.

"I wasn't sure if I should join you at the door," she mumbles against my neck.

I press a kiss to the top of her head before I reply, "I'm glad you didn't. If you did, it wouldn't have tipped me off she's watching me... us. Were you close enough to hear her?"

Maia shakes her head. "No, as soon as I heard who was at the door, I came up here."

I nod and continue. "She didn't mention the DNA test, but she must know about it. But how?"

"Blaine will find the leak."

"I know. What are your plans for the rest of the day?"

"I don't have any."

"Do you have any assignments coming up?"

She smiles. "I'm joining Madeleine on her interviews tomorrow. She has meetings with four potential clients."

I frown. "Why does she need security?"

"Normally, Christoph goes with her. After the incident with Miss Goldberg, Jake has been leery sending me anywhere. It keeps me working, and Madeleine still has the appearance of security. I'm sure Christoph likes to spend his day with her, but it isn't necessary anymore. I appreciate the accommodation."

"Truth be told, I do too. I know you're capable, but my need to protect you increased the second I felt him move. I'm sure you think that's silly."

"No, I don't. Until recently, we haven't been together for you to see the changes in my body and my ability to take a risk for a client. Our bosses are family, and given the scare, they're adjusting to protect our little guy as much as me."

"Would you be upset if I moved in here until we find a home?" Deep down, my request is more about possessiveness and fear my mother will return.

"I can take care of myself, Nolan. Sharon doesn't scare me."

"I know you can, but it doesn't prevent me from freaking out."

"I would love for you to move in. The only thing you truly do at the bunkhouse at this point is sleep and dress. It's been that way since I moved here. I mean Lane, Finn, Callan, and Sawyer are great, but I'm awesome."

He grins at me. "True. I'll work on bringing my clothes tomorrow. We should finish our conversation we started about your job yesterday."

"Nothing really to talk about right now. I'm going to talk to Jill this weekend. She may have some insight or a lead for me. Plus, I'm going to do some research and truly consider going back to school in the fall for my degree. Is that something we could pull off?"

"We'll figure it out."

"Why don't you go downstairs and run off some anger?"

"I can think of a better way to expend my energy."

"Oh really?"

"Yes. You interested?"

"Hell yes!"

I set her on her feet and follow her downstairs as she strips off the limited clothing she has on as she goes.

CHAPTER FOURTEEN

MAIA

Parking in front of Christoph's home, I adjust my clothes. Thankfully, Madeleine, Callie, and Norah have extensive maternity wardrobes and graciously allowed me to borrow the items I needed. To be fair, as much as Madeleine's suits and dresses are gorgeous, she possesses generous curves that I sadly lack.

"Morning, Maia," Christoph greets me at the front door.

"Hi, Mai." Liz peeks around his legs.

Squatting down her level, I say, "Hi, Liz. How are you?"

She twists her hand as if to say "so-so."

I giggle softly, and Liz joins me. Then she steps around Christoph and hugs me.

"Let's go inside and get Mommy," Christoph suggests.

Liz grabs my hand and tugs me inside. Christoph and Madeleine purchased this dilapidated farmhouse and the attached farm. They renovated the main house for themselves. When the company added the gym and client training to the services we offer, Christoph and Jake updated the cottages at the rear of the property for clients to use while they're training.

Madeleine sweeps into the kitchen, perfectly coifed and ready to go. Her perfection isn't annoying like most similar women. It's who she is, a professional powerhouse in a male-dominated field. She's the president of Scala Talent and Sports Management, and she's damn good at it. "Morning, Maia. How are you feeling?"

"Morning. Pretty good, thank you."

"*Anamchara*, Jack's here," Christoph informs her. The endearment means "soul mate" in Gaelic. Jack, her driver, moved from New York City when she moved her home base to DC.

"I'm ready." She lifts Liz, kisses her cheeks, and hands her to Christoph, who kisses her softly, then shoos us out the door.

"Morning, almost Mrs. Anderson." Jack is an older gentleman, and I surmise former military or law enforcement given his posture and the way he carries himself. Plus, Christoph coaxed him here to be her driver.

Madeleine smiles widely. "Morning, Jack. Have you met Maia?"

"Yes, we've met. Nice to see you again, Miss Park."

"You as well. Please call me Maia."

He replies, "I'll try. Miss Wilton has been trying to get me to call her Madeleine for years." Jack closes the rear door and settles into the driver's seat.

"Time to share, Maia. How are things going with Nolan?"

"Okay, good, and incredible." Normally, I would wait until girls' night, but Madeleine can't attend.

"Now you must tell me. Start with the okay and go from there."

"The okay is more with him not us. There are some issues with his family. It isn't my information to share, but he feels it's necessary to deal with it before the baby arrives."

"I understand. It isn't news now, but when we learned about Collin, only Jake was aware." Collin is Christoph's younger brother. He didn't know about him until a year ago.

"I met him at the summer celebration at the farm. Is he still at Fort Meade?"

"Yeah. He visits Betty, Christoph, and Liz whenever he has leave. What about you and Nolan as a couple?"

I attempt to hide my smile. "We have a bunch of things to work out, like where to live and whether or not I should get a new job. Please don't say anything to Christoph. I'm still mulling my options. It's a lot to ask the guys to make sure at least one of us is home for the baby. Plus, our little surprise made us have some hard conversations. The main theme that keeps popping up is… I want Nolan. Apparently, the two of us have been pining for one another separately for some time."

"Ooooh, that means the incredible is—"

"Yes, the sex is absolutely the incredible."

"Block your ears, Jack," she instructs.

"Did you say something, Miss Wilton?" he replies with a wink.

"While my experience is sparse, no one comes close to how Nolan makes me feel."

"Unrequited feelings seem to combust into an inferno, or so I'm told."

I laugh. "The stares you and your future husband shared nearly set the room ablaze at Callie's wedding."

Madeleine's face turns bright red.

"No need to be embarrassed. I mean, you are marrying him in a few weeks."

"Best decision I ever made was asking him back to my hotel that night."

"Flying to Australia may very well be the same thing for me."

"Have you and Nolan talked about marriage?"

I shake my head. "Sort of. We've talked about it in the abstract with other people. What I mean is, we both want to get married but wanted to do it before having children. I don't see us pulling a wedding off before our son is born." Immediately, I cover my mouth with my hand.

"A boy! How exciting? Was it supposed to be a secret?"

I shrug. "I guess not, Nolan knows, and we aren't doing a gender reveal or anything like that."

"I won't share. You could always elope. I've considered running away with Christoph numerous times in the last few weeks. Planning a huge wedding, continuing to kick ass for my clients, and rocking my mom duties is a lot."

"Did you want a small wedding?"

"Not really. My clients are family to me, and they want to be present equally as much as I want them there. I made it clear no work would be discussed once I clock out the day before and until we return from our child-free-honeymoon nearly two weeks later. My second-in-command, Valencia Halden, and Simon can handle anything one of them throws at them in my absence."

"Simon is a hoot."

Madeleine smiles as Jack pulls into the driveway of her office building. He pulls the car along the sidewalk and opens the rear door. "Have a wonderful day, Miss Wilton and Miss Park. "

"Thanks, Jack," we reply in unison and head inside.

"Good morning, Miss Wilton and Miss Park. Here are your packages that arrived after Mr. Dumont this morning," the receptionist greets us.

I accept the packages and thank her.

"Please call before showing Mr. King, Mr. Fleming, Mr. Cappelli, or Miss Kimball to the conference room," Madeleine requests.

"I will. Have a lovely day."

Madeleine breezes past the desk and power walks to her office. "Hi, Simon."

"Morning, Mads. Hi, Maia. You're especially glowy today."

"Thanks, Simon." I appreciate he hasn't guessed or surmised about my pregnancy. It makes me like him more. Then again, Simon is the epitome of perfection and class as far as personal assistants are concerned. In fact, it wouldn't surprise me if congratulatory flowers arrive at my condo tonight after I return.

We enter her cozy but professional office, and Madeleine busies herself with her email. I take a seat on the couch and open my laptop. I peruse the homes available in the area until her first appointment arrives.

Lucia, Madeleine's junior assistant, shows Cian Fleming and a frail girl into the conference room. If I had to guess, she's probably eight. He's an Irish-born *futébol* player for the New England regional soccer team. He fired his agent when the contract negotiations were not going smoothly after his trade from a Florida-based team.

"Mr. Fleming, it's a pleasure to meet you." Madeleine extends her hand to him. "And you are?"

"Penny, short for Penelope. It's nice to meet you, Miss Wilton."

She's clearly attended one of her father's business meetings before. Her manners are on point.

"Do you miss Florida?" Madeleine asks her.

"No. I like having seasons and snow on the ground in the winter. Plus, my new nurse is amazing."

Surprise materializes on Madeleine's face. "I see."

"It isn't really a secret. I have lymphocytic leukemia and transferred my treatments to Maine. Nurse Scarlett is awesome and doesn't care who my dad is. Kind of like you and her." Penny points in my direction.

"Hi, I'm Maia. It's nice to meet you. Would you like to sit over here and color or chat with me while your dad and Madeleine meet?"

She casts a look at her father who nods slightly. "Yes, thank you."

We shift to the far end of the conference room. For nearly an hour, we chat and decorate mandalas with colored pencils.

Mr. Fleming approaches after wrapping up with Madeleine. "Thank you, Maia."

"You're welcome. Penny is awesome."

A proud and sad smile graces his face. "She is."

After they leave, we grab a quick drink, and Madeleine immediately rolls into her next three meetings without stopping. I don't know how she pulled this off when she was pregnant with Liz. I'm exhausted, and I'm truly watching the door at this point.

After her final meeting of the day, Simon sweeps into her office with a coffee for Madeleine and chocolate for me.

"Thank you, Si. Can you call Jack, please? I'll be ready in about fifteen minutes."

"You're a rock star, Simon," I offer.

"Of course." He winks at me, sets down a water as well, and leaves.

"You must be tired. I forgot how draining office days are when you're not sleeping," Madeleine offers.

"How did you pull it off?"

She laughs. "Christoph and Simon culled my schedule as much as they could and added breaks between meetings without my consent. I appreciated the effort though."

"They're good guys."

"Yeah, they are."

We settle into the back of the car, and Jack drives us to Madeleine's. After a quick goodbye, I settle into my car and head home.

Nolan is waiting to open my car door as soon as I park in the garage. He offers me his hand and draws me into his arms. His soft lips settle on mine for a sweet kiss.

I could get used to this.

"How was your day, beautiful?" he asks after adding some space between us.

"Long and exhausting, but otherwise fine."

"I thought that might be the case. Do you want to shower or eat first?"

"You made dinner?"

"Yes. Did I overstep?"

My eyes flutter closed. "No, thank you. I'm not used to being taken care of, that's all."

"Start getting used to it. I'm in, all in."

"Okay. I would prefer to eat first, please."

"As you wish," he murmurs and leads me inside.

After a delicious dinner and relaxing shower, I fall asleep within minutes of curling up on the couch with Nolan.

A few days later, Nolan has left for his assignment with Miss Gomes. At first, I was upset. I mean, he's leaving again. However, we need to work, and it includes travel. Besides, now I won't feel badly about going to girls' night. We haven't had one in a few months.

With my drink of choice—pink lemonade—on the floorboard, I drive to the compound. Callie is hosting tonight. I input the code at the gate and park near the bunkhouse and walk up the hill.

The door flies open when I reach the top step. "Yay! You're here!"

"Hi, Jill. Am I late?"

"No. Javier is on assignment, so I had dinner with Norah and Jake." She ushers me inside.

"How is school?" Jill is a special education teacher at an elementary school.

"Pretty good. They've settled into the routine since holiday break. Before I leave, can we chat about the requirements for being a teacher or owning a daycare?"

"Sure. How are you feeling?"

"Better. Most of my morning sickness has passed."

"I wish," she mutters and immediately covers her mouth with her hands.

"Welcome to the pregnant club. I think there's another member in our group of friends as well." I offer.

"Me too. I'll let her share though."

Callie comes downstairs. "Hey, Maia. Thanks for getting the door, Jill. Sutton decided my shirt needed to be dirtier."

I giggle. "Where is she?"

"Connor is changing her, and then they will be out the door."

"How is your house so quiet with three babies under four living here?" Jill asks her.

Callie points toward the office behind me, which has been turned into a main floor nursery of sorts. "Amara and Myers fell asleep the moment I put them in their carriers to leave."

"I'll happily take any tips you may have," I add.

"Call anytime, Maia," Callie offers.

With a flourish, Connor loads up his children, kisses Callie, and he's gone. As he leaves, Norah and Alex step inside. We greet one another and take a seat in the living room with drinks and two charcuterie boards, one complete with crackers and cheeses and the second with sweets, including small truffles and miniature cheesecakes. Silence hangs over us as we dig into the platters.

"How are you feeling, Maia?" Alex whispers beside me.

"Much better."

Alex stares, waiting for me to share more.

"Spill, Maia. We want all the dirty details about you, Nolan, and the little nugget," Norah chimes in.

I huff, knowing full well the bonds of girls' night are sacred. Similar to the mantra "What happens in Vegas, stays in Vegas."

"I'm feeling much better. We're having a boy."

"You know we need more than that!" Callie says from behind the island in the kitchen.

"Nolan and I are working on us as a couple. The rest isn't mine to tell, and I won't violate his trust in me to share it with you despite how much I love each of you."

"Awww. Maia and Nolan sitting in a tree," Alex starts singing.

The room devolves into laughter.

I rebound, asking, "Anyone else have news to share?" I gaze toward Jill, then Norah, and back again until Jill breaks.

"We're having a baby too!"

Cheers erupt in the room to the point where we almost don't hear Norah add.

"Us too!"

"All these new additions are going to make Cruz weepy, especially his own," Callie suggests.

We laugh and continue to catch up for the next few hours. It doesn't seem like that long, but it is. The boards are clear, and our glasses have been emptied and refilled. As I make the rounds to say goodbye, I realize Jill and I haven't talked.

"Are you free tomorrow?" I ask, hugging her.

"Yes, want to come over for brunch at ten?" she offers.

"Sounds perfect! See you then." I make my way out the door and to my car. After silencing the alarm at the condo, I reset it and collapse onto the bed. I send a text to Nolan, knowing he's working, and go to sleep.

My phone wakes me the next morning.

Nolan: Hi, beautiful. I hope this doesn't wake you. I'll be home by dinner.

Me: Morning. It's good you texted. I'm going to be late.

Nolan: For?

Me: Brunch with Jill. See you later. xoxo.

I send the text before overthinking the x's and o's I added to the end. I should tell him I'm falling for him. Not true. I fell a long time ago and gave him my whole heart as well. Only he doesn't know… yet. Now and over the phone isn't the right time to share either. Rather than think about my message to Nolan, I jump out of bed and hurry through the shower.

Although I'm eating with Jill, I grab some fruit on my way out the door. The ride to their home isn't long. I park along the curb and ring the bell. Jill rushes to the door, opens it, and scurries away, her words, "Come in," trailing after her.

I laugh and close the door behind me. Their home is a cozy and gorgeous craftsman. Jill fixed it up herself with a bit of help from Jake. "Smells amazing, Jill."

"Thanks. Sit. I only need to plate this."

"A bagel would've been fine."

She smiles and slides a plate with colorful food in my direction, including eggs Florentine with toast, fruit, and some type of hash with sweet potato. "Eat."

I dig in and savor the first bite. "Ohmigod! This is delicious!"

"Thanks. I assume the topic of discussion for today is hush-hush."

I shrug and continue shoveling food into my mouth. It's that good. "You know before Blackthorne I was working a bunch of retail or food service jobs. When I was hired, I focused on the work here. Before that, I was in survival mode. Now—"

"Now you see an opportunity to become what you truly wanted to be… which is?"

"A preschool teacher."

"I can see that."

"Do I need a degree?"

Jill shakes her head and replies, "Not for preschool or daycare, but there are certifications you need to earn. You can do it while you're working though. If you want to be a teacher, then you need a bachelor's in education and then pass the exam."

"The reality is both of us can't be away on an assignment when the baby is born."

"Makes sense. Have you talked to Jake and the guys about this?"

"Not yet. I wanted to see what the options are first and then decide if I truly want to go to college right now on top of a new baby and looking for a house."

"I'm glad I don't have to do that with Javier."

"Honestly, I think Nolan will agree to any affordable house I choose. In that arena, we're simple. I never had more than I needed until Connor's rooftop. Nolan's requirements are fairly simple. He wants a nearby park and good schools. I would like a fenced yard. It doesn't need to be like the farm though."

Jill laughs. "My brother's property is gorgeous, but too much for me as well. Come to think of it, my neighbor passed away a few weeks ago. I'm sure his family is looking to sell his home. I can give you his son's contact info if you want."

"That would be great!"

The entry sensor for the front door chimes. "*Cariña*, I'm home," Cruz calls from the entryway.

Jill jumps off the stool, runs, and crashes into him. I take his arrival as my cue to leave.

I rinse my plate and put it in the dishwasher.

"Hi, Maia," Cruz greets me.

"Hey. I'll be on my way. Thank you for chatting with me, Jill. I would love the contact information when you get a chance." My only inclination when Nolan returns is to hurriedly remove his clothes, which is exactly my plans for later today. Cruz has just returned from an assignment. I'm sure Jill feels the same way as I do. "No rush on the phone number. Tomorrow or the next day will be fine."

Jill hugs me and laughs. "No problem."

I step outside and make my way home.

CHAPTER FIFTEEN

NOLAN

Another delay? This assignment has been nothing but issue after issue. Interestingly, it has nothing to do with our client. Outside forces are not falling into place and haven't for the past few days. Before stepping into a relationship with Maia, the hour of my arrival home never concerned me, not the length or the lateness when I arrived. Now I don't want to leave at all. On top of those issues, the results of the paternity test are sitting in my inbox. My self-control is off the charts. I refuse to open them until I'm home.

While I highly doubt Blaine is wrong, I can't pinpoint how well I'll handle the results. I need Maia beside me when I open them. Sitting back, I close my eyes and will this flight to land.

"Sir," a soft, feminine voice filters into my mind. "Sir."

I open my eyes and look up at her.

"The flight has landed. You can deplane now." She turns toward the back of the plane.

Reading between the lines, I interpret her meaning. *Get going I want to go home.* She doesn't need to tell me twice. I rise, grab my bag from the overhead compartment, and hustle down the carpeted aisle. Each step takes me closer to holding my woman and child in my arms. The rush of thinking about Maia as my better half and mother of our son never gets old.

The drive from the airport to the condo is about forty miles. I exceed the speed limit by enough to cut it down to thirty minutes. Pulling into the garage, I hurry inside, calling her name. She doesn't answer immediately. Bounding up the stairs to the roof, I find her curled up on the chaise with her book against her chest, sound asleep. My instinct is to run my hands over her from head to toe, but I refrain. Instead, I take a seat across from her and wait for her to wake.

Opening the reading app on my phone, I scan the pages while I wait. Maia has influenced me to learn to enjoy books more. It certainly helped when I found a few authors I love with the lending library at Norah's store. It's one of the many ways Maia makes me a better man. You would think with my uber-rich upbringing, reading would've been thrust upon me. Mother didn't care for me and my sister. Our nanny and the household staff raised us. It's the last thing I want for my child—hopefully children—with Maia. My attention returns to the book, and I dig into the story. While Maia prefers thrillers and a splash of romance, I lean toward military suspense. Almost an hour later, she greets me.

"Hi." Maia pushes up to sitting, setting her feet on the floor.

I set my phone on the ottoman, move beside her, and sweep my hand around her neck, drawing her closer. "I missed you so much."

"I missed you."

"Does it feel weird to say it out loud?"

She smiles at me, and it lights me up from the inside. Always has. "I shared my feelings without words every time you came home since we met."

I wrinkle my brow at her.

She continues, "What happened after every assignment before the party?"

I run through a few examples. Each time, the one of us returning has dinner with the one who was home. If we were on the same job, we grabbed takeout and shared it to spend time together. "We had dinner together each time."

"Yeah. I wanted to be with you and spend time with you. It wasn't the right time for us."

"It is now." My words are steady and forthright.

"Yes." Leaning forward, Maia eliminates the space between us and plants her lips on mine. At first her kiss is light and soft. Then it turns hard and greedy.

I consider giving in and stripping her clothes off up here but pull back instead. "As much as I want to continue this, we need to talk about a few things."

She pulls her lower lip between her teeth.

"Stop. You know what that does to me."

"I do." She winks and releases her lip. "Want to go first or second?"

"Ladies first."

Maia shares what she can about her time with the girls, including Norah's and Jill's pregnancies as well as her conversation with Jill earlier today.

"Do you want to go to college?"

"It would be a lot to handle at once, right? Plus, there are levels, I guess. I wouldn't need a bachelor's if I choose preschool instead of kindergarten."

"Maybe, but if you want to go back to school, you should. Whatever you want, we'll make it work."

"Really?"

"Of course. I understand why you didn't go before, as well as your reasons to choose a different career after our son is born. My only goal is for you to be happy."

"I'm happier than I've ever been with you and our son. These decisions are simply avenues to make our life together better. As long as we have you, I don't need anything else."

"I'm here and always will be. However, it may get harder before it gets easier."

"We can handle harder… together. What happened?"

I lift her into my lap and reach for my phone. "The results are sitting in my inbox."

"You didn't open them?" The concern in her voice is palpable.

"I needed to be with you to do it. I trust Blaine, and it's likely merely a confirmation, but—"

"It makes it real when you verify the results."

"Yeah. It'll confirm what my mother is and how I don't know where I came from."

"She may not have made the best choices and isn't a nice person for that matter, but she's your mom. How you handle the results is up to you."

"What would you do?"

She inhales sharply and kisses my lips lightly. "Leaving me here to fend for myself is unforgivable. I was a child, but I survived. Would I prefer my parents were alive and well even if I don't want a relationship with them? Yes, but it isn't an option. You may not have been left to fend for yourself, but you were in a different kind of survival mode. You can't wish your mother made different choices. The only people who matter are sitting on this couch."

I love you, Maia. The words run through my heart and mind, but I can't bring myself to say them aloud. Each person I've said those three words to have abandoned me in some way, except for Lara. Yet I know without any shred of doubt, I love Maia and have since the moment we met. After a deep, settling breath, I unlock my phone and scroll to the email containing the results.

Maia threads her fingers with mine, and I read through the words in front of me. The samples indicate specimen A is not excluded as the father to a percentage of 99.9 percent.

Confirmed. The senator is my father. Now what? So many questions swirl in my mind. Does Michael know? Is Lara his as well?

"What do you plan to do with this confirmation?" Maia asks softly.

"I want to get to know him and his wife. Start building a relationship with him if he's willing."

"Okay, and your mother?"

I pinch the bridge of my nose. "I'm angry and don't know what to do with it."

"Rightfully so. Whatever you decide, I'll be beside you."

"Thank you."

"What would you like to do in the meantime?"

I glance at my watch. It's too late to call. "I'll call in the morn—" The trill of my ringtone interrupts me. The caller ID shows Wentworth's number. "Good evening, Mr. Wentworth." I put my finger to my lips and use speakerphone.

"Mr. Dalton. I apologize for the late call, but the senator requested I reach out as soon as he read the results. Are you free to meet with him on Tuesday afternoon at his residence in DC?"

"Yes."

"Miss Park is welcome to join you."

"We'll be there. Please forward the information when you can."

"Will do. You're confirmed for Tuesday evening. The senator and his wife are looking forward to meeting you."

"As am I. Thank you, Mr. Wentworth."

I end the call and meet Maia's gaze.

"How does he know about me?"

"I agreed to a background check in addition to the paternity test. It doesn't surprise me his investigator is as good as Blaine."

Maia shakes her head. "Me either."

With questions still swimming in my mind, we head inside and to bed. Terror is a funny thing. I'm not afraid to meet him. However, the answers to some of my burning questions could alter my life exponentially.

As promised two days later, a car arrives precisely at three in the afternoon. My collared shirt feels like a vise around my neck.

"Deep breaths," Maia whispers as she threads our fingers together.

"Good afternoon, Mr. Dalton and Miss Park. I'm Jason."

"Good afternoon," I reply and guide Maia into the back seat of the town car.

Jason nods and closes the door behind me before retaking his seat. "The ride should be about forty minutes."

I shift in the seat and sidle closer to Maia.

"Do you want to change your mind?"

Linking our hands atop my thigh, I turn and whisper, "No. I need to this for us. For our son."

The ride passes wordlessly, but Maia draws circles with her thumb on the top of my hand. Not only is it soothing but a reminder of her presence. Fighting my feelings for Maia took monumental strength and fortitude. Now it takes the same attributes to fight for us.

Jason pulls in front of a gorgeous townhouse in Georgetown. The cobblestone walkway and stairs lead to an arched entryway. He escorts us to the door and rings the bell.

A gorgeous blonde wearing an emerald pantsuit answers the door. She's classy with little makeup and her hair skimming the top of her shoulders. I surmise she's Mrs. Phillips. "Mr. Dalton, Miss Park, please come in. Thank you, Jason." She ushers us inside. "Edward is running late. He should be here soon. Can I get you a beverage?" She pauses midway down the hallway, exposed brick on one side and a perfectly appointed living room with an ornate fireplace as the centerpiece of the room on the other. She turns to face us again. "I'm sorry. I skipped a step. I'm Sera. It's a pleasure to meet you both."

"You as well," Maia answers for us. "Please call us Nolan and Maia."

She leads us into a chef's kitchen with an expansive marble island and luxury appliances, including a droolworthy double burner range and oven.

"Your kitchen is amazing. Do you cook?" Maia asks.

Sera laughs. "Actually, Edward is the cook in our relationship. What would you like to drink?"

"Coffee for Nolan, and I'll take a water please."

I squeeze her hand in thanks. The opulence doesn't shock me, but Sera's ease with having me here is surprising. Immediately, I chastise myself for judging her.

We take a seat at the island, and she serves us. "What do you do for a living, Nolan?"

"I work in personal security."

"Wonderful, and you, Maia?"

"Same actually."

Sera wrinkles her eyebrow.

Maia continues, "I'm considering other options for after the baby is born."

Senator Phillips's arrival effectively ends the awkward conversation for now.

"Sera?"

"We're in the kitchen," she replies, effectively warning him to put on his game face.

Ugh! Stop judging them. He steps into the kitchen and promptly kisses his wife lightly on the lips. His stature strikes me. He's tall with dark hair that has hints of silver at his temples, and he's equally as fit as I am. Do I see a resemblance? Not sure.

"Mr. Dalton. Miss Park. Thank you for coming."

"We understand how delicate the situation is. The formality isn't necessary, Senator," I offer.

Sera sets a cup of coffee in front of him and takes a seat beside him.

"I'm sure you have questions, but if you would allow me to speak first, I would appreciate it." The senator requests.

"Of course," I reply.

"I'll give you some background. When we were in law school, Sharon and I dated for almost two years. She broke off our relationship within hours of meeting Michael Dalton, claiming she had been unfaithful to me with him."

The mere fact neither of my parents were faithful both during their marriage and during her relationship with the senator doesn't surprise me in the slightest.

He continues, "It's my understanding, Sharon had a daughter a few months after their wedding and prematurely."

"Yes, my sister, Lara."

Maia covers her hand with mine.

"I reached out to Sharon and requested proof of Lara's parentage. I was concerned your sister may be my daughter. Lara isn't my child. Three years later, Sharon and I ran into one another at an annual board of trustee's dinner for our law school. She indicated Michael filed for divorce because Lara isn't his daughter. Before you ask, I only know she isn't mine." Sera slides closer to her husband and links their hands on the white and gray Carrara marble.

I acknowledge his words by dropping my head slightly. It only begs the question: Who is Lara's father? *I need to tell her. I don't want her to marry Paul for the wrong reasons.*

"Fast forward about eight months, Sharon showed up at my office. She was distraught over her divorce close to being finalized. We had dinner, and she stayed in my guest room for a few days. We fell back into our old ways as far as intimacy, except we were careful. More careful than during law school, which is ironic, I know."

"She never told you about me?"

"No. I understand how difficult it must be to hear me disparage your mother."

I shake my head vehemently. "Not really. I believe you. Never once in my life do I recall a time when Sharon was honest with me or put me ahead of her own desires. She wasn't honest after I learned Michael isn't my father. In fact, she actively thwarted my attempts to learn about you. I'm surprised she didn't attempt to throw money at me to keep quiet." I pause and notice my hand is trembling.

Maia whispers, "You good?"

I kiss her temple and murmur near the shell of her ear, "Yeah. I need to do this for us." I turn my attention back to the senator. "I'm not here to ruin your chances of becoming president. I want to know you and your family, especially since we're starting our own." I raise Maia's hand to my lips and kiss the back.

"Congratulations to both of you," the senator states.

"Thank you. I'll do whatever is necessary. As painful as it may be knowing the truth, if you need me to stay away until after the election, I'll do it. If you choose to get ahead of the story, we're prepared for that as well. As I mentioned, Sharon and Michael do not know about this meeting. She attempted to get me to back off a few weeks ago, imploring me to stop digging. She admitted on our doorstep that you had no knowledge about me. Her reaction will likely be unpleasant for everyone involved, including your wife."

"My wife and I have no secrets, Nolan."

"I didn't mean to suggest you did. Sharon will go after who she perceives is the weakest link. She'll offer them money to keep my true parentage a secret. It wouldn't surprise me if she stooped to blackmail or coercion to get what she wants. She'll try Maia first and then your wife."

"Why does it matter to her at this point? You're a grown man who is about to become a father."

"It isn't about me at all. Sharon will see her dirty little secret and your candidacy coming out as an opportunity to smear you and make herself look like a victim."

"The victims are you and my husband, though," Sera adds with disdain in her voice. Her shoulders drop before she replies, "Mrs. Dalton has nothing to offer me."

The senator turns toward her. "I know, Sera. How about we talk to Weston and Abigail to get their opinions?"

Watching my father interact with his wife is strikingly similar to the Blackthornes and the Michelsons, including Jake and Connor. He's attentive and listens to her. His admission about secrets would lead me to believe they're honest and forthright with one another. Exactly how Maia and I are. My father and his wife are couple goals.

"If I may, who is Abigail?" I ask.

"Yes, sorry. Abigail Whitman is my campaign strategist and communications director," the senator replies.

"I appreciate your candor. If you feel she would be helpful, then by all means."

"Thank you. Would you be willing to join us for dinner? I would like to learn more about you and your life. I planned on preparing pasta carbonara if the menu matters."

"We would love to. It appears we have a love of cooking in common."

My father's—weird to say that, even in my head—smile widens. "Well, perhaps you should assist me. Sera is not a fan of the kitchen, a place I happen to love."

"Interesting, Maia agrees with her wholeheartedly."

"In that case, why don't the ladies refill your drinks and keep us company while we cook?"

"I'm in… after I use your restroom," Maia admits.

"It's down the hall, second door on the left," Sera directs her.

Over the next few hours, the four of us spend time getting to know the basics about one another while we enjoy the perfect carbonara.

"I'll reach out after I speak with Abigail, not only to share her thoughts but to plan another get-together," my father states as we walk toward the door.

"Sounds perfect."

"We would appreciate your discretion until we create a plan," he requests.

"Of course. I wouldn't have offered otherwise. Truly, I want to know you and your wife. I have no interest in anything else." It bears repeating.

Like Sharon, I'm confident the senator and his wife are well off. I refuse for him to believe his wealth and status are the only reason I'm seeking him out.

"It was a pleasure meeting you both," Maia states.

Sera moves in for a hug, and my father shakes her hand.

"Take care of her, Nolan," my father directs.

"I will."

Jason is waiting with the rear door of the car open.

"Good evening, Jason," Maia states.

"Miss Park, Mr. Dalton, good evening to you. The drive will be a bit shorter given the time."

Like our trip into the city, the ride home is eerily silent. I have so many things floating through my mind, I'm not sure where to start. Luckily, Maia knows me well. I'm a ponderer and need to organize my thoughts and emotions before hashing them out with her. She simply supports me in the quiet with her hand twined in mine.

CHAPTER SIXTEEN

MAIA

The next morning, I wake and find our bed empty. *Our.* It rings true in my mind. After the initial devastation of Nolan asking for time, I'm glad we're headed toward a family instead of only coparenting. Tugging his hoodie overhead, I pad into the kitchen, hoping to find Nolan. He isn't there. The coffee maker is warm, but the stove is cold. I listen at the top of the stairs for the treadmill but hear silence.

Water in hand, I climb the stairs to the roof and find Nolan with a notebook in his hand.

"Morning."

"Morning. Are you ready to talk now?"

He shrugs. "Yes and no. I'm floored by how last night went. He has every right to shun me to protect his family."

"You are his family, Nolan."

"True, but my existence could ruin his lifelong goals and dreams."

"You don't know how he feels, do you?"

"No, I don't. You're right."

Giddiness trickles through me. "Oooooh, say that again!"

He leans in and kisses me hard before adding, "You're right."

"Honestly… how are you feeling about meeting your father?"

He takes a few deep breaths. "Weird to call him 'my father,' but it's true. He was gracious and not angry with me. If he was, it didn't come across. I appreciate his admission about sharing every detail with his wife. It would be difficult to keep any of this from you, nor would I want to. The sheer number of things we have in common is overwhelming. Not only is he a closet chef and a good one, but he's also a martial artist like us. Obviously, he's smart and well read. We didn't discuss politics, but his platform from his website would lead me to believe we agree on most things."

"It's a start, right?"

"Yeah. I'm looking forward to spending more time with them. Although, it will be difficult while he's campaigning."

"I would agree completely, except he needs to be around for votes on the senate floor. I'm sure you could schedule a meeting or dinner."

"Good point."

"Did you say 'I'm right' twice in one conversation?"

He hauls me into his arms. "No, I absolutely didn't. I said you had a point. A point and right are not the same thing."

"Mm-hmm. Sure they're not."

"What time is it?" he asks.

"Seven, why?"

"We need to get ready for the meeting and prepare a list. We need food in our refrigerator."

I frown. "Fine. I like 'our.'"

"Me too. I'm sorry it took me so long to see it."

"Nothing to be sorry for. I understood and mostly agreed with your position."

He arches his eyebrow at me. "Mostly?"

"I agreed being a couple wasn't the right move for us despite our underlying feelings for one another. Too much was at risk. It allowed us to build a stable foundation of friendship before we jumped off the deep end into a relationship." I'm madly in love with him and yet can't say the words. *Why?* I'm terrified he will change his mind.

"Acceptable pivot."

"You're incorrigible. You hid your feelings from me too." *Still are as far as sharing them aloud in words.* He takes care of me without me asking. Little things like making sure I eat, setting up time for me to hang out with Alex, and pushing me to consider college. *Pot meet kettle, Maia.*

"You're right. We should—"

"Twice in one morning."

He huffs and leads me inside to get ready for our meeting. With a few minutes to spare, we take our seats in the conference room after speeding past Gemma at reception.

Christoph and Connor make quick work of the meeting and hand out our assignments for the next two weeks.

"You are free to go, except Maia and Nolan."

Alex hugs me from behind. "I'll call you later. I have a thing with Reese's class. Love you."

"Have fun. Love you too." In this moment, I realize we need to schedule time together. Not only is her relationship progressing, but so is ours. Keeping my friendship with Alex is a priority.

Lane, Finn, and Callan grab handfuls of food as they hustle out the door.

Christoph motions for us to sit again. "We wanted to discuss the review of your assignment with Miss Swisher."

"Her recommendation of you and our company has yielded a few new clients."

"Great," Nolan states. "What about Cole Foster?"

"Surprisingly, he was courteous and also gave a glowing review despite the situation and how it played out."

"Meaning?" I ask.

Connor adds, "She dumped him. I can understand how he might not provide positive feedback."

"Fair. Ian was professional and helpful," Nolan replies.

"How was your meeting with your father?" Christoph steers the conversation back to the present.

Nolan tilts his head in question. "How?"

"Did you really think Senator Phillips would invite you to his home without checking with us first?" Connor asks.

"No, I guess not."

"Who do you think provided his background checks?" Christoph retorts.

Nolan shakes his head. "It was surprisingly easy. Now my feelings about my mother are a different story."

"Understandable," Christoph offers. "How did you leave it?"

"He's going to talk to his campaign strategist and get back to us. As I mentioned to him, I don't want to derail his campaign or make unnecessary waves." He takes my hand in his. "I wanted to start our life with a clean slate concerning our pasts, if you will."

"I know you haven't read the schedule yet, but, Nolan, you're unassigned at the moment and Maia is going to join Kelly Barnett in New York City Wednesday through Friday this week."

"Okay," we reply in unison.

"Please keep us informed of future meetings with your father and what choices you make regarding going public with this information."

"We will," Nolan answers.

"We're set unless you have questions or concerns," Connor states.

"Thanks. I'll let you know about my father." Hand in hand, we leave the conference room.

"Do you have any plans for the rest of the day?" I ask him.

"Only groceries. What do you want to do?"

"Take a drive through some neighborhoods to narrow down the radius before I call Jake's realtor. Jill mentioned her neighbor, Mr. Appleton, died and his family is selling the house."

"Being neighbors with Jill and Cruz would be awesome," Nolan admits.

"Yes, it would."

"As long as by the end of the day there's food in the fridge, I'm game."

"Perfect." I take his arm and lead him across the street to Mille's. I'm surprised my weight hasn't ballooned, considering the sheer amount of chocolate this little boy makes me crave.

We drive for three hours in and out of the surrounding neighborhoods, including out as far as Christoph's farm.

Nolan parks in the lot of the grocery store and turns toward me. "Do we agree to avoiding the area around Chestnut Street and Mechanic Way?"

"Yes. I loved the area near Jill and Cruz's house."

"I did too. Let's get some groceries and then chill at home."

With a tad of desperation, I ask, "I know we're picking up groceries…."

"But?"

"Can we have Chinese for dinner?"

"Whatever my lady wants, she shall have."

"Awwww. Thank you," I reply, then pepper his cheek with kisses.

With a smorgasbord of Chinese food, including Moo Shu pork, dumplings, and fried rice, we set up around the firepit and enjoy the gorgeous evening.

CHAPTER SEVENTEEN

NOLAN

Maia's assignment with Kelly Barnett gives me the opportunity to finish moving into the condo and plan the perfect first date. Unfortunately, only as it pertains to restrictions our son would put on her, I can't take her on her ideal first date. Her ideal first date is a day at the nearest amusement park complete with all the bad-for-you, though delicious, food and every roller coaster imaginable.

I've planned everything. Now my woman needs to get home safely. In my head, I know she can take care of herself. The scuffle when she was assigned to Miss Goldberg sent my protective streak into overdrive. Not true. When the words 'I'm pregnant' left her lips, my world stopped spinning for a moment. Processing her words, my need to shield her increased one thousandfold. I may not have voiced my opinion to her yet, but I want her to stop working for Blackthorne. I did the moment she shared about our son and still do. I appreciate our bosses are giving her puff assignments, but we both can't put ourselves at risk after our son is born. A text interrupts my thoughts.

Jill: Jonah dropped off the keys. Everything will be set for your date.

Me: Thanks, Jill. You're the best.

Jill: I love cooking for others. Possibly choosing our neighbor is a bonus.

Me: I hope so too.

I smile, knowing the house will be perfect and decide to run off some of my energy. Almost an hour and a long run later, I pause the belt on the treadmill and down a water.

As I climb the stairs, my phone rings. "Good afternoon, Mr. Wentworth."

"Mr. Dalton. Are you and Miss Park available for dinner on Wednesday evening to discuss our strategy?"

"Yes, we'll be there. May I ask what your team determined would be best?"

"Of course. The senator would like to get ahead of the story rather than wait for after the election. Your meeting is to discuss how and when to go public with the information."

"Understood. Thank you for calling."

I exhale and smile widely. I text Jake the information about our meeting next week. As I do, a message from Lara comes through.

Lara: Are you free this evening?

Me: Are you okay? Yes, I can be free.

Lara: I'm not sure. I'm safe. Can I stop by?

Her update concerning her safety makes me feel a tiny bit better, but not enough.

Me: Of course. I add the address next.

Lara: I can be there in an hour.

Me: See you then.

Worry courses through me. I hustle through the shower and dress casually. I grab a protein shake to tide me over until dinner.

Lara knocks on the door slightly later than expected. "Hey. I'm sorry for barging in like this."

"You're always welcome. Are you okay?"

Her eyes close tightly, and she wraps her arms around me. "Not sure."

"Did Paul hurt you?"

"No, Paul is… he would never hurt me physically."

Momentarily satisfied, I usher her upstairs. "Want a drink?"

"A coffee would be great." She sets her Chloé bag on the granite and takes a seat.

While the coffee brews, I polish off my shake and grab more water. "What has you worried?"

"I went to get a copy of my birth certificate to prepare for our wedding."

I cover her hand with mine and wait her out. Lara is the contemplative one between us.

She continues, "My father isn't named."

Damn! I scrub my hand down my face. Lara will keep my confidence until the senator releases his statement. "I need to institute our childhood cone of silence." When we were young, it was a way to make sure Lara and I would always have the other's back.

"Absolutely. Do you know who my father is?"

I shake my head. "Not exactly." I share with Lara the details of my parentage, when I learned, and where I am now.

"Senator Phillips is your father, but not mine." A statement, not a question.

"Yes. We're working to share the truth with the press before the election."

"Does Mother know you know?" She buries her head in her hands for the ineloquent question.

I laugh. "No need to worry about formality with me, Lara."

She shakes her head. "I know. I'm confused and flustered. How can I find out the truth?"

"I can ask our investigator to look into it for you. Please know, Sharon will see it coming a mile away, or at least she'll be tipped off like she was when I started digging for information. I don't know how. The only thing I can be sure of is our investigator wasn't the leak."

Without hesitation, she replies, "Yes, do it. I need to know."

I thumb out a text to Jake about Lara and her father. He replies to both texts at once. Redirecting my attention to Lara, I ask, "My next question is going to seem callous, but... after learning Michael isn't your father, do you want to marry Paul?"

Her shoulders slump, and she stares at me with both shock and relief on her face. "Yes. No. I don't know. Paul is a nice guy."

"But?" I prod her to continue.

"He's boring as hell. We have nothing in common, except the status of our families—a family that isn't mine."

"You have a great job and earn a high salary. You don't need Paul. If you love him, fine, but don't marry him because Michael arranged it for you."

"You're pretty smart, little brother."

I roll my eyes at her. "When I learned Michael wasn't my father, I ran away, as you already know. Now I'm working on building a family of my own with Maia."

Lara cants her head in question.

"I guess Sharon's stab was to confirm. She showed up here, telling me to stop digging into my father. She correctly accused me of keeping information from her. I didn't acknowledge Maia's pregnancy."

"Ohmigod! You're going to be a dad. Wow!"

"Yeah, the fear is real."

"Why didn't you call me?" A hint of sadness is woven into her question.

"As I shared in the last thirty minutes, I've been busy. You're going to have a nephew this summer."

"I'm so happy for the two of you. Where is Maia, by the way?"

"She's on her way back from an assignment. She should be home within the hour."

"It's settled. I'm staying to congratulate her. Feel like cooking dinner with me?"

"Yes. Let me verify her arrival time." I pull out my phone and text her.

Me: Hey. Lara stopped by. When will you be home?

Maia: Hi. Is she okay?

Me: She will be.

Maia: I'll be home within the hour. Xoxo

Me: We'll make dinner.

I set my phone down. "Maia will be home soon. Let's get started." I invite Lara into our fridge, which thankfully is stocked to my specifications. We start one of our childhood favorites that Donna prepared regularly.

Laughing and reminiscing, we make dinner and set the table.

"I miss spending time with you," Lara mumbles.

"Same. Let's schedule another visit before you leave."

"Yes."

The entry sensor chimes, and I meet Maia at the top of the staircase and relieve her of her bags. After a sweet kiss, I greet her properly. "Hey, gorgeous."

"Hi." She plucks off her shoes and immediately hugs Lara. "Nice to see you again, Lara."

"You as well. Congratulations! I'm excited for the two of you."

"Thank you."

"Why don't you wash up? This will be ready in ten minutes," I suggest.

Maia kisses me again and rolls her luggage down the hall.

"You two are super cute together, and your son is going to be gorgeous." Lara literally grins from ear to ear. Genuine feelings ooze from her pours.

I smile and hug her. "Thanks, Lara. When I get the report, I'll share it with you and we figure out the best move for you."

"First, I need to stall my wedding," she shares.

"You picked a date?"

"Sort of? The wedding will be at the club over the holidays."

"Is that what you and Paul want?"

She frowns. "No, we don't." My sister wrinkles her nose. "I don't. Paul would marry me tomorrow if it fit in his schedule."

"All I can offer is this. If I were you, I wouldn't marry someone Michael chose unless you truly see yourself being happy building a life together. If it's solely because Michael deems him worthy, walk away."

Lara nods, and Maia joins us. As the three of us dine on chicken piccata over angel hair pasta, we catch Maia up on the reason for her visit. Afterward, I wash the dishes, and the girls gush about all things baby. Despite her exuberance, I can see Maia is exhausted. As soon as Lara leaves, I escort her to our bedroom, peel off her clothes, and tuck her into bed. She's sound asleep when I return with my book and a water for her.

Bright and early the next morning, I work through my Tae Kwan Do cadence before preparing breakfast for us. Maia wakes earlier than I plan. The water is running in the en suite bathroom.

"Please get back in bed," I call from the kitchen.

She giggles before replying, "Okay."

I round the island with a tray of breakfast and coffee and carry it to the bedroom.

"You're sweet to me, Nolan. Are you joining me? I couldn't possibly eat all this." The tray is overflowing with food, including pancakes, bacon, scrambled eggs, fruit, and juice.

"Yes, I'm joining you." I set the tray over her legs and carefully slide in beside her. "I know what you're thinking, you can take care of yourself."

Her mouth drops open, and her hand points to her chest. "Me?"

"I realize it's weird and new, but you wanted me as your other half. This is me taking care of you. Please let me."

"Okay." She digs into her plate without another word. When I'm almost finished, she asks our plans for the day.

"I'm offended. You forgot about our date."

"Of course not. I would never."

"You definitely did."

She scowls at me. "Fine, you're right."

"Today's my day to be right. Sweet!"

"Where are we going?"

I wink at her. "It's a surprise. I will tell you that I didn't plan what you believe is the ideal first date."

"You know what my perfect first date would be?"

"You've shared numerous tidbits of boyfriend information unwittingly over the last few years. Each detail is seared into my brain."

"Did I now?"

"Yes."

"Please share my ideal first date with me," she demands.

I lay out her ideal date at an amusement park with the most thrilling roller coasters in the country as well as her desire to try each sugary, sweet, and delicious confection, including funnel cake and deep-fried Oreos.

Her lips purse together, and she considers my answer. "I don't recall telling you that, but it's spot-on."

"I've been paying attention since the day we met."

"What else have you learned?"

Placing a kiss on her temple, I catch her gaze and reply, "I'm not divulging every detail. You'll just have to wait and see when I use the next bit of information later today."

"Fine. What time do I need to be ready for our date? What is the dress code?"

"We're leaving at three. Leggings and a hoodie will work."

"I'm excited for our date, Nolan."

"Me too, beautiful. Me too." We enjoy our breakfast before I wash the dishes. "I'm going to the gym. I'll be back before our date. Your first surprise should arrive any minute now."

"All in, huh?"

"Yes. All in." I kiss her tenderly and back away. Her pregnancy is obvious now, and her silky camisole fits snuggly around her fuller breasts.

If I don't leave, I'll strip her clothes off and savor her for the rest of the day.

When I tug open the front door, Alex and Reese are poised to knock.

"Hi, Uncle Nolan."

Alex nods, and they slip inside.

"Hey, Reese. Thanks for coming."

"Are you kidding? A home spa morning will be perfect."

"Glad you're excited too." I hop into my car and head to the farm. Hopefully, one of the guys will be available to spar. I park near the barn and find the gym silent. Without a second thought, I start hiking to the point. It's one of the places Maia and I would go to sort out family issues or to be alone. The late spring air is filled with sweet scents from the grass and wildflowers lining the path.

I sit on the ground and lean against the tall oak near the point to spend time in the quiet. For most people, to fully be in their head requires solitude. Not me. I prefer to have Maia beside me when I tackle life's obstacles. Today though, there is nothing for me to contemplate. Each avenue of my life is moving forward, and for the first time, I'm truly happy. The birth of our son and a future with Maia will only add to my life.

I hike back to the barn and come across Jake and Norah.

"Hey, Nolan. Everything okay?" Norah asks.

"Yeah. Killing time before my date."

Jake nods but says nothing. Probably because he already knew and didn't share with his wife. Surprising? Maybe a little. Then again, he wouldn't violate our trust by gossiping. It's not who he is.

"Have a nice afternoon. I need to make a stop before I pick up Maia."

"You too."

I pull away with a wave, which both return. With her favorite flowers in hand, I slip into the basement and change for our date. Sneaking back outside a few minutes before three, I ring the bell.

Maia answers the door with a huge smile on her face.

"Hi, beautiful. These are for you." The bouquet includes most of her favorite blooms, for example ranunculus, hydrangea, and roses in bright, bold colors. Maia brings color and light into my life. The flowers are a reflection of her.

She's struck silent. "What else did I unwittingly share with you?"

"Hopefully, everything. Your nails are perfect!"

"Reese is quite the nail polish expert. Do I have time to put these in water?"

I lift one finger, asking her to wait. I hop down to the basement and grab the vase I purchased for her. She shakes her head and climbs the stairs. Once the flowers are set, I escort her to the car.

"Where are we going?"

"Are you going to be able to contain your excitement?"

"I'll try."

"We're going to tour Mr. Appleton's house."

Sheer glee pours over Maia. "Really?" She can't help but squeal.

"Yes," I answer.

Despite the fact I'm driving, she peppers my cheek with kisses. After taking her fill for the moment, she resettles into her seat. Glee rumbles through her for the rest of the drive.

Hopefully, my gamble will be worth it. I park in the driveway and send a text to Jill. She asked that I text her an hour before we were ready to eat dinner. With the key in hand, I escort Maia up the front steps. The large front porch has a pair of wooden rocking chairs. I open the door and flick on the lights. The foyer is quaint with a formal dinner room to the right and a study to the left. The interior has been updated within the last five years. The kitchen is gorgeous with a granite island and high-end appliances, which is a plus for me.

Maia takes in each detail of the house as we wander through. Her silence is concerning. While she's quiet to most people, Maia has always been expressive to me. This house has three bedrooms plus a master on one level. She has peeked into each room and thoroughly inspected the master suite and the middle bedroom. Lucky for me, she hasn't been outside.

I wrap my arms around her shoulders from behind. "What do you think?"

"It's perfect," she whispers and dips her head to kiss my forearms.

"I agree. Come with me." I release her and thread our hands together. "There's more." Leading her through the sliding door, I reveal the next part of our date.

"How did you...?"

The patio is adorned with string lights and a table set for two. "While you were on assignment, I worked with Jonah and asked to show you the house and put in a conditional offer."

"Conditional on what?"

"Conditional on you loving this house as much as I do."

"Meaning?"

"If you sign right here"—I point to the last page of the contract—"we will become the owners of this house before our son is born."

A tear rolls down her cheek. "Really? Just like that. You would buy this house for me."

"I knew the moment we learned it was available and after the approval of the neighborhood during our drive. If you love it, it's ours."

She kisses me deeply, then asks, "Where do I sign?"

I laugh and point to the line for her signature. She signs her elegant signature beside mine. "What's next on our magical first date?"

Now it's my turn to laugh. "On our first official date, we bought a house."

"It appears we did."

"Dinner shall be here momentarily." As the words pass my lips, Jill and Cruz step through the rear gate with our dinner.

"Thank you, guys!" Maia exclaims.

"I love cooking for my family." Jill casts a look in my direction. She knows the entire plan, considering she vouched for us with Jonah.

I nod.

She continues, "And neighbors!"

Maia smiles and takes a seat in the chair I pulled out for her.

"The appetizer is bruschetta with artichokes, followed by a Caesar salad. The entrée is pork braciola over linguine. I'll be back later with your dessert. Enjoy!"

"You guys are the best." Maia smiles as they leave.

Ravenous, I dig into the food. It takes me a bit too long to realize Maia hasn't said anything else.

"You okay?"

She looks up from her plate. "Yeah. I'm taking a page out of your playbook."

"Taking a minute and absorbing the awesomeness of our date?"

She giggles. "Yes, something like that."

Over the next hour, we chat about the house, moving, what we need as far as furnishings, and potential baby names.

"Nolan Jr," I suggest.

"No. It needs to be unique."

We toss ideas back and forth until Jill delivers dessert packaged for us to eat at home.

"You need to warm it in the microwave for a minute at most and top it with the gelato before eating. See you again soon, soon-to-be neighbors."

"Thank you for this amazing first date meal, Jill."

Jill blows Maia a kiss and disappears from sight.

"Ready to go home, beautiful, and have dessert?"

"Sure, but you should know, I don't kiss on the first date."

Containing my laughter is impossible. "Buying a house while already carrying my son is allowed, but a kiss isn't?"

"Exactly," Maia manages before dissolving into a fit of giggles.

After devouring the decadent chocolate confection Jill baked, my gorgeous woman did kiss me on our first date, plus so much more until the wee hours of Sunday morning.

CHAPTER EIGHTEEN

NOLAN

After the weekly meeting, we revel in the fact our assignments are daily and not far away. I'm sure the guys selected us for these jobs on purpose. My gratitude is immeasurable. Maia is spending three days this week with Madeleine before her wedding.

I'm working with the guys at Christoph's farm to finish the buildings for the new hires during training. Normally, it's not a regular assignment, but we're family and I'll help out wherever necessary. The four new hires will be joining the team at the end of the week and will move into the new level of the bunkhouse Jake has been working on. One will replace Alex on Connor's team, and the other three will be joining Jake's team. It allows Alex to complete their training while Christoph and Madeleine are on their honeymoon.

I join Alex at the Anderson farm after the morning meeting, and Maia heads home. The ride is about forty minutes to Christoph's. When I arrive, I opt for the rear entrance to save the half-mile hike from one end of his property to the other.

"Hey, Nolan," Alex greets me.

"What's up? You're helping out here today?"

"Yeah. I wanted to discuss the candidates with the guys, and here I can hold them captive while making progress on the cottages."

"Who did you hire?"

"The guys chose Shea Tobin, Lucien Culpepper, Nico Calderone, and Marcello Herrera."

"Do you know any of them?"

"Don't think so."

Armed with paintbrushes, we get started on the walls of cottage two.

With each stroke of paint on the wall, the space looks brighter.

"How are things with you and Maia?" Alex asks.

"Excellent. We found a house."

"She mentioned it. I mean with your relationship."

"We went on our first date two days ago. In the eyes of most, we're taking it slow. The problem is, I know without a doubt, she's it for me." *I've always known.*

"Except you're terrified to say the words because her not saying them back will crush you."

I stare over at her, mouth agape. "How on earth did you peg that?"

"Maia is my bestie too. She's lucky enough to have two besties, one of each gender. She was traumatized when her parents left her to fend for herself. How could they leave her here? I'm sure she questioned their motivations daily. No, I *know* she questioned their choice daily. Would she have been better off going to Vietnam with them? Maybe. She'll never know how different her life could have been. She may not have met you or be pregnant with your son. Our bestie is afraid to share her feelings with you because she did it once and they let her down spectacularly. She doesn't want to feel the nagging, hollow ache if she's wrong about you again."

"She isn't though. Maia stated her desire to be with me and raise our son together, but she hasn't said the words."

"I know. You can't say the words either because you don't know if what you're feeling is love."

I pause with the long, handled roller halfway up the wall and look at Alex. "Are you a shrink?"

"No. The feeling of comfort, security, and the gnawing ache when something goes awry, that's love. When you would make a choice to absorb harm, whether physically or emotionally, for the other person without a second thought, that's love. When you and Maia come to a point where a compromise needs to be made and you both give a little rather than give up, that's love. Allowing Jordan and Reese in … giving my heart to them was worth it. Is it soul baring and difficult? Absolutely. It's also worth taking the leap."

"How can she not feel my love for her?"

"She might. I'm sure she realizes the meals and the little things you do for her are to show your love. The words are equally as powerful though."

"I understand your point."

"When the time is right, you'll say those three little words. Until then, keep doing what you're doing. When the turmoil with your family and the decisions she needs to make are settled, it'll click into place."

"Thanks, Alex."

We finish painting the living area and bedroom before she tackles the bathroom and I work on taping the galley kitchen. By dinner, we've almost finished this cottage. We head our separate ways, and I ponder Alex's words on the drive to our condo.

Each word and piece of advice is on point. As soon as things settle with my father and our plan, I'll share my feelings with Maia, out loud and in boldface letters.

When I arrive at the condo, I note two Blackthorne vehicles along the curb. *Not a good sign.* After parking, I hustle inside.

"Maia," I call out.

"We're in the kitchen."

I find Jake and Connor sitting at the island when I crest the stairs.

"Is everything okay?"

"Yes and no. Have a seat," Jake suggests.

I ignore him, circle the island, and kiss Maia's cheek. Then I lean against the counter across from him with an expansive island between us. "I'm good standing here," I reply after threading my fingers through hers.

"Blaine finished his report on your sister, Lara Dalton. She was right to question whether Michael is her biological father. He isn't."

The words are a relief but also stab into my chest. Not only do I feel bad for Lara but myself as well. We were both subjected to Sharon's manipulation our entire lives. "Was Blaine able to determine who her father is?"

"Yes. This is the part where you should sit."

I wave him off. "I'm fine here, but thanks."

"Your choice. The person who leaked the details of you reaching out to Senator Phillips was Weston Wentworth."

"Why?"

"He's Lara's father," Jake offers.

Maia tightens her grip on my fingers.

I blink at them a few times before processing his words. "It makes sense. I've been working with him to figure out how to handle the revelation about my father. Weston is the inside man, if you will. Did he use his job to remove his name from her birth certificate more expeditiously than a regular citizen?"

"Yes. Blaine found footage of him paying off a clerk."

Now what?

Jake continues, "I used my friend at the Secret Service to reach out to the senator directly. I'm expecting a return call from him within the next thirty minutes. I recommend you call Lara and share this revelation with her before your mother attempts to do damage control."

I nod and drag Maia into the office. Before I dial Lara, I draw her against me and kiss her breathless. "How are you, sweetheart?"

She smiles, sets her hands on my chest, and replies, "I'm feeling good. You?"

"Still working it out in my head."

"Okay." She attempts to leave the office.

Hauling her against my hip, I unlock my phone and call my sister.

"Hi, Nolan."

"Evening, Lara. Where are you?"

"I'm out to dinner with a few friends in the city. Why?"

"Could you go somewhere private and discreet, please?"

"You're scaring me."

"Nothing to be scared about. I have information for you. The information you asked me to obtain." I hear her excuse herself from the table and then the commotion of her exiting the restaurant.

"Go ahead, Nolan."

I share with her the details Jake provided me, including the little detail concerning Wentworth using his position in the senator's office to remove himself from Lara's birth certificate since Sharon showed up at our condo.

A string of curse words flow from my sister's lips. Stifling a laugh is a virtual impossibility. I've never heard her curse before. "Holy hell, Lara! Good for you."

"How do I use this information?" she asks, her words barely audible.

"Completely up to you." I imagine her gazing at her engagement ring. It's highly likely Paul is out of the loop as far as her parentage and very well may feel marrying Lara is best for his career and maintaining his social status. "First, you need to decide if Paul is the man you want to spend your life with. Then, the rest will fall into place."

"You're the best brother a girl could ask for," she states.

"A fact that will never change."

"Love you, Nolan."

"Call me when you want to talk more. Love you, Lara."

She ends the call, and we join the guys in the kitchen again. Within minutes, Jake's phone rings.

"Good evening, Senator Phillips," he answers the call. He explains the situation and who is present. After receiving permission, he sets the phone on speaker.

My father—still weird to say aloud—greets Maia.

"Good evening, Maia. How are you feeling?"

"Good evening. Fairly well today. Thank you for asking."

After greeting me, he allows Jake to continue relaying the details he's learned.

"I understand. What do you recommend, aside from firing Mr. Wentworth?"

"Are you willing to share what you decided regarding your relationship to Nolan and how you plan to proceed in revealing your relationship to one another?"

"I was going to discuss this with him and Maia at our meeting on Wednesday. Nolan, may I speak freely with Mr. Blackthorne and Mr. Michelson on the line?"

"Yes." I appreciate the request, but it wasn't necessary.

"Mr. Wentworth recommended holding off until after the election to bring our relationship public. Whereas Ms. Whitman felt getting ahead of the story now would provide a sense of transparency for the voters. My inclination was to wait until after the election while getting to know you during that time. Now, I'm wondering what Mr. Wentworth could've gained if I opted for his recommendation."

"If I may?" I interject.

"By all means," the senator replies.

"It's fuel for future blackmail. He can tank your campaign with one well-placed phone call. If you follow Ms. Whitman's suggestion, you'll be able to control the narrative."

"Salient points, Nolan. What is your opinion?"

"At this point, I don't see the benefit in waiting. It takes away his leverage. We should release the statement first, then fire him."

Senator Phillips laughs. "I'll have Abigail draft a statement and send it to you for approval before releasing it."

"Thank you. I'll be looking for it."

"Good night."

I drag my hand down my face. Leveling my gaze with Jake, I ask, "Will this impact my ability to work for Blackthorne?" A notion I hadn't considered before now.

Connor answers this question. "Undetermined at this point. During the last one hundred and twenty days of the general election, Senator Phillips and his wife will be afforded protection, if they choose. If elected, the senator and his immediate family would receive protection until the election and thereafter. You would be a case of first impression. As far as I know, no other immediate family member of the sitting president has ever worked in personal security before or after taking the oath of office."

I nod and glance at my phone when the notification comes through twenty minutes after our call. I read the text twice with Maia reading over my shoulder before I turn it toward Jake and Connor.

"Are you sure?" Connor asks.

"Yes, if I needed someone to look out for our safety, I would choose this company. It starts with vetting this statement about my true parentage."

Both men take their time reading and rereading the press release before recommending two simple tweaks to protect how long I've known about my relationship with the senator and a way to tone down the underlying anger toward Sharon for hiding my paternity for this length of time. I reach out to Abigail with the proposed changes. Her email response is quick. She indicates she'll make the changes and release the statement immediately. She'll reach out to schedule a dinner as well as a public event for us to join the senator after the statement is released. While she would've preferred it be simultaneously, it isn't possible any longer.

"Aside from extra vigilance going forward, how concerned should we be about this address getting out?" I ask the guys.

"It shouldn't. The condo is still in my name," Connor asserts.

"Good point," I admit.

"If necessary, you can use the guest suite at the farm until your house is ready for occupancy," Jake offers.

Maia thanks him. "Hopefully, it won't come to that."

"Despite the press release requesting privacy, it may not happen," Connor adds.

"True, this isn't ideal. I'll take a look at his campaign schedule and let you know which event we plan to attend," I offer.

Jake speaks up next. "Thanks, Nolan. We won't keep you any longer." Jake hands Maia a set of keys for a company SUV. "Use the company vehicle instead of your car for travel to Madeleine's for your assignment the next few days. You can ride with Maia in the morning and then home. The following day, there has been a slight change. Both of you will work on the cottages and then go to her appointment."

I nod and escort them out. Maia hands me a drink when I return to the kitchen. "Thai?"

"Sure."

"Want to talk about the fact Sharon will show up here tomorrow?" she asks while ordering our dinner through their app.

"No. Honestly, I'm more worried about Lara than us. We can handle ourselves. Not only does my sister have to decide if she wants to marry Paul but deal with the fallout of not keeping the peace."

"Doesn't Lara have her own money?" Maia questions.

"She does, but I'm not sure how much Michael subsidizes her lifestyle."

"I didn't realize he was paying for her."

I shake my head. "I don't know for sure Michael is paying her bills. I know she has a trust fund though, and she may not want to give it up."

"When does Lara get access?"

"After she marries Paul."

Maia scoffs at the notion. "Wait, Lara is entitled to her trust fund only after she marries an appropriate and preselected man?"

"Yup."

"Wait, does the same type of trust exist for you?"

"No because Michael knows I'm not his son whereas he believes Lara is his daughter."

"Michael and Sharon are despicable."

"I agree with you. To be fair, Michael knew about me."

"Don't make him out to be the good guy. Both broke their vows, which isn't acceptable."

I'm saved from adding my opinion by the delivery driver ringing our bell. We spread our dinner on the ottoman. After eating, we turn in early to prepare for the potential storm brewing outside our walls.

My phone rings at midnight. When I look at the screen, I see it's my mother. I force the call to voice mail. When it immediately begins ringing again, I note it's my mother again. Then silence my phone. Maia needs her rest. Satisfied we won't be disturbed, I set my hand on her belly and curl around her.

CHAPTER NINETEEN

MAIA

Before the alarm sounds, I slip out of bed and downstairs to the gym. I slowed down on my running during my last trimester and focused on walking and easy stretches. My yoga session this morning is needed, given I'll be sitting for the remainder of the day in Madeleine's office.

After my workout, I climb the stairs to the kitchen and down a bottle of water and some yogurt before waking Nolan. He didn't sleep well last night. Each toss and turn woke me or reminded me both of us were awake. With a cup of coffee for him in hand, I pad down the hall.

"Morning, sweetheart," he grumbles when I sit beside him on the bed. The sheets are twisted around his calves. His muscled torso and distinctive V-cut at his hips are readily available to be gawked at. His perfection is patently unfair. The hair on his head is mussed, and his eyes are sleepy. "Don't look at me like that," he warns.

"Like what?" My voice emerges sweet and syrupy.

"Like you want to lick me from head to toe."

I wink at him. "If I do, would you stop me?"

He pauses, and a small grin curls at the corner of his mouth. "Probably not."

"I want to do exactly that, but I know we don't have time before work. It's already seven. Drink up."

"You let me sleep?"

"Yes, you needed it. I'll be out in ten minutes."

"I don't know what I would do without you."

"Same." My stomach balls up in knots. Those three words are on the tip of my tongue. I love him to the depths of my soul. Yet saying that out loud to a person who could decimate me with rejection, the thought paralyzes me with fear.

Ready to take on the day, we both wake our phones. A slew of notifications ring out. While Nolan checks his, I scan mine.

Alex: Ohmigod! Are you two okay? How are you feeling?

Me: Morning. Hanging in there. Wasn't ready for it to be public yet.

Alex: Understandable. Call if you need backup or company.

Me: We will.

After deleting some unwanted emails, I move beside Nolan. "Any issues?"

He shakes his head. "No, there are a few options for when we can join my father on the trail. We can check them out tonight."

"'Kay. You sure there's nothing else?"

"My mother left a voice mail when I didn't answer at midnight. Then radio silence."

"You're worried." A statement, not a question.

"Yes."

"We can handle anything together."

"We can, but I'm done being tested and threatened by people outside of our family—Lara, found family, and you, I mean." I splay my hands on her abdomen to include our nugget as well.

"Me too. We need to go in case there's traffic."

We walk downstairs hand in hand and step outside. The radio silence since her voice mail should have been heeded as a strong warning.

How did she get here so fast? Did she speed up the interstate in the middle of the night?

"Nolan Edward Dalton, how dare you?" Sharon bellows.

"Mother, how did you get here so fast?" he asks her.

Her response is forceful but wavering. "I was staying at the Davenport."

"My statement about seeing you was clear. The only reason you're here and seething is you must know I uncovered another of your dirty little secrets. During your first uninvited visit, you told me to stop digging into my father because he didn't know about me. Only a select few people knew I was seeking answers. The only untrustworthy outlier was Weston Wentworth. He's your inside man. Connecting him and Lara took a few keystrokes."

I take a deep breath and discreetly text the guys, shielded by Nolan's body.

Me: Sharon showed up at the condo. We're going to be late.

Jake: Roger. Do you need backup?

Me: Probably not. She's alone.

Then I refocus on Nolan's conversation with his mother.

"You didn't tell her, did you?" Her voice sounds both resigned and aghast.

"The only family member who has been honest and forthright with me for my entire life is Lara. Yes, she knows."

"You're going to ruin everything!" Sharon charges toward Nolan.

Without any inkling of concern for himself, he shifts with an elegance and grace unlike anyone else and pushes me back as far as his arm will extend.

Conflicting emotions flood my brain. I can take care of myself—a fact he's cognizant of—yet he's protecting me and our son. Despite being beside me during a few hairy assignments and both surviving injuries, he insists on protecting me. *He gets a protector too. One for his body and, more importantly, one for his heart.* Each day my feelings deepen for this complex man.

"What are you talking about? There's more?"

Sharon narrows her eyes at him as if the next shoe will impact Nolan. "If Lara doesn't marry Paul, we'll be bankrupt."

Nolan shakes his head. "How?"

"We're broke. Your fath—Michael is overextended on the yacht, the house in the Outer Banks, and the townhouse in Georgetown. Paul's company is set to take over the commodities firm. If they don't marry, the deal is off."

He pinches the bridge of his nose. "I may not have an MBA or a business mind, but it seems to me you need to sell some extraneous possessions. The choice needs to be Lara's. The last thing she should do is bail you and Michael out. Hell, an arranged marriage should've never been on the table, debt or no debt, merger or not. You've lied to her since the day she was born. It's despicable you would consider using her for your own survival. Please leave and don't come back here."

"We'll be destitute! How can you do this to me?"

Destitute! Ha! She doesn't know what the word means. Destitute is couch surfing and scurrying away in the dead of the night because you know the marshal is coming to evict you the next day. Destitute is eating the remainders of your customers' dinners they were willing to throw away.

Nolan fires back immediately. "Me? I've done nothing to you. In fact, it's the other way around. Own your choices and fix your problems, Mother, without using me or Lara to do it."

"I'll ruin you, your knocked-up hussy, the senator, and his Stepford wife."

Nolan takes a few steps closer to Sharon. "Don't you ever speak to her again. Don't think about her at all, as a matter of fact. Leave and don't come back."

"We will get what we want, Nolan. The only question is whether Lara will be cast off like you."

"Exactly how do you plan on accomplishing your goal? You don't have any more children willing to marry for money. Do you?"

Fury bubbles up on Sharon's face. "Lara will do my bidding and save this family. Lord knows, you and your fake girlfriend...."

Containing my anger toward Sharon increases the longer she hurls insults at me and Nolan. I set my hand on my abdomen when our son kicks up into my ribs. While I'm distracted, Sharon makes a move and skirts around Nolan.

She grabs my forearm and squeezes tightly. "You aren't getting a dime. I know you got knocked up at the engagement party intentionally once you realized we had lots of money. Jokes on you."

I twist in her hold and bend her arm behind her back. Leaning closer, I whisper, "Nothing you can say to me or about me will change who you are. Unlike you, I would never trap a man by bringing an innocent child into this world intentionally. You saw dollars signs with Mr. Dalton at the end of law school and deceived him into believing Lara was his daughter. Then your marriage nearly collapsed when your husband learned the true reason you chose him. You ran to Senator Phillips and duped him as well. You lied to him about birth control, didn't you?" I release her arm and step backward, adding space between us.

"How could you know...?" Her words trail off.

"A strong hunch, which you just confirmed." Before I finish speaking, a company SUV screeches to a halt in front of the condo. "Do not come back here, Mrs. Dalton. You are not welcome." Ideally, their arrival will hasten her departure.

Anger seethes from every pore. "How dare you? Your parents didn't want you. Now, look at you. Poor little Chinese girl knocked up by the broke rich boy."

Tears burn in my eyes. I stifle them. She will not get to me. Sharon Dalton knows absolutely nothing about me or my family. I may not agree or understand my parents' choice, but I've thrived and made something of myself while she graduated with honors from a prestigious law school and did nothing but disgrace her marriage and family before it even began.

Connor and Jake advance up the sidewalk.

"Mrs. Dalton, I strongly suggest you leave before we contact the authorities," Jake states, crossing his arms over his chest.

"Ah, the illustrious Mr. Blackthorne. Your reputation precedes you. Good luck keeping those two in line. They are disloyal gold diggers." Mrs. Dalton throws daggers at us with her eyes as she weaves between the guys.

"Well, the company is as exceptional as the employees. Nolan and Maia are two of my finest team members. Good day, Mrs. Dalton," Jake offers.

She huffs, looks from Nolan to me, and walks away, exasperated with the situation.

In equal measurement, Nolan backs me toward the entryway as Sharon moves away. The instant she pulls away, he turns and his hand skims over the length of my body. Once he's done a quick assessment, he checks my forearm. "Are you okay?" His voice is soft and laced with fear.

I cup his cheek with my hand. "I'm fine. What about you?"

Anger oozes from his pores. "She didn't touch me," he growls.

Connor interrupts. "Let's go inside for a few minutes and regroup."

The guys follow us inside and direct me to the couch. I shake my head but heed their request. Fighting them will do no good, nor will failing to use the offered ice pack either. A brief rest to calm down is probably a wise decision. As I sit, Nolan sidles beside me with a bottle of water and a snack before addressing the events of this morning. He shares the content of our discussion, specifically about Lara and the merger with Paul's company.

Connor speaks first. "How do you want to handle this?"

"I need to talk to Lara. Is anyone unassigned?"

"Lane and Sawyer are unassigned," Jake shares.

"As soon as I locate her, can you send one of them to secure her until this mess is handled?"

"Yes. Call your sister, and I'll call Sawyer," Connor replies.

Nolan nods, rises from beside me, and calls Lara. Connor calls Sawyer.

Jake immediately takes Connor's spot beside me. "Please let me look at your arm."

Lifting the ice pack, he checks it over and sees for himself a doctor isn't necessary.

"Thank you for coming, Jake."

"We're family. We take care of our own."

"Do we need to relocate?" I mumble.

"Do you want to?"

"No, hell no! I won't bend to that woman."

Jake shakes his head. "Easy, Maia. I wasn't going to suggest you should. I see the protective mama bear mode extends to Nolan too."

"It always has."

"I know. You two were inevitable from the day you met."

A knowing smile overtakes my face.

He continues, "I would recommend parking in the garage. In fact, we're going to take your other car and leave a company SUV."

I nod when Nolan returns. "Lara is staying at the JW Marriott in DC. I told her to stay in her room and wait for Sawyer. I texted her a photo."

Connor rejoins the conversation. "Norah is going to meet Sawyer at Christoph's farm with his go bag. He should get to Lara in under two hours. We'll work out a more detailed plan after he arrives, considering her work and other commitments."

"I don't know what to say, except thank you," Nolan offers.

Connor replies, "None are necessary. Christoph had Lane escort Madeleine to her office today. He will work with her tomorrow as well."

"Should we skip the wedding?" Nolan asks.

It doesn't surprise me. Nolan always puts others before himself.

"No, absolutely not. Simon will rule the door with an iron fist."

We laugh.

"Yeah, he will," I add. "What do we do in the meantime?"

Jake answers, "I'll keep you in the loop about Lara."

Nolan nods and hands Connor his keys. The guys leave. Before he relaxes, Nolan pulls the SUV into the garage. When he returns, he sets the security system and plops beside me on the couch.

"Come on." I stand and extend my hand to him. "We're not wallowing our free day away."

"I'm intrigued," he states after sliding his hand into mine.

I lead him into the master bedroom and turn on the water in the massive tub. Despite knowing he'll hate it, I add jasmine bubble bath to the water and point sternly at the tub. "In you go."

"I have one condition."

I tilt my head, urging him to share his request.

"You need to join me."

"Planning on it." I step out of my shoes, which are starting to kill me as my pregnancy progresses. Stripping out of my dress, I lay it on the vanity. It's then I feel him watching me.

Wordlessly, his gaze travels from my face to my toes, and incrementally his stormy, hazel eyes climb, leaving heat and desire behind.

"What are you thinking right now?" I ask, my voice soft and uneasy.

He reaches over the edge of the tub and extends a hand to me. "You're stunning. You were before, but now, carrying my son, you're a goddess."

I carefully climb into the tub and recline against him. His hands collapse around me, one over my breasts and one on my belly. The hot water is soothing, and we succumb to the pull of relaxation. In here, we're safe and secure. Inwardly, I scowl, wondering what else….

"Stop worrying about her."

I shake my head against his chest. "I'm worried about you and Lara, not Sharon."

"What about you?"

I crane my neck to meet his gaze. "Regardless of my disdain for your mother, what can she do to me? I may hate her—sorry, but it's true—but I'm confident she won't physically harm her grandchild, one she will never see, but nonetheless, I don't see her stooping to murder."

"Perhaps there is a grain of civility in her, but we aren't taking any unnecessary risks," he warns.

"Fine." I twist and straddle him in the rapidly cooling water. Impaling myself on his hardened length would be delicious.

"Maia, we should move into the bedroom."

"We've never done it in the tub."

He arches an eyebrow. "We can… after our son is born. For now, bedroom."

I purse my lips and climb over the edge of the tub. After a quick dry off, we dance to our bed, spending the rest of the morning and into the afternoon tangling our sheets.

We stumble to the kitchen for food and then to the rooftop to handle the updates from Jake regarding Sharon and Lara.

"Good ahead, Connor," Nolan answers the call on speaker.

"Lara is secure. Sawyer will remain with her until the situation is resolved. Paul has been informed, but Lara has requested time to speak with him before making any other decisions."

"What exactly does that mean? What decision has Lara made?"

"Sawyer will shadow Lara until she makes the necessary decisions for her engagement or Sharon has been sufficiently handled."

Nolan shakes his head. "Fine. I'll call her later or tomorrow."

"Understood. Let us know if you need anything or want backup," Connor offers.

"Thank you," we reply at once.

I exhale slowly after ending the call. "What do you say to making some baby decisions?"

"Like what?"

"We need to pick out a crib, bedding, and perhaps talk more about a name for our son."

"Sounds like the perfect way to fill the rest of our day."

With the tablet propped in front of us, we scour the baby stores for crib options. Choosing the furniture is easier than I anticipated. The bedding, on the other hand, is still up for debate a few hours later. We don't begin to discuss names until dinner is being prepared. We've tossed around a few ideas, but no decisions have been made.

CHAPTER TWENTY

NOLAN

The next morning, I slip out of bed and reach out to my father. "Good morning. I apologize for calling so early in the morning."

"Morning, Nolan. I'm an early bird. What can I do for you?"

"We would like to schedule a dinner with you and Sera. During the meal, we can go over your campaign schedule and choose an event or two for us to join you."

"Are you free on Wednesday evening?"

In two days. "Yes, we're free."

"Great. If you would like to wait until after your son is born, we can do that as well," he offers.

"Thank you. I'll talk it over with Maia. However, I'm sure she will want to move forward."

"Great. Would you like Jason to pick you up?"

"We can drive. For now, we are using Blackthorne vehicles."

"Understood. We'll see you in a few days."

"Perfect." I end the call and stare at the wall for a few moments. I have no basis for building a relationship with my father. Nothing went well with Michael for obvious reasons.

"All you need to do is be yourself and get to know one another," Maia says, taking a seat beside me.

"How do you always know what I need to hear?"

She kisses me and says, "It's a gift."

"What time is your appointment?"

"Two."

I nod. "Are you up for a trip to the farm?"

She wrinkles her nose at me. "Why?"

"I need to get in the ring."

"Sure, I can walk the dogs out to the point."

Thirty minutes later, I park and kiss Maia. With her fully charged phone and a water bottle, she rounds the house and calls Tank and Sabre. The dogs happily trot to her side. Jake waves as he crosses to the gym.

Over the next hour, I spar with Jake and Lane. Neither of them are forgiving or go easy on me. The three of us collapse on the mat, staring at the ceiling.

"Feel better, man?" Lane asks.

"Yeah. Thanks."

"Anytime. I'm going to need some time to recover though. You had a lot to work out," Lane observes.

I turn and look at him. "I did. Still do, but I'm working through it."

"Everything set for this weekend?" Jake asks.

"How do you know about this weekend?"

Jake sits up and looks over at me. "If the shower is meant to be a surprise to anyone other than Maia, you've failed. Alex is on top of the baby shower and roped all the ladies into the planning, except Madeleine. Alex didn't want to add more pressure with the wedding in two weeks."

"Makes sense. As far as I know, Alex is set and has given the ladies their tasks."

"Good," Jake states.

Ten minutes later, the three of us peel ourselves off the mat.

Maia breezes into the gym. "Hi, guys!"

"Hey, Maia," Lane greets her. "How are you feeling?"

"Good. Thanks." She turns her gaze to me. "We need to leave for you to have time to shower."

I nod. "Coming."

"The dogs are in the backyard," she tells Jake.

"Thanks, Maia. See you later," he answers.

I hustle home and hurry into the guest shower while Maia showers and changes in the master. If I'm anywhere close to her naked, we won't arrive on time. Within forty minutes of arriving home, we're back out the door headed to her appointment.

After waiting an extra hour, Dr. Flagstone indicates Maia is fine, and we schedule her next appointment in two weeks. As she gets closer to the end of her pregnancy, the visits increase in frequency.

As we leave the office, my phone rings. Discreetly, I answer Alex's call. If Maia hears her, she will catch on to the surprise.

"Hello."

"Hey, Nolan. Are you alone?"

"No." One-word answers are all she can have right now.

"Got it. Everything is set for the party on Saturday at one. I'll have the guests there by noon."

"Sounds perfect!" I end the call abruptly, hoping Maia doesn't ask who it was. Thankfully, she doesn't. After a simple dinner, we snuggle on the couch until Maia falls asleep.

Bright and early the next morning, we head to Christoph's to work on the cottages. Maia is going to spend the day with Betty and Liz. Neither need security, but there truly aren't any assignments the guys feel comfortable sending her on with my angry mother prowling around. We're going to leave from here and head to dinner with my father and his wife. Each time I think about him, I address him as my father in my mind. Eventually, it won't feel foreign.

Christoph sends me to cottage four today. The solitude of painting alone is welcome. Focusing on my relationship with Maia and our son is truly everything I want. Unfortunately, I don't have the luxury of narrowing my focus as I wish. Sharon hasn't pulled anything again. Lara has shared the details about her father and the merger with Paul. As suspected, Paul was out of the loop as well. He was not aware his mother and Sharon were consorting along with their husbands. A marriage of these two families would set up the Dalton and Goldman families for generations.

While they haven't broken off their engagement, Lara and Paul elected to push off their wedding. My thoughts spin, increasing my pace, while I roll silver gray paint on the bedroom walls. When I finish the bedroom and shift into the living room, Maia appears at the threshold.

"I brought you some lunch."

"Hi, beautiful. How are Betty and Liz?"

"They're a hoot. Liz toddles around after her in the greenhouse for flowers and veggies."

We eat a leisurely lunch, and then Maia slips away to allow me to finish the living room before dinner. A few hours later, I step out of the shower and dress for dinner. When I emerge, Maia is waiting for me on the porch.

"Ready, sweetheart?"

"You look nice."

I chose charcoal pants and a dress shirt. "Thanks. You're beautiful as always." Arms linked, I escort her to the passenger seat and round the SUV.

She's unusually quiet.

"What's on your mind?"

Her eyes meet mine.

"I know you as well as you know me. Please share."

She smiles. "A few things…. I was thinking about the baby's last name and also the conversation I had with Jill. She said there's a job opportunity at her school in the fall. No degree required, but I'll need to take a few certifications concurrently while I work."

I pause, process her statement, and tackle the easier one first. "Amazing! Do you want to apply?"

"Yes and no. Jill kind of hinted the job is mine if I want it. It's to be her assistant in her classroom."

"Wow! Even better. What are your reservations?"

"I don't truly have any, but I wanted to talk to you."

I consider pulling over, but I know it isn't a wise choice. Threading my fingers in hers, I squeeze her hand. "You should chase your dream of being a teacher. Hold on to it. We will be beside you every step of the way."

"Really?" A few tears roll down her cheeks.

"Without question. I'll miss being on assignments with you, but you should have everything you ever wanted in your life, including your dream of being a preschool teacher. I'm proud of you, Maia."

She smiles widely at me. "Thank you."

"What do you mean our son's last name? It should be mine." We talked about first name options, including Joseph and Ethan, but not his last name.

Maia twists and tightens her grip on my hand. "Not what I mean. Yes, he should have your last name, but which one? Do you want to change your name?"

My chest constricts when I consider her question. "I don't know."

"Okay. Will you think about it?"

"Yes, I will. Do you have a preference?"

"No. My only desire is for our son to have the same last name as you. If you keep Dalton, fine. If you change it to Phillips, that's fine as well. We can change his later, if necessary."

Her name is going to change as well. "I'll consider my options."

"Thank you." The remainder of the ride passes in comfortable silence. She makes a good point. It also makes sense for me to decide before the baby is born. Parking along the curb, I hustle around the car and open Maia's door.

"There's a photographer at ten o'clock," she states when I reach her.

"I see him. At least they're across the street. Hopefully, the attention will die down."

"It'll take some time."

I shrug. We're greeted by the security at the front door. With Sharon's threat and revelations about Wentworth, my father requested a security detail given the sheer access Wentworth had regarding his schedule, routes, and personal information. Once they usher us inside, Seraphina greets us.

"Lovely to see you both again. Maia, you look beautiful."

"Nice to see you as well. Thank you, Sera."

She's dressed more casually for this dinner than the last one. Rather than a suit, presumably from the office, she's wearing pants and a cream-colored, three-quarter-length sweater with chunky bracelets. Normally, a detail like that wouldn't register, but the clinking draws my attention.

"Good evening, Nolan. Maia. Please come in," my father greets us. "Would you like a drink?" He's wearing suit pants and a dress shirt with an apron over the top.

"Iced tea?" Maia asks.

"Right this way. I set some appetizers on the island." We gather and talk the entire evening on varying topics from books to movies. When my father and I begin discussing sports, Maia and Sera's eyes glaze over.

"Not a sports fan, Sera?" I ask.

She shakes her head. "Never had time to learn or fall in love with one unless you consider riding show horses as a sport."

"I can see an argument on both sides similar to cheerleading," I offer in reply.

"Fair point." Before we leave, we select a campaign event in Maryland to attend in a few weeks. We step outside after our meal and find the street is blissfully empty of photographers. Whatever the reason, I'm grateful.

I usher a sleepy Maia into the condo and tuck her into bed. With a cold beer, I climb to the rooftop and ponder her question from earlier today. *Do I want to change my name?* Mentally, I make a list of pros and cons. Changing to my rightful birth name, in my opinion, is my choice. It isn't as if Sharon gave me her maiden name, which was Mencia. It wouldn't maintain the status quo with Michael. Would my father be amenable to me changing my name? Do I need to ask? Before I think better of it, I call him.

"Nolan, are you all right?"

Internally, I berate myself for intruding. "I'm sorry. I didn't mean to disturb you. I can call back in the morning."

"Nothing to be sorry for. What's on your mind?"

"I realize my thoughts may seem out of place and be inopportune, however... how would you feel about me changing my last name?"

"Your desires aren't misplaced. You're about to become a father and you want the world around your son to be perfect. The upheaval with your childhood impacts you on a fundamental level, your name."

"I don't want to adversely impact you in any way. It's the reason I felt talking was appropriate."

"It boils down to one question. Do you want your son's surname to be Dalton?"

No. "No, but is it appropriate for me to change mine and give it to him?"

"I understand the conflict you're trudging through. If I thought for one moment in the last twenty-plus years you could be my son, I would've fought for you. Sera and I would've fought for you at any time during our marriage had we known. Your choice to change your name will not impact me negatively at all. The decision is yours."

The angst and tension in my mind and heart dissipate the instant his permission is bestowed upon me. "Thank you for picking up. I'm sorry for calling so late."

"Both Sera and I are available for you, Maia, and our future grandson whenever you need us. Call, we'll answer."

A promise that may be difficult to keep when he's elected, but it was offered, nonetheless. "Thank you. Good night."

"Good night, Nolan."

I end the call and decide how to proceed. I trudge downstairs into the office and print the necessary paperwork. In the wee hours of the morning, I crawl into bed beside Maia.

After preparing breakfast for us, I grab the petition and hustle to the circuit court before heading to the cottages.

CHAPTER TWENTY-ONE

MAIA

The weekend arrives, and I'm ecstatic to spend time with Nolan. Near nine, my arm finds a cold spot in the bed where he should be. I frown but know he wouldn't leave without telling me. I shuffle to the bathroom, brush, and slip his zippered hoodie on. With a water and fruit in hand, I search for him. It doesn't take long. I find him sweaty and catching his breath on the bench in the gym.

"Morning."

"Hey. Did you get some sleep?" he asks.

Sleeping comfortably has been increasingly difficult the last few weeks. I've tried the suggestions from the girls. Norah suggested a body pillow, which has been helpful. Callie swears by a white noise machine, and Madeleine recommended sleeping in loose-fitting shorts and a fitted but not tight tank. "I have for the past few days. You haven't though."

"No, I haven't."

"Want to share why?"

"Maybe later. We're going on a date."

"We are?"

"Yes. First, we're getting pedicures, and then we're coming home. You're having a girls' day with Alex."

A huge smile grows on my face. I was excited to spend time with him, but I haven't spent time alone with Alex in a while as well. "Thank you! Thank you! How much time do I have?"

"Our appointment is at ten."

I lean over, kiss him, and scurry upstairs to get ready. The salon is about fifteen minutes from the house. Kimber, the owner, leads us to a private room and assists me into the chair. Within minutes, the courteous staff is hard at work massaging my feet while Nolan's are soaking.

"I can't believe you chose this," I state.

"Why wouldn't I want to relax with you?"

"Relax, sure. Get a pedicure? I'm surprised is all."

"Fair. Close your eyes and relax." The foot rub and lavender-scented salts help soothe me. Once my nail polish—a soft pink to match my dress for the wedding—dries, we head home to get ready for my date.

Before he parks in the garage, I ask, "Are you going to share where we're going?"

He shakes his head. "Nope. Your girls' date is a surprise."

"Fine, what is the dress code?"

"A dress, please," he requests.

After a short kiss, I step into the closet and pull out a few options. There's an A-line, ankle-length dress in yellow and a T-length dress in powder blue. I opt for the blue and join Nolan in the living room a little past noon.

"You look gorgeous," he says as I twirl in a circle.

Not really my style, but today I feel pretty good considering I slept well last night.

Nolan escorts me to the SUV in the garage.

"What are you going to do while I go out with Alex?"

"Jordan and I will probably shoot pool at the house or relax outside."

"You relax?" I literally laugh out loud. "You don't know how."

"I do know how, but things are on edge right now."

I cover his hand with mine and gaze out the window as we head to meet Alex.

Nolan is attempting to discreetly text Alex while driving.

"Want me to text her and let her know we're almost there?" I offer.

"Sure."

Me: We'll be there in ten.

Alex: Yay! See you soon!

"All set."

A few minutes later, Nolan pulls into the gated driveway and parks right in front of the house. It's odd though, the street is lined with cars. One of the neighbors must be having a party.

Then a thought occurs to me.... *They wouldn't, would they?*

"Please tell me you didn't?"

Feigned confusion takes residence on his chiseled face. "What are you talking about?"

Certainly without question, I'm walking into a party ambush. "You know I'm not a fan of surprises, Nolan."

"Yes, I'm aware."

"Am I walking into a baby shower?" Tears trickle from my eyes as he parks in front of the house.

Nolan swipes the tears away. "If you were?"

I pout and meet his gaze. "I don't like surprises."

"I know. Alex doesn't either, but sometimes you have to let the people who love you do things for you and accept them graciously."

People who love me. With a huff, I pull out my phone and text Alex.

Me: I love you for this but please call off the surprise part.

Alex: Did Nolan crumble like a cookie?

Me: Lol. No, I noticed the cars and overdressed attire for girls' only.

Alex: You got it. Love you.

Me: Thanks.

After allowing me a few minutes to compose myself, Nolan hustles around the car. He curls my arm around his, and we ring the doorbell.

Alex answers the door, and Reese sprinkles me with confetti.

"Sorry, Auntie. I was looking forward to the confetti," Reese states with a sheepish look on her face.

"Thank you for toning it down, sweetie."

"Welcome." Reese hugs me before rushing away.

Alex links her arm through mine and leads me into the kitchen. Jordan ices a gorgeous cake with blue buttercream. "Hi, Maia. I'll only shoulder a portion of the blame."

"No worries, Jordan. I'm sure your fiancée dragged you along kicking and screaming." I wink, and we join the rest of the guests outside.

Alex has outdone herself. Who knew my bestie was an expert party planner? There are tables set at the edge of the grass with drinks and finger foods. Delicious desserts fill another table, offset by the drink display. The gift table is overflowing. Come to think if it, the party thrower is Jordan. I would bet on a mixture of Jordan and Alex.

"She's here!" Jake exclaims.

"Hey, Jake." I greet him with a hug and a wave to Norah and Ben who are rolling a ball on the grass.

"We had a bet you would beg off completely," he shares. "It's twenty bucks I'll happily fork over."

"What's with our family betting on things?" I ask aloud.

Madeleine joins the conversation. "Like what? The perfection of Alex for Jordan?"

I laugh and greet her. "True." I'm glad Alex took a risk on Jordan and Reese. She's happy and deserves it.

"How are you feeling, Maia?" Madeleine asks.

Christoph, her almost husband, slides his arm around her waist with a watchful eye on Liz and Ben on the grass.

"Pretty good. Thanks to all of you, I slept well last night. Plus, the prenatal pedicure and foot massage this morning was heavenly."

Madeleine laughs. "Glad to hear it."

"What about you?" Nolan asks.

"I'm past the point of stressing. Each and every detail has been checked, double-checked, and triple-checked, and paid for. Simon and Lucia will hide any issues from me going forward. The rest is slowing down enough to enjoy each moment of our wedding day."

"Good for you. I'm looking forward to getting dressed up. It'll likely be the last time for a while," I offer.

Alex shakes her head. "No way, honey. There will be more events forthcoming to get gussied up for."

"Did you pick a date?" Glee seeps out of my pores.

"We did. We're going to have a small ceremony before preseason and our trip to Columbia."

"Sweet!" I'm ecstatic for my bestie. However, there's a nagging thought in the back of my mind. *No!* We're buying a house and having a baby first. Then we'll worry about a wedding. *Right? Right!*

Nolan leans closer. "We'll get there too, Maia." He always knows. The front door opens and draws my attention.

Without hesitation, I hurry to greet Lara. I hug her close while Sawyer closes the door.

"I can't believe you're here."

Lara grins. "I wouldn't miss this! I'm crazy excited for the two of you. Nolan will be an amazing dad, despite his concerns otherwise."

My nose wrinkles before I reply. "Yes, he will."

Nolan and Sawyer greet one another before we switch. "Hey, Sawyer. How's it going at the hotel?"

"It's fine. I'm used to it. It's better than the bunkhouse. Plus, the Marriott is plush as far as chain hotels go."

"True. Any issues?"

Sawyer shakes his head. "My presence may be overkill, but Lara is easygoing and content staying put for now."

Lara works remotely, which has been helpful given the circumstances.

"Good. How is she holding up?" I ask him.

Lara answers instead of Sawyer. "I'm going to be fine, Maia. Paul and I agreed to take a step back from wedding planning. The details of the merger were heavy for him to handle. He didn't know our parents were conspiring, much like I didn't. To be fair, I knew Paul was chosen for me. I didn't know about the merger or the financial implications. I can't even bring myself to call her my mother at this point."

Nolan throws his arm over his sister's shoulder. "Let's have some fun and save the chat about our family dysfunction for our lunch next week. You are free to go anywhere on the property."

Lara casts a glance at Sawyer, who nods in agreement with Nolan's instructions. I appreciate the effort by both of them.

"Yes, let's." She smiles and allows Nolan to lead her toward the rest of the guests. Once Lara is situated, Jill and Cruz join our group with hugs. Jake and Christoph step away to chase the kids around.

"Hey! You look beautiful," Jill offers.

"Thanks. How are you feeling?" I ask.

Cruz slides his arm around her waist and draws her close.

Jill glances left and right before replying, "I feel fantastic, unlike Norah."

I frown. "Are you going to find out the gender?"

"Yes," Cruz answers, "I want to know."

Madeleine laughs. "Why?"

"He or she needs the perfect name," Cruz responds empathically.

"Okay, then. Good luck with him, Jill," Madeleine warns.

"I'll do my best."

I glance around the backyard and find Alex walking around with string. "What is she up to?" My question is directed at Nolan.

"It's one of the shower games we felt she could get away with. Each guest takes a length of string. The one closest to the circumference of our baby will win a prize," Nolan explains.

"Okay, what other games are we doing?"

"I'm surprised you're interested. Blindfolded diaper changing when Alex finishes with the string," he answers.

"I was never against a shower, just the surprise part."

Nolan shakes his head and leans closer. "Not true, beautiful. You aren't a fan of people doing things for you or accepting gifts. You want to do everything on your own."

He's absolutely right. "Maybe true."

"Completely accurate. Look around," he murmurs near the shell of my ear.

I comply and causally glance around. Found family surrounds us. My interview with Jake three years ago was the beginning of my family. On the same day, I met Nolan. Each new team member offers another helping hand or giving heart.

"Every person here, beginning with me, is here for you and our son. Please know without a doubt, I'm going to be beside you to raise our child. Along with your happiness, our family simply wants to share in our joy."

Tears roll over the balls of my cheeks. Alex approaches as he finishes pouring his heart out to me. She glares at me. "You made her cry."

I shake my head. "Happy tears."

"Okay. You're forgiven." She turns to me. "Ready for the first game, Maia?"

"Sure."

"First, we need to measure your belly and find a winner," Alex admits.

Alex grabs the blue string and wraps it around me at the fullest part of my belly and pinches the ends where they meet. After cutting, she has me walk around and compare it to the strings the guests have. One after the other, they don't measure up. So far the closet is Sawyer, with a handful of people left to go.

"How, Sawyer?"

He shrugs, and I note Lara watching him intently. Can't blame her. Sawyer is tall and handsome in a wholesome country-boy kind of way. It makes sense considering he was working on his family farm before taking this job.

We finish checking the others and bring the closest two entries— Sawyer and Reese—out near the pool. Alex hands me the string and they measure theirs against it. By the slimmest of margins, Sawyer's is near spot-on.

"Sorry, Reese," Sawyer mumbles.

"No problem. It was fun. Mom, what did he win?"

"First, I need to know. How did you accurately predict her belly size?" Alex pointedly asks.

Sawyer blushes fiercely. "I apologize in advance, Maia. I'm exceptional at estimating size for when our cattle are pregnant."

Our friend group dissolves into laughter. I even catch Lara laughing. Instead of jumping into the next game, Alex has me take a seat and unwrap the mountain of gifts from our family.

"Nolan." The tone of my voice is indicative of my displeasure.

"Yes? Why do I get the feeling I'm in trouble?"

I raise my shoulders. "You registered without my input?"

"Nolan, Nolan, Nolan." Jake grips his shoulder. "First rule of a relationship, communication is key. Be careful with making decisions on your own, or they may bite you in the ass. Right, Norah?"

"You know better," Norah replies from our right with the kids corralled in a large playpen. Only Amara isn't in with them because Cruz is happily feeding her off to the side.

The rest of the crowd laughs, and I tear into the gifts. The pile of wrapping paper is as tall as my waist. We make the rounds, hugging and thanking everyone. Despite not having any input, the daddy-to-be covered our bases from the crib to the onesies with cute sayings. The best part is the guys are loading two company SUVs with the gifts and bringing them to Jill's. It's silly to move it to the condo and then to our house in under a month.

A huge smile graces my face when I hug the guests as they leave. After waving to the last guest, I collapse on the couch between Alex and Reese. "I don't know what to say."

"You are the most determined woman I've ever met. This little guy is going to have an amazing life with you as his mom," Alex offers.

"Hey, what about me?"

"Hush, Nolan. Right now, it's about Maia. As I was saying, you turned terrible circumstances into a steady career, and you're building a safe home for your son. He's lucky to have you."

"You're wrong there, Alex," Nolan interjects. "All of us are lucky, not just our son."

"I concede your point," Alex offers. "Don't get used to it though."

Nolan points to his own chest and says, "I would never. Ready to go home?"

I nod and stifle a yawn. "Thank you for throwing my nonsurprise party, Alex."

"You're welcome. Love you."

We say our goodbyes and head home. After we park in the garage, Nolan asks, "How mad are you?"

"I'm not angry. I would've preferred to know in advance, but I appreciate the effort to make it a surprise despite my dislike of the same."

"While we were celebrating, the attorney called. We should be able to close two weeks early."

"That sounds lovely. First, though… I need to sleep until tomorrow. Want to join me?"

He raises an eyebrow.

"Sleep now, Nolan. Then perhaps morning sex, because thank-you sex isn't happening right now."

He chuckles. "I'll hold you to it," he warns, as if sex with him at any time of the day is a deterrent.

"I expect nothing less." I shuffle to the bedroom, stripping off my dress as I walk. Sinking into our bed is exactly what I need after the amazing but tiring party.

CHAPTER TWENTY-TWO

NOLAN

One of my worst fears is realized a few days later. A barrage of notifications hit my phone first thing in the morning. Headline after headline, internet links on repeat, and well-meaning voice mails from the guys and Lara. The splash on the financial papers accuse Michael of defrauding his customers, extortion, and attempting to get insider information to cover the losses. Sharon is mentioned, but the extent or her knowledge of involvement is unclear at this point. After skimming the first few articles, I decide silencing email and push notifications is the way to go. Before I set my phone aside, I text Lara.

Me: Morning. Still up for lunch?

I join Maia on the rooftop on this gorgeous sunny day. "Morning." I kiss her and settle beside her.

"Morning. How bad?"

"Bad. I expect calls from Jake and probably Abigail on my father's behalf soon."

"Okay. Are you still planning on meeting Lara for lunch?"

"I texted her. Hopefully, I can persuade her to come here. It'll give Sawyer some time off and no worries about photographers."

"Makes sense."

"Still joining us?"

"Up to you. I understand if Lara wants the meeting to be only the two of you. I'll be fine up here or inside while you discuss."

I attempt to allay any discord between Lara and Maia, but she cuts me off.

"I know it isn't about me. Lara is in a tough spot, like you are. If you want to handle this only you and your sister, it's fine with me."

She's everything. "Thank you. I'll be in the gym."

Maia nods, and I head back inside. Before jumping on the treadmill, I scan my texts again and note a reply from Lara.

Lara: Sure. Sawyer said there would be better.

Me: Okay. See you at one.

With my schedule for the day settled, I run and run until my legs give out. Normally, sparring would better serve to exhaust me, but getting into the ring isn't an option today. I find Maia scouring lists of baby names when I step into the kitchen. I prepare a quick protein shake for both of us to hold me over until lunch.

"Find anything you love yet?" I ask as I approach her with the smoothie in hand.

"Thanks. Gross, you stink! Go take a shower," she states.

I laugh, kiss her head, and scurry away. At the threshold of the bedroom door, I retreat and ask about the names again.

She shrugs. "I like Devin and Collin, but Collin is Christoph's younger brother's name, right? Also, we need to figure out our furniture and get started on packing."

"Devin is nice. Collin too, it is a little close. Sure, after lunch with my sister."

She continues scrolling. After showering and dressing, I join her in the office. Somehow, she is now surrounded by lists.

"Beautiful, what are you doing?"

She pouts and frowns before replying, "I started making lists of what needs to be done to move and for the baby and for the hospital and for dealing with my new job and...."

"Relax, Maia. Why didn't you tell me you were stressed?"

Tears pour from her eyes, enough to fill a bucket. Before her pregnancy, Maia hadn't been weepy, at least not in my presence. I scoop her into my arms and settle with her in my lap on the couch in the office. Holding her as close as possible, I wait for her to calm down some.

"Why didn't you tell me you're stressing about things?"

Her words are muffled against my chest. "I didn't want to add more for you to worry about."

I press a lingering kiss to her head and exhale before adding a sliver of space between us. "We're a team, Maia, for everything. No more worrying. We'll start with one thing at a time."

She wipes her tears and nods furiously. "What do you want to start with first?"

I shake my head. "No. Is there one item you can knock off the list, right now?"

A small smile curls at the corner of her lips.

"Which one?"

"I want to take the job and give Jake my notice."

I pull out my phone and dial on speakerphone.

"Hey, Nolan. Everything okay?" Jake asks when he answers.

"This call isn't about me. I'm meeting with Lara in a little while. It's about Maia."

"Hi, Jake," Maia interjects.

"What can I do for you?"

Maia exhales slowly and squeezes my hand. "I don't know how to say this. Taking a risk on working for you was one of the best decisions I've ever made. You've taught me more than I could imagine about business and myself." Maia closes her eyes and says, "I found a new job working with Jill. I need to resign from Blackthorne."

"Congratulations, Maia! I'm happy for you. More so, I'm proud you decided to chase your dream of working with children."

"You're not angry?"

Jake laughs. "We're a family. The sole reason I'm angry is I'm losing one of my most tenacious and gritty employees. Jill will be lucky to have you working with her and her students in the fall."

She exhales slowly before replying, "Thank you, Jake."

"Of course. I'll see you at the wedding. Nolan, please update me after you meet with your sister. I assume you're going to relieve Sawyer for the day?"

"Yes, that's the plan. While I have you on the phone, how much longer do you feel security is necessary for Lara?"

"I would say another week or two until the media circus dies down regarding Michael and Sharon Dalton. It's only a matter of time before the media seeks her and you out for comment."

"Understood." I end the call and look at Maia. "I'm crazy proud of you."

"That was nerve-racking."

"Why?"

She rolls her eyes at me. "I made a huge life decision without stewing on it for months."

"Good. You're reaching for a job in your chosen profession instead of one for survival. It's a huge deal, sweetheart. Anything else we can tackle before Lara arrives?"

"Not really. I can't do anything about the hospital yet; it's too early. While you talk to Lara, I'll bring up some storage totes and pack unnecessary items in the office."

"I'll get the totes for you right now. No lifting, please."

Her eyes flutter closed. "I promise not to overdo it."

With a sweet kiss to her forehead, I set her on her feet and carry four empty totes upstairs for her. After I set them down, Sawyer and Lara arrive.

"Hey, come in."

I bro hug Sawyer and hug my sister.

"I'll be back to pick you up later, Lara," Sawyer offers.

"Okay. Thank you."

He retreats down the front stairs.

I lead Lara into the kitchen and usher her to one of the stools. "How are you?"

She looks tired and wrought out. I suspect she's thinner as well. "I'm tired of the bullshit. I've looked at the situation over and over from many different angles. The more angles, the angrier I become."

While Lara talks, I prepare lunch. "Completely understandable."

"The merger is off. Paul's parents' company backed out in writing two days ago. Then this morning the charges against Michael and Sharon were announced. Michael's firm has suspended him without pay pending the investigation. Their entire net worth has been squandered, and there isn't a chance they will break even after the fire sale of property and other items. Our mother is broke."

"I'm not surprised. Are you?"

"No, I didn't know about the fraud. However, it was clear they were overextended. It's why they lost their minds when we asked for a longer engagement. I knew marrying Paul was a business deal, and I was willing to sacrifice my happiness for our family."

Fury boils in my veins. "He isn't our father."

"No, he isn't. However, he treated us differently from the beginning."

I drop my head, conceding her point. I set a plate in front of her. "I'll be right back." With a plate and drink in hand, I bring lunch to Maia in the office. When I peek my head inside, I find her sound asleep on the couch. Tiptoeing out, I return to the kitchen.

"Is Maia okay?"

"Yeah, she fell asleep. Where was I? Yes, you're correct. Michael did treat us differently, but it doesn't change the fact you don't have to marry to help him."

"True. Sawyer said something similar."

Surprised she talked to Sawyer, I press on anyway. "It boils down to what you want. Do you see yourself with Paul for the rest of your life? Do you love him?"

A wistful look passes over my sister's face. "I love Paul, but not in the enduring love and friendship to span years kind of way. It isn't all-encompassing and heart-stopping agony when something goes wrong."

"That type of love is the kind you want?"

"Yes, you found it with Maia. I want a love centered around one man who is not only my lover but my best friend. Paul is wonderful, but he doesn't make my heart flutter or my panties wet with a few well-placed kisses or naughty words."

My sister's words strike a nerve. *How will I know it's love?* Everyone around me sees it, but saying those words are nearly as terrifying as becoming a father in four weeks or less. "Damn! I never heard you speak quite so honestly, Lara."

A flush of pink brightens her face. "Well, my middle name isn't appropriate for nothing." She laughs softly between bites of the chicken rice bowl I made for us. "Sharing those thoughts out loud is enough for me to hide for a little bit before dating again."

"Did you call off the engagement?" Immediately, I glance at her ring finger. The gaudy ring is still perched on her hand. I know my sister, and she would never pick an engagement ring as ostentatious as the one on her hand.

"Yes, but we haven't shared it publicly yet."

"Do you have a plan when that will be?"

She shakes her head. "Paul wants to wait until the press coverage dies down."

"Makes sense."

"While I don't mind having company, how much longer will Sawyer need to shadow me?"

"I talked to Jake earlier. He estimates about two more weeks."

"Not terrible. I'm sure there are more important clients Sawyer could be working with."

"No." My words come out more forceful than I intend. "Sorry, having Sawyer with you is for my peace of mind."

"It's fine. I'm not convinced Mother will leave me alone considering she still believes I'm her last hope of survival."

"Laughable, if you ask me. Though you're right, it does offer a bit more comfort regarding your safety."

"Understandable. Can we go back to your statement from before?"

I frown at her.

"You haven't told Maia you love her, have you?"

Silence blankets the room. "I've never said it to anyone before, not a woman, not family. How will I know?"

Lara covers my hand with hers. "It's how I know Paul isn't the love of my life. I can go days without thinking about Paul. I would bet you couldn't go an hour before she was pregnant."

"Okay, so?"

"Nolan… love is knowing at the end of the day if your head is next to hers in your bed, you'll sleep well. Love is deciding to show up and disagree but never quit on each other. Love is wanting to see her for only five minutes but driving an hour to do it. Love is knowing without a doubt you would scorch the earth to get to her—your family."

Maia embodies each quality Lara is describing.

Lara continues, "Every person around the two of you can see how deeply you love one another. It's written in how you look at one another and how you act around each other. Sharing those three little words out loud tells Maia you aren't afraid to stand beside her when times are smooth, but more importantly, when times are tough."

"Like she is for me now?"

Lara raises her hands as if to say "Duh!" She clears her plate and climbs to the rooftop to read until Sawyer returns. Before she disappears up the stairs, she turns toward me. "Don't force it, Nolan. She knows, but I'm confident hearing the words are important to her as well."

"Thanks, Lara."

After settling my thoughts, I slip into the office and sit beside Maia. She's still sound asleep. I consider waking her but decide extra sleep should win over food. I set a kiss to her forehead and whisper, "I love you," knowing she won't hear me.

About an hour later, Sawyer returns to the condo. "Hey. Thanks for the respite."

"You're welcome. Have you talked to Jake?"

Sawyer nods. "Yeah, he's thinking another week or two. Whatever Lara needs is fine. She's easygoing as far as having a shadow. She's not fussy and content staying in. I'm the same way, so it works out."

Interesting. Sawyer and Lara? Nah. I shake the thought away. He's a great guy, but she's barely single. "She's upstairs."

Sawyer seeks Lara when Maia appears in the doorway of the office.

"Hey, sleepyhead. Feeling better?"

She wipes her eyes. "I didn't feel poorly, but the nap was perfect. Did Lara leave already?"

"Not yet," Lara replies with Sawyer right behind her.

"Just wanted to greet you. I hope you're doing well. He's not a pain, is he?" Maia hooks her thumb in Sawyer's direction.

Lara laughs softly. "Nah, we're both chill and comfortable with limited movement."

Sawyer glances in my direction and shrugs.

"Hopefully, we can get together again soon." Maia and Lara hug. Then she hugs me before Sawyer escorts her out the front door.

I lock my arms around Maia and ask, "Hungry?"

"Yeah, but I can have a small snack until dinner arrives."

Confusion reigns on my face. "Arrives?"

"Yeah, the bean wants Thai."

"As you wish." I coax her onto one of the stools and prepare a snack for her—a plate of cheese, crackers, and grapes. "Up for furniture browsing?"

"Yes, absolutely. Which rooms do we need to furnish immediately?"

After some discussion, we narrow it down to the master bedroom and living room for now. We scroll through a few websites and put a few options in the cart.

Shortly thereafter, I grab our dinner and join Maia in the living room. While we eat, we decide on the bedroom, but are still torn between two options for the living room. I wrap my arms around Maia, and we sit in the quiet until we turn in for the night.

Quite early the next morning, my phone vibrates on the nightstand.

"Hello."

"Good morning, Nolan. It's Abby."

Fear shoots through me. "Is everyone okay?"

"Yes. We had a phone call scheduled to discuss the campaign event, didn't we?"

Inwardly, I shake my head. "I thought it was tomorrow. No problem at all." I slip out of the bedroom, and we discuss the order of the speakers and our seating on the stage. Abby recommends a few color choices for my tie and Maia's clothes.

"Aside from the Secret Service, will there be additional security on site?"

"Yes. Hotel security will also be present."

"Do you know how many?"

She hesitates to answer. "Umm. Yes, but—"

"It's okay. It's a hazard of my job to be interested in the planning of this type of event. I'm sure the plan is solid."

"Thank you. I'll speak with the senator and see if he's willing to share the information with you beforehand."

"Thank you. We'll meet the senator and his wife at the hotel before the procession next week."

"Great."

"Let me know if anything changes. Have a nice day, Abby."

"I will. You too, Mr. Dalton."

Not for long. When I filed the petition, the clerk indicated it could be as soon as four weeks, which is soon. Dressed for painting and moving furniture, I smile inwardly. The guys have kept me local in case Maia needs something, but also my father's campaign impacts which assignments they can send me on. I'm grateful and prepared to have a discussion with them after the election to determine if I need to resign as well. Interestingly, knowing I may have to step down because I learned he's my father doesn't anger me. I wonder how different my life would've been had I known the truth years ago.

CHAPTER TWENTY-THREE

MAIA

For the past few days, I've stowed items into totes and stashed them in the gym during the day while Nolan and the guys finish the cottages. We're scheduled to close in a few weeks. As far as the indictment for his parents, the interest in us and Lara has been dying down.

As the clock ticks to the end of the day, I'm getting increasingly giddy. We're checking into the hotel this evening for the Anderson wedding tomorrow.

"Sweetheart, I'm home." He hops onto the top step and sweeps me into his arms. After a blistering kiss, he rushes into the bedroom. That kiss felt different than previous ones. Before I make it into the room, he's stripped down to his boxer briefs. He slips out of his remaining clothing and steps into the steamy shower. For a moment, I consider foregoing the opportunity to be with Nolan. I push the crazy thought out of my mind and leave my clothes in a pile on the tiled floor. I bracket his waist with my hands and press a row of kisses along the middle of his back.

"I thought you wanted to get into the city as soon as possible tonight."

"I do, but I want you to fill me first."

Nolan arches an eyebrow at me. "Absolutely, but not in here."

I frown. "Because?"

While he considers his words carefully, he soaps up and rinses his body quickly. "I don't want to take any extra risks. The chance—though slim—we could slip in here is high enough for me to hurry you out of the shower and bend you over the love seat near the fireplace instead."

"Umm, hell yes!" I wink at him, push the door open, and towel off immediately.

I arrange the pillows and set my hands on the arm of the love seat facing away from the bathroom door.

Nolan growls when he finds me waiting for him. "You weren't kidding?"

"Not at all."

He stalks toward me with an unmistakable heat in his eyes. "How wet are you, beautiful?"

"Touch me and find out."

Nolan drags one hand from the back of my knee, over the curve of my ass, and to the small of my back at the same time as the fingers of his other hand slide through my core. "You're soaked."

"Yes." The single-word reply is filled with anticipation and yearning wrapped into one syllable. "I need you now!"

He laughs. "No foreplay?"

"I'm not against it, but hard and fast now, then slow and sensual later."

Wordlessly, Nolan buries his length into my core before pulling out completely.

I groan and glare over my shoulder.

After another laugh, he fills me again and meets my backward thrusts with equal force. A surge of bliss has my inner walls contracting around him. As soon as the nausea ended, my sex drive skyrocketed, and the ecstasy has increased to earth-shattering proportions.

"Don't stop... holy hell."

At my command, he drills deeper into me until he lengthens within me and I feel him explode into me more forcefully than ever before. He lowers his head and kisses each knob of my spine as high as he can travel.

"Another shower before we leave?"

"Sure."

We maneuver our overnight bags into the back of the SUV after washing and redressing. I settle into the passenger seat, and Nolan drives toward the hotel. The ride into the city takes longer than expected. After checking in, we collapse on our huge bed until our breakfast arrives, per the bride and groom's request.

Madeleine rented the entire hotel for their nuptials. Instead of staffing the restaurant with servers, a late brunch was to be served in each individual guest's room. Hors d'oeuvres and cocktails are set to begin at three.

Nolan and the rest of the Blackthorne staff are taking turns checking the security at the hotel. No one without an invitation will be admitted through the front door.

I finish dressing and meander down to the ceremony. The courtyard in the center of this hotel has been turned into a French country garden complete with flowers and greenery.

"Hi, Simon and Lucia. You two look gorgeous."

Simon kisses my cheeks. "Speak for yourself. You're the most gorgeous pregnant woman I've ever seen."

"Keep the compliments coming. I don't feel gorgeous today." I feel tired and heavy. My feet look like I stuffed them into elf-size shoes.

Lucia shakes her head. "No way, honey. Your dress is perfect. The A-line hem with crystals along the bodice and the thigh-high slit accentuates your cute bump."

"You're both too kind. Where are Nolan and I sitting?"

Simon smiles. "You're seated in Atlanta."

"Thank you." Madeleine has the tables designated with locations where something significant occurred in their relationship. Madeleine and Christoph met for the first time at Callie's last concert in Atlanta.

Not only does Madeleine deserve to have her wedding how she wants it, but the guest list is a veritable who's who in the sports and entertainment world. In the recesses of my mind, I knew Madeleine was a big deal. I didn't know quite how big until I read the list of guests.

Of course, Jordan and Alex will be here, but his teammates Cameron Beau and Tyson Beck are also the bride's clients. Carter Luther and his wife, as well as Bryce Hillman from the DC team, are beside them as well. They are chatting with a tall, fit man, presumably a football player, but I can't place him. The stunning blonde on his arm is Elsie Snow. She's an A-list actress and recently wrapped a movie with Ellis Barnett. Normally, the star power at one of these events doesn't get to me. However, glancing around this room, I realize how lucky I've been to work at Blackthorne. A small twinge of sadness passes through me, but teaching was always my dream.

I take a seat near the front along the aisle and wait for the ceremony to start. After Christoph and Madeleine are married, we'll be escorted into the ballroom through a covered tunnel for privacy.

"Sorry, I took so long," Nolan whispers when he takes a seat beside me.

"Any issues?"

"No, but I got some fabulous news."

My eyes widen, urging him to continue sharing.

He molds his hands around our baby. "Do you remember our conversation about my last name and whether I wanted to change it?"

"I remember talking about it some but not making any decisions."

"It was a difficult topic for me. Anyway, I had a conversation with my father about it as well. As of yesterday, my last name is now Phillips."

Processing his words leaves me momentarily speechless. "Really? That's amazing. Why didn't you tell me?"

"I didn't want to add to the stress you were putting on yourself."

"I appreciate that, but I would have liked to be there for you while you were waiting."

He drops his head. "I didn't realize it was that important to you."

Own your feelings, Maia. "You are my world. You're everything to me. I—"

He cuts me off. "Me too, but...."

"You don't trust the words." Burying the sadness is difficult. Without a quiver of doubt, Nolan loves me. Not hearing those three little words though is understandable and heart-wrenching as well.

"No. Not one person who has said them to me in my entire life means them and stays."

"I do. I will."

Anguish mars his face.

"I won't now, but not saying the words doesn't make it any less true. You show me with your actions."

"Like?"

"Making sure I eat, attempting to extricate Sharon from our life on your own, clearing the stray shoes to help me avoid tripping, working on the cottages instead of taking an assignment that would require travel."

"You knew about that?"

I drop my head. "Those three little, but significant, words are equally as important as how you treat me. I won't hurt you or leave. When you're ready to say them out loud for me and the world to hear, I'll accept them. The only person in the dark is you. Not only do I see it, but our found family and friends do as well."

"I'm terrified."

"I kn—"

The ceremony music interrupts our conversation. The guests rise and watch Madeleine walk down the aisle with her mother. The sight is stunning, considering the turmoil Madeleine endured with her family. I glance at Christoph and see him visibly teary-eyed. Jake and Connor are beside him.

"You're stunning." I overhear Christoph from my seat. Madeleine's lace gown skims over her curves perfectly. It's classy and understated, much like the bride herself.

"You look pretty dashing yourself. What do you say we make this official and have a rocking party to celebrate?"

"Yes," Christoph replies.

Less than fifteen minutes later, the officiant declares, "It is my distinct pleasure to introduce for the first time Mr. and Mrs. Christoph Anderson."

The guests hoot and holler as they walk through the tunnel into a private room. We mill about in the courtyard until the entrance to the ballroom is open. Rather than follow the crowd, Nolan leads me into the hotel lobby and guides me to sit on one of the couches.

"I'm truly sorry, Maia."

I slide my hand up his sculpted chest and cup his jaw. "I'm not angry. Thinking about it more, I may have made the same choice if the situation were reversed. However, I would prefer to discuss major things before we do them going forward."

"I promise. What do you say we join the reception, enjoy amazing cuisine, and dance slow and close on the dance floor?"

"Yes, let's."

He rises and extends his hand to me. When I take it, he kisses the back and wraps my arm around his. When we step into the ballroom, we are greeted warmly by Miss Goldberg.

"Hi, Maia."

"Demi, nice to see you again."

"Kellan, please meet Maia and—"

"Nolan." The guys shake hands. "Pleasure to meet you."

"So, how are you doing since the premiere?" I ask.

A smile grows on her face. "I was more worried about you."

Kellan adds, "Please accept my apology on behalf of my brother. He's overprotective and acted without all the pertinent information."

Intriguing statement, especially in line with the fact that Aidan, his brother, is the lesser imposing of the two men. "Much appreciated," I reply. We chat a bit about their current projects and the gorgeous venue Madeleine chose. "It was great chatting with you."

"If you would excuse us, I need to escort Maia to our table and handle something for the groom," Nolan offers. Smiling cordially, Nolan guides me to our table. "I'll be back soon." With a kiss to my temple, he disappears.

With my lemon water in hand, I glance around the room. When I turn to the far end of the room, I spot Miss Swisher headed in my direction.

Without hesitation, she leans down and hugs me. "You look amazing! How are you feeling?"

"Thank you. You look beautiful as well. I feel good overall. How about you?" Her emerald dress molds to her generous curves.

"Things are good. The storm from the end of filming passed, and thankfully, he is respecting my decision to be single."

"Good for you."

"Thanks. One day I'm going to find my other half like you did with Nolan. You two are couple goals." A hint of sadness passes over her face. Remembering a lost love perhaps?

As the words pass her lips, Nolan slides his arm around me from the side and kisses my cheek. "Hi, Rachel."

"Hey. How are you?"

"We're great! We found a home, and our little guy will be here soon. There are still some issues with my family, but progress is progress. What about you?"

"Like I told Maia, things have calmed down."

"Did you reach out to the one that got away?"

"No. He's happily married. I won't intrude in his relationship. I made the wrong choice and ownership is on me. Eventually, I'll find someone who makes me smile as brightly as you two do for each other."

I set my hand on her forearm and squeeze. "Thank you."

"Excuse me for interrupting," Simon joins our group, "but the photographer is ready for you now." Miss Swisher nods, and Simon whisks her away. Madeleine is taking family photos with everyone, including her clients.

When the newlyweds are happy with the images, they line up and make their grand entrance. The staff immediately serve a delicious four-course meal. Madeleine and Christoph are having their first dance after the meal, which strays from the norm slightly. The DJ shifts from classic jazz during the meal to their wedding song. Once their first dance is complete, the music flows smoothly into upbeat songs.

Nolan rises to his feet and extends his hand to me. "Maia, may I have this dance?"

I giggle and slip my hand into his. When we reach the dance floor, the music fades into a slow jam.

Nolan draws me as close as he can. His arms surround me as if they were built for the job. "Exactly where I want you."

"Exactly where I want to be." *For the rest of my life, if he'll have me.*

"Can you promise me something?"

Pulling back, I add enough space so I can stare at him. "What?"

"Promise me we're going to raise our son together. Promise me he won't ever have to feel the angst and turmoil we have. My father and I have made strides in getting to know one another and uncovered numerous similarities, but… I don't want our son to know the despair of feeling unwanted or unloved."

"Never." *Neither will you if you let your guard down completely.* As my response leaves my lips, his fingers bruise my skin, marking me as his.

"What do you say to tangling the sheets in our room?"

I tug my lower lip between my teeth as I consider his offer. "Yes."

"But?"

"We can't leave until they cut their cake."

"Fine, but as soon as the cake is served, we're out the door for a night of decadent, sexy time in our room."

"Yes."

Almost an hour later, we offer congratulatory wishes to the happy couple. We hurry away like teenagers sneaking out of prom for the after-party. It isn't as if the others don't know what we're up to. We spend the rest of the night sharing our love for each other without words.

CHAPTER TWENTY-FOUR

NOLAN

We leave Dr. Flagstone's office after her most recent appointment. Our baby is measuring perfectly. Maia has been having contractions for the last few days, but the doctor jokingly indicated these were practice ones. Maia wasn't smiling. Our next stop is the Blackthorne office. Our attorney agreed to meet us there to close on the house.

"Hi, Gemma," Maia greets her.

"Look at you. The cutest pregnant woman I've ever seen," she gushes.

Maia smiles. Inwardly, she's brushing off the compliment. "Thank you."

Gemma continues, "Attorney Colgate is in the smaller conference room. She was early."

I thank her and escort Maia through the door.

Camille Colgate is a friend of Jake and Norah's. She's tall with just enough curve and fiery-red hair. Cami is comfortable in a courtroom and hanging out at the farm with the kids and animals. "Maia and Nolan. Ready to get started?"

"So excited!" Maia shares.

Cami laughs. Over the next hour, we sign our names nearly one hundred times. It's an exaggeration, but it feels like that many. When she flips the last paper over, she hands Maia the keys. "Congratulations!"

"Thank you," Maia replies and accepts Cami's hug.

Cami whispered something I couldn't hear, which I'm sure was by design. Maia replies softly as well. Both ladies laugh.

As we leave, I open Maia's door and round the car while making silly faces at her. She giggles and smiles. "What do you say to a picnic meal at the house?"

"Sure. Can we bring a load of stuff over now instead of saving it for tomorrow morning?"

"No, you aren't doing anything. Not today or tomorrow. The guys will be available to help in the morning."

She pouts, sticking out her lower lip, knowing full well it usually gets me to crumble.

"Nope, not this time."

Maia frowns. "I want to sleep in our new home tonight."

"You'll survive until tomorrow."

She crosses her arms over her larger chest and says, "Fine."

"Will candy cheer you up?"

Her eyes dart in my direction. "Maybe." There's no maybe involved. Her favorite candy bar always cheers Maia up.

"Want to wait here or come in with me?"

"I'll stay."

Taking my time, I peruse the shelves in the store despite having already preordered candy for Maia. Plus, it gives me time to check on the guys' progress.

Connor answers on the first ring. "Hey, Nolan."

"What is the status?"

Connor chuckles. "Is she nearby?"

"No, but I don't put it past her to sneak up on me."

"True. We finished moving your furniture into the house, and the delivery window extends for another hour."

"I can't thank you enough."

"No thanks are necessary as long as there will be pizza and beer later today."

"A deal is a deal. Maia and I will be home soon."

"Later."

When I check out, I notice Maia standing on the sidewalk shouting at someone. Maia is the most nonconfrontational person I know. Whoever she's arguing with is obscured by a massive tree. As I approach, I hear Maia.

"I have nothing further to say to you."

"Well, you can listen you gold-digging slut."

Fuck! My mother. *Why did she have to pick today?* I step between them. "You have no right to call Maia any derogatory names considering your choices, Mother."

"I'll call her whatever I like," she retorts.

"No, you won't." I open the car door and close Maia inside. She'll be able to hear our conversation, but at least there will be somewhat of a deterrent to her speaking to Maia.

"What do you want? There's no reason for you to come here and bother my family."

She cackles. "Your family. Ha! You don't know the meaning of the word."

"Completely your fault, isn't it, Mother?"

She stares at me dumbfounded. My tone and words were entirely unexpected. Until now, I have been mostly respectful to her. Today and with her treatment of the woman I love, no more.

"What do you want, Mother? Last time I'm going to ask."

"Thanks to you and your sister, I'm broke. I have no money to pay for my room and food."

"I had nothing to do with you losing your cushy lifestyle. You're begging me for money? That's rich. I don't have the kind of money you need, and I'm not bailing you out."

"Except you do," she mumbles.

"No, I don't. My job pays enough to support myself and my son."

"You truly are an idiot. How did you not get some of the brains between your father and I?" *Which one?* The stray thought pops into my head.

Her words are out of spite and don't hurt as much as she believes they will. "Calling me names isn't going to help your cause, Mother. What are you talking about?"

She huffs before sharing. "When you and your sister were born, my parents created a trust for each of you." Sharon Dalton neé Mencia was born with old money. It's surprising to me she chose Michael over the senator. Edward Phillips, my father and future president, is old money while Michael was new money. The chasm was deeply rooted like *The Great Gatsby*.

"No reason for me to believe you. Why wasn't I told before now? It's mighty convenient, isn't it?" My maternal grandparents sold their vineyards and their patented distinctive grape blend to a conglomerate. They live in Florida half the year and Tuscany the other half and have for as long as I can remember.

With shaky hands, my mother reaches into her Gucci handbag and extends a stack of papers in my direction. "My parents didn't share the creation of the trust with me. When I told them about your impending fatherhood, they requested information to contact you. Why now? Well, you're entitled to the funds when your first child is born."

"Thank you for bringing this to my attention. I'll have my attorney review it."

She scoffs. "You don't have an attorney." She waves off her own words as if having a personal attorney matters. "Knowing this, would you be willing to loan me funds to tide me over?"

"No. As I said earlier, I will not help you."

"It must be nice to have all the power. It feels exhilarating, doesn't it? I recall that feeling well."

"No, it doesn't."

"It doesn't?"

"No, because I'm not you. Whether or not this turns out to be true is undetermined."

"You don't trust me?"

"Why would I? You have lied to me my entire life. Again, thank you for sharing this with me. Maia and I have somewhere to be. Good afternoon, Mother." I round the car and open the driver's door.

"How dare you?" she exclaims. "I'm going to end up on the street!"

"I highly doubt that. I suggest you reach out to Nana and Papa for help. It won't be coming from me." Without another glance, I sit in the driver's seat and pull away from the curb.

A few miles of scenery pass before Maia speaks. "Are you okay?"

"I don't know. Did you hear our conversation?"

"Most of it."

"We can talk about it later. Can you call the pizzeria near the house and order enough to feed the guys and their better halves?"

"Sure. We havin' a party?"

"Sort of. It was supposed to be a low-key surprise. I know you don't like them, but we are sleeping in our home tonight with our personal items."

She wrinkles her nose and tears flow from her eyes. "Oh, Nolan! Thank you." Maia leans over the center console and peppers my cheek with kisses.

"Get to orderin'. The guys have been waiting longer than planned because of our unexpected visitor."

Maia pulls out her phone and orders enough pizza for our guests. Then she takes my hand in hers. "I'm crazy proud of you. You were respectful—which she doesn't deserve—and you didn't cave."

"It was difficult not strangling her. My blood was boiling in my veins when I heard her call you.… It isn't remotely true."

"As long as we're on the same page, I don't care what she says about me."

"We are on the same page, but I care.… Well, that's not true. I care she disrespected you. Her words are hollow and untrue."

"Okay."

I pull into our driveway and smile over at Maia. "Are you as excited as I am?"

She shakes her head like a giddy schoolgirl. With a quick kiss, I hurry around the car and escort her to the front door. Cheers erupt when we cross the threshold.

Maia walks around our fully furnished home with the girls, including Reese. Joining the guys on the porch, I twist off the cap to a beer.

"Whoa, Nolan. What happened?" Connor asks.

"My mother accosted us outside of the store." I share the details with Connor, Jake, Cruz, and Lane who have gathered around me. The remaining staff members are on assignment. Jordan is at an off-season training retreat with his college teammates in Florida.

"Isn't a trust fund a good thing?" Cruz asks.

I shrug. "It could be, if it's real, but she attempted to use it as leverage to get money from me."

"You think she's lying?" Jake asks.

Taking a pull from my beer, I respond, "I wouldn't put anything past her. Misleading me about my father and Lara's, hiding her financial issues, choosing Lara's fiancée to help save the family from bankruptcy… falsifying a trust… it wouldn't surprise me."

"Understandable," Connor offers.

"Can we put it aside for now? If it's true, great. If not, nothing for me changes. The reality doesn't affect today. We have amazing friends who are like family. I'm getting to know my father and his wife. Most importantly, Maia and I are going to be parents."

"To Nolan and Maia." Jake raises his glass.

The ladies rejoin us and toast us as well. The pizza arrives shortly thereafter, and we hang out in our backyard. Near seven, they leave to pick up their kids. Both the Michelsons and the Blackthornes are watching their grandchildren at the farm.

Our house is empty except for the two of us. I slide my arms around Maia from behind in the kitchen.

"This was a perfect surprise," she admits.

I press my lips to the nape of her neck. "I'm glad you approve. What do you say we christen our new home properly?"

"Hell yes!"

After setting the alarm, we hurry upstairs, leaving a trail of clothes to our bedroom.

A few days later, we arrive for the staff meeting at the office. The only staff members present are me, Maia, and Lane. Jake shares the schedule and dismisses Lane.

"Have you had time to read the trust?" Jake asks.

I take a deep breath. "Yes. Does it make sense to me? Not entirely."

He extends his hand in my direction and scans the document printed on thick paper stock. "Your grandparents own Mencia Wines?" Jake is a wine enthusiast. I shouldn't be surprised he knows who they are. I knew they were a big deal, but they sold their company fifteen years ago and have been blissfully retired since.

"Yes?"

"I may not be an attorney, but I've read enough contracts to know this is a big deal." Without hesitation, Jake opens a line and dials a phone number.

"Good morning, Mr. Blackthorne. How can I help you?" an older woman says, answering the call.

"Hello, June. How are you?"

"We're well. I'll see if she's available."

Less than a minute passes before another voice comes on the line. "Morning, Jake."

"Thanks for taking my call, Ana."

"I always do." Anastasia Fielding works at a large firm in DC.

"One of my employees was informed he's the beneficiary of a trust upon the birth of his child, a triggering event that is set to occur within the next few weeks. Do you have time to meet with him in the next few days?"

"I have an opening this afternoon. Who is the settlor?"

"The settlor is The Mencia Family Trust," Jake informs her.

She fails to hide her surprise. "Can you hold a moment while I check with June?"

"Of course."

"Is that a good thing or a bad thing?"

Jake lifts a shoulder in question. "Don't know."

Attorney Fielding returns to the line about five minutes later. "Are you able to establish a secure conference call link?"

"Yes. Give me fifteen minutes." Jake ends the call. In a flurry of activity, he turns the conference room walls opaque, pulls down the screen, and sends the link to the attorney.

She appears on the screen. "Good to see you, Jake."

"You too. Please meet Nolan Phillips, formerly Dalton, and Maia Park."

"Pleasure. Mr. Phillips, the trust Jake is speaking of was drafted by my father for your grandparents. Do you understand the parameters of the trust?"

I reply, "No, not at all." My gaze meets Jake's, and I ask him directly, "Did you know?"

"No. I recognized the firm logo. Ana is my personal attorney. I didn't know about this connection."

She shuffles a few papers in front of her. "Your grandparents didn't sell their company, though they led your mother to believe they divested themselves of it. Your mother's current financial and legal issues are not the first time this has occurred. Sharon and Michael were rescued by your grandparents about fifteen years ago."

More secrets and lies. At the same time, they were renewing their vows? When the antenuptial agreement was executed?

Attorney Fielding continues, "They put it in a trust for you and Lara. It's currently managed by a group of advisors."

Maia twines her hand with mine beneath the table.

"What does it mean for me?" I manage.

"The terms stipulate, upon attaining the age of thirty-five or the birth of your first child, you're entitled to income and other benefits as an owner of the corporation. Forty percent of the Delaware-based company belongs to you. Lara will receive her forty percent upon attaining age thirty-five or having a child, whichever occurs first. Your grandparents own the remaining twenty percent."

I own a controlling interest in Mencia Wines? "I see. What do I need to do now?"

"My firm will prepare transfer documents for execution when the triggering event occurs."

I nod. "Then?"

"Then you will meet with your grandparents and determine the best role for you in the company. It can be merely an owner or something more intensive," she informs me. "What's your contact information, Mr. Phillips?"

I rattle off my contact information for her.

"I'll get started on this." She moves her mouse to wake her computer. "I would like to schedule a meeting in two weeks." She suggests a date and time.

"We'll be available."

She ends the call, and I slump back into my chair.

"Now what?" I mumble.

"One step at a time," Maia replies.

"If I may?" Jake asks.

"It's why we came here," I answer.

"I suggest you take some time to process this fortunate turn of events. Then focus on your first public event with the senator."

I'm shell-shocked.

Maia speaks for me. "Thank you, Jake. I'm sure you have other things to handle. We'll be on our way soon."

Jake drops his head, gathers his files, and leaves us in the conference room.

"Nolan," Maia whispers.

When I don't immediately turn to face her, she cups my jaw and aligns my gaze with hers.

"How can I help?"

"My grandparents are billionaires," I mutter with disbelief lacing my tone.

"Okay. It appears you and your sister are as well. Calling me a gold digger makes more sense."

I frown at her. Those words should never be in the same novel when describing Maia, let alone coming out of her mouth. "Why?"

"Even if she's telling the truth about the trust, she had to know your grandparents cut her off after bailing her out. Sharon knew you and Lara would inherit everything."

I laugh heartily. "Especially considering she did nothing to foster a relationship with either of us."

"Would it have mattered?"

I grip the back of my neck and reply, "No, not at all. What do you say to chocolates and a long soak in our huge tub at home?"

"Absolutely."

"Then we can go over the security protocols for the event in a few days." I lean over and kiss her deeply. Without her, I would crumble under this pressure.

CHAPTER TWENTY-FIVE

MAIA

"Nolan, the car is here. We need to go," I shout from the kitchen.

He comes out of the bedroom with a suit jacket on his arm and three neckties in his hand. I chose an A-line navy dress with matching jacket. It fastens with a small bow at the top of my bump. Bump isn't the appropriate word any longer. The Braxton-Hicks contractions for the last week have made it abundantly clear we're closer to the end than the beginning. Although the contractions, I've experienced today are increasing in intensity.

Upon arrival at the hotel, we're escorted to the penthouse suite. Sera greets us. The senator is on a call near the window. "Good morning." She hugs us both. "How are you feeling, Maia?"

"Huge."

Nolan scoffs and rolls his eyes. "Stop, you're gorgeous."

Sera nods and offers us pastries and coffee. "There has been a short delay. Senator Carmen's flight was held up."

"No problem," Nolan replies while preparing a cup of decaffeinated coffee for me and one for himself.

Once he ends his call, the senator greets us. "Thank you for coming."

"We wouldn't miss it."

The four of us catch up and chat about the baby while we wait. While we wait with Sera, a few contractions have grabbed my attention. However, I've been able to keep Nolan and Sera in the dark.

Thirty minutes later, Agent Timothy and Agent Southerland accompany us to the entrance of the ballroom.

Nolan's phone vibrates in his pocket. He plucks it out, notes Jake is calling, and sends the call to voice mail. We take our seats on the stage. A strong contraction builds at the base of my spine once we're seated. It's harsher than the previous ones.

"You okay?"

"Yup." A tiny white lie. There isn't a chance we're going to miss this event. I scan the room in a grid pattern. I may not be working at Blackthorne anymore, but it's second nature.

Senator Carmen takes the stage and gives a rousing speech touting Senator Phillips's education and clean energy platforms. As he nears the end of the introductory speech, he introduces Sera, Nolan, and me before turning the podium over to the guest of honor.

My phone vibrates in my pocket, but I don't check it. Once it stops, Nolan's does the same. He glances at the screen and sees Jake is calling but doesn't answer.

"Something is up," Nolan whispers.

"Yeah. Want me to go find out?"

He shakes his head. While the senators are shaking hands, I continue my scan of the room. It's ingrained in me. I'm watching the people in the room. To be honest, Jake's calls only add to my vigilance.

"Nolan, check ten o'clock," I warn. A man with an oversized coat, not necessary for being indoors, is overly agitated.

"Got him." Nolan stands and shares his concerns with the senator. I'm sure his intention is for his father to step behind the podium, which would offer more protection.

As he's sharing the information, supporters for his opponent barge into the gathering. The supporters have signage and are shouting their candidate's slogan.

"You're going down, Senator Phillips!" a burly man shouts from the middle of the pack. He reaches back and pulls a pistol from a shoulder holster.

How did he get past the metal detector? "Gun!" I shout. Nolan covers his father, and I push Sera behind me. Two shots ring out in the ballroom. A streak of stinging pain rips through my shoulder.

Chaos follows the shots. The noise levels crescendo and then fall quickly as the constituents and the protestors scatter. Nolan secures his father and Sera behind him, then the Secret Service converges onto the stage.

Panic materializes on his face when he sees me on the floor with blood gushing from my shoulder. "Are you crazy?" He uses his jacket as a compress. "You promised not to take any unnecessary and extra risks. Why would you do that?"

"Not crazy. I love you and don't want to be without you. You recently found your father. You deserve the time to get to know him and Sera."

"You would sacrifice yourself—" he swallows the lump in his throat. "—for me?"

"Yes, without reservation or hesitation."

A myriad of emotions dance on his face, including love, fear, and a bit of anger.

Hotel security wrestles the gunman to the floor and out of the room.

"Sir, we need to get you and your wife out of here," Agent Timothy instructs him.

"No. She needs medical attention." The senator's voice is strangled with emotion and fear as he points toward me.

"You first, then her," Agent Southerland reiterates.

"No, I'm fine. She's carrying my grandchild. Get medical in here. Now!"

Agent Southerland radios for emergency medical personnel. Within seconds, they're escorted in the rear entrance of the ballroom.

"Sir, you need to be secured," an agent states.

"No, I'm not leaving until she's on her way to the hospital," he demands.

"Not an option, sir."

"Dad."

The senator's head snaps to Nolan's.

"Go. It's required. I'll update you as soon as I can."

Sera squeezes my hand in support and smiles before the agents escort her and the senator to safety.

My other hand tightens like a vise grip on his as a contraction tears through me. "Nolan. Nolan," I call his name more than once. "Nolan," I shout again.

"What?" annoyance laces his tone given the situation we find ourselves in.

"My contractions… water broke," I manage.

"Now? Are you sure?"

The puddle soaking my dress should be enough evidence. I roll my eyes and deal with the pain tightening my abdomen. "Yes!"

Medical personnel surround me once they leave.

"What's your name?" one EMT asks me. She has a bright smile and perfect skin.

"Maia."

"Hi, I'm Tasha. That's Nancy." She indicates her partner on my other side. "How far along are you?"

"She's thirty-eight weeks," Nolan supplies, fear moving across his face with the realization he's going to a dad soon.

Tasha checks my shoulder. "The bleeding has stopped. It appears the bullet went straight through. How long have you been having contractions?"

"Braxton-Hicks for the last week. The intense ones since this morning around nine."

"How close together are they?" Tasha inquires.

"Now, about every seven minutes or so."

"Maia, why didn't you tell me?" Nolan asks.

"We weren't missing this event for contractions."

Tasha laughs softly. "When did your water break?" She moves to my feet.

"A few minutes ago," I answer.

She acknowledges my answer and states, "I'm going to check your progress now."

I drop my head and squeeze my eyes shut. Another contraction grips my attention. My only hope is I'll make it to the hospital.

She lifts the hem of my dress and removes my panties. Tasha speaks in hushed tones to her partner before addressing me. "Maia, we're going to shift these dividers around you to offer some more privacy. You're fully effaced and crowning. It's time to have a baby. When the next contraction comes, bear down and push. Dad, you can hold her foot or hand whatever she prefers."

I reach my hand out and draw him closer. He presses a kiss to my sweaty forehead. When the contraction spikes, I take a deep breath and push.

"Good, during the next contraction when you're ready, go again," Tasha instructs in her smooth voice.

I follow the same pattern two more times with Nolan watching me in awe.

"On the next contraction, baby will be here," Tasha assures me.

A wailing cry fills the room after another strong push. I've never heard a sweeter sound. A few tears roll over the balls of Nolan's cheeks.

Tasha speaks next. "Dad, would you like to cut the cord?"

Nolan can only nod and follow her instructions. After cleaning him up a bit, they set him on my chest, and I'm dumbstruck with love and fear. A flurry of activity swirls around us. The EMTs transfer me onto a stretcher and transport me to the nearest hospital.

When we arrive, they escort me to the emergency room to allow the doctors to check out my shoulder wound.

"Go with him. I'm fine," I reassure Nolan.

"You're amazing. I love you. After they fix up your shoulder and check him out, we need to decide on a name." Nolan rushes down the hall after our son, likely not realizing what he said.

A tall, rail-thin doctor enters the curtained area. "I'm Dr. Omar. We're going to take you for a CT scan as soon as you're up to it. The bleeding has slowed, but we want you to catch your breath before putting you through more stress. The nurses are going to clean the wound and administer some antibiotics. The on-call obstetrician will be here to check on you as well. Tasha indicated the birth was uncomplicated outside of the shoulder wound, correct?"

"As far as I know."

"Perfect." Dr. Omar leaves.

For a few moments, I'm alone. Worry for my son sets in until I recall Nolan is with him.

The curtains shift, and Dr. Flagstone steps in. Surprise must be evident on my face. "Hello, Maia. I work at this hospital as well. I hear congratulations are in order. Sorry I missed the birth. How are you feeling?"

Considering I had my son quickly in a hotel ballroom with a bullet wound in my shoulder, I feel pretty good. "Not terrible. I would like to get up, but Dr. Omar suggested I wait a bit."

"Understood." She examines me while the nurse prepares to clean my shoulder. "Everything looks fine. In addition to the antibiotics, they will administer Pitocin. When you're comfortable, you can go for the CT scan. I'll check on you after they bring you to the maternity ward."

"Thank you."

"I'm looking for my sister, Maia Park!"

Alex. I turn to the nurse cleaning my shoulder. "Could you allow my sister in, please?"

"Of course." She peeks her head between the divide. "Miss, your sister is in here."

"Thank you so much, Nurse."

Nurse Phyllis eyes Alex suspiciously. There isn't a chance the fiery Latina is truly my sister, but she doesn't object.

"Ohmigod! Look at you! Where's Nolan? Is the baby…?"

"The baby is fine. Nolan is with him."

Phyllis loosely covers my shoulder. "They will be down soon to take you to radiology."

"Thank you."

Before Alex can ask anything further, Nolan arrives pushing a bassinet with our son, followed closely by a nurse. He parks our son beside the bed and kisses my head. "Hey, gorgeous. I pleaded for a trip down here to be with you until your transfer. Hi, Alex."

"Can you hand him to me?"

The nurse interjects here. "First, let me handle the security check and give you the matching mom's bracelet."

I rattle off my name and date of birth. She verifies it on my emergency room bracelet and adds another to match Nolan and… our son needs a name. Once she's done, Nolan sets him in my arms and remains beside me while I memorize his perfect nose and long eyelashes.

"I'm going back out to the waiting room to give everyone an update," Alex states.

"Everyone?"

"Absolutely. It took a herculean effort to leave Reese with the guys. She wanted to be the first one to meet your little guy. Nolan, please text me when you're in a room on the maternity floor."

"I will," Nolan replies.

As soon as Alex leaves, I'm whisked away for my scan and brought to my private room.

"Can we choose a name?" I ask once the nurse leaves my room.

Nolan hands me our son and curls into the bed beside me. "You're anxious about him not having a name?"

"A little."

"You have one in mind we haven't discussed yet, don't you?"

I wrinkle my nose. "Perhaps."

"Let's hear it," Nolan urges me to share.

"I wanted a name that includes both of us somehow."

"What is your suggestion?"

"Parker Nolan."

Leaning over, he presses a sweet kiss to my lips. "I like it. What do you think of Parker Edward?"

I smile at him. "Perfect."

"Yes?" He rises from the bed, walks to the whiteboard, and changes Baby Boy Park to Parker Edward Phillips.

"Knock, knock," one of the maternity ward nurses says.

"Hello, Maia. How are you feeling? I'm Katie."

"Hi. Sore, but otherwise ecstatic."

"From your shoulder or the birth?"

I smile at her. "Mostly the birth."

"Okay. Dr. Omar indicated your wound was a through and through with minimal soft tissue damage. In short, you were incredibly lucky. He wants to close the wound with some stitches before you have guests."

I nod and turn my attention to Nolan. "If you want to take him to them while my shoulder is stitched up, that's fine."

Nolan shakes his head. "No. They can wait and visit both of you at once."

"I see." I turn back to Katie. "The sooner you can close this, the better then, please."

Over an hour later, my shoulder is stitched up and bandaged. Nolan notified Alex, and a stream of guests make their way to meet our son. It's packed in here, but I love it. The girls and I chat while the guys stick to the edge of the room. Reese sits at the bottom of the bed examining Parker with delicate precision. I may never get my son back.

"Auntie, he's so stinkin' cute and tiny! Whenever you need a break, I'm available to watch him for you," she states firmly.

"Noted, sweetie."

Alex chuckles behind her.

"Uncle Jake?" After Jordan hired Blackthorne to handle Reese's security, Alex pieced together similarities in Jill and Jordan's stories. After some investigation, Jordan learned he has two sisters, Jill and Julianne. Their relationship gave Reese a huge family overnight.

"Yes, Reese?"

"You can check him out now, but I'm not giving him up yet," Reese admits.

He laughs. "Understood." Jake gazes down at Parker and then turns his serious eyes toward me and Nolan. "What is the first rule in the Blackthorne handbook?"

Nolan drops his head, but responds, "Always answer the phone." It isn't the first rule, but the gist of the rule is communication is key.

"To be fair, we weren't working," I offer to bolster our choice to ignore the call.

"True, but we may have been able to avoid your shoulder injury," Jake retorts. "The man who shot you is an avid supporter of the senator's opponent. Today wasn't the first time he's been arrested at a rally, nor his first gun charge. However, it's the first time he was motivated to injure someone."

"Who was the target?" Nolan asks.

"Your father," Jake replies. "He intended to eliminate the competition, if you will. He's been arrested and will be subject to a host of charges, including attempted murder, possession of a firearm without a permit, inciting a crowd, and other charges they can prove."

"Works for me."

Slowly, our family leaves, and I take a short nap. When I wake, Nolan is still right beside me.

"Hey, beautiful. How are you feeling?"

"Not bad. I would like to get up and walk around before dinner arrives."

"Okay. I fed Parker about thirty minutes ago and wrote the details on the paper like the nurse suggested." Nolan stands beside me and guides me to the floor.

I tug on a robe Alex brought me and slowly walk around the room. It isn't a huge space, but I'm not capable of remaining still for long.

"Are you up for more visitors?"

I frown and run through who could be left. "Yes, that would be nice."

Nolan dials and works out the details.

Parker deserves to know his grandparents. The Phillips may be the only ones willing to nurture a relationship. When he wins the election, it may require more work, but it'll be worth it for our son.

After thirty minutes on my feet, my dinner arrives. I take a seat on the couch beside Nolan, and we dig in. When we're nearly done, there's a knock at the door.

Agent Southerland enters and sweeps my room. "Congratulations, Miss Park. Mr. Phillips." He radios his partner, presumably Agent Timothy, the room is clear. Within five minutes, Edward and Sera cross the threshold. Both hug us and inquire about me.

"How are you feeling, Maia?" Edward asks.

"Sore, but otherwise fine."

"And your shoulder?" Sera asks.

"Minimal soft tissue damage, through and through," I reply.

"Wonderful," Sera replies, "No, not wonderful—"

I set my hand on her forearm. "It's okay. I understand."

"Thank you for protecting us," Sera whispers.

"You're welcome." I did it because I'm trained to. More accurately, I did it because I want Nolan to have time with his father and stepmother. I may not have the opportunity, but he should hold onto them with both hands. Perhaps I wouldn't take the second chance with my parents. Having the option to do so would be nice though.

While we talk, the senator wanders over to the bassinet and stares down at my son. He's mesmerized. "May I?"

Sera rises and stands beside him.

"Of course," Nolan answers.

Edward lifts his first grandchild into the crook of his arm. "What's his name?"

"Parker Edward," Nolan shares.

A wave of emotion overcomes him when he realizes we gave our son his name. "Thank you."

"We may not have been able to start at the beginning, but you and Parker can."

"I would like that," the proud grandfather admits.

"We would as well," I respond.

Perhaps being a presidential hopeful affords more leeway. Edward and Sera stayed for a few hours, well past official visiting hours. Before they leave, we agreed to join them for lunch after I'm discharged and ready for company.

CHAPTER TWENTY-SIX

NOLAN

The last few months have been a whirlwind of activity. If I thought my life changed the moment I shared my heart with Maia, I was wrong. Parker is growing by leaps and bounds, and outside of our little family, the chaos has increased.

"Maia, time to eat before work."

"Coming," she calls from the bedroom.

Minutes later, my gorgeous woman joins me and Park in the kitchen. He's cooing in his vibrating chair. "Sit. Eat," I demand.

"Fine, pushy. At least it's Friday." She kisses our son's head as she passes by and devours the breakfast burrito I prepared for her.

With all the changes in my life, I've taken a leave of absence from Blackthorne to care for my son and figure out my next steps. I have plenty of options, from continuing to work for Jake or shifting to a role in the wine company.

"Time to go, beautiful." I kiss her deeply and hand her a packed lunch.

"You're the best ever. Are you sure you don't want to be a stay-at-home dad?"

"It's an option. Have a great day at school. We love you."

"I love you both." She bounds down the stairs into the garage and disappears for work.

"What do you say to some tummy time while I take some calls?" I ask my son, who certainly can't answer me. He looks at me with wide eyes teeming with trust. "Good." I laugh out loud and move him to the mat in the office.

At little after nine, I take the first call of the day. "Good morning, Lara."

"Hey, Nolan. How is my cute nephew?"

I smile although she can't see me. "He's perfect. Are you surprised? I'm not."

She chuckles. "No, not at all."

"How are you?"

The turmoil in our family has been a lot for her. Unlike my father, hers hasn't been receptive to forming a relationship with her. It's been difficult. "Fair. Parts of my life are terrible."

"Your dad?"

"Yes. Parts are pretty good."

"Your bigger job." Lara has expanded her business as a charitable foundation creator.

"Yes. The option to use the Mencia name to help the charities is invaluable."

"Good. Your personal life?"

"Paul and I are officially unengaged. I hope he finds the right woman for him. It wasn't me. I've been on a few dates, but I'm not looking to rush into another new relationship right now. Single Lara is where I want to be. What about you?"

"I'm working on plans for Maia and me. As far as work, I have a telephone conference with Papa Mencia later this morning."

"What's the topic?"

"I want to see what options are available for me at the company. Being home with Parker is fantastic, but I need to work, or I'll go stir-crazy."

"I couldn't sit around either. Have the lawyers reached out to you?"

"Which ones?"

"Michael and Sharon's."

I scoff. "Yes, but I haven't returned their call, nor do I intend to. I want nothing to do with either one of them. In my opinion, the further we stay away, the better. I don't have any knowledge regarding their financial affairs or business dealings."

"Unfortunately, I do, at least as it pertains to my potential marriage to Paul and the merger."

"Fair, but did you know any details about the actual deal aside from your tacit agreement to marry Paul?"

"No," Lara replies. "Aside from sharing the information with the lawyers, I have no intention of assisting them further."

"Glad to hear it. I need to go. Parker is ready to eat."

"Bye, Nolan."

I end the call and settle onto the couch to feed Parker. Once he's full and has a dry diaper, he takes a nap in the portable bassinet. With the monitor attached to my hip, I call Alex to solidify my plans for making Maia mine… permanently.

"Hey, Nolan."

"Hey. Before you ask, your nephew is milk drunk and sleeping."

She laughs. "Everything is set for part one. I'll be at your house tomorrow morning to watch Parker for you."

"You're the best friend we could ever ask for."

"Awww. Fine, I'll share her. Same goes."

After my call with Alex, I chat with Papa Mencia about my options. With my mind flooded with choices, I lace up and head into the basement. When we moved into the house, we outfitted the basement with an exceptional gym. Not only do we use it, but driving to the farm isn't truly an option anymore with Parker.

A few miles in, he fusses a bit but doesn't wake. I finish mile three and scamper upstairs. I hedge my bets and hustle through the shower. Luckily, he doesn't wake until I finish. After feeding him again, I pull out dinner ingredients and set out the items Parker needs for his day with Alex tomorrow.

Near four, Maia arrives home and immediately scoops Parker up from his chair. Once he's in her arms, she kisses me.

"I see. I'm second fiddle now."

She wrinkles her nose. "No, he was closer to the door."

"Hardly." I kiss her before guiding her to the couch, and she sets Parker in his chair facing us. "How was your day?"

"Great. I love working with Jill and her students. Jessie, Kate, and Stevie are loads of fun. The way they adapt to the world is fascinating. We have a new student named Billy. He has dysgraphia, which causes problems with handwriting, such as problems forming letters, writing on a line or in a box, or even sharing his thoughts in writing."

"Wow! How do you and Jill work with his challenges?"

"Mostly practice and keeping him calm when he falters. We use talk-to-text as well. It allows him to express himself, and the words appear for him. Then we attempt to write the words as well."

"Cool." I wrap my arms around her waist and pull her closer.

"What about you? How was your call with Papa Mencia?"

"Good, I guess."

"Meaning?"

I huff. "I was hoping he would be more forceful with me."

Maia laughs softly. "Liar."

"No, truly." I grip the nape of my neck with my free hand. "I never subscribed to the billionaire attitude or bank account. Now that I have it, I don't know... I'm not making sense."

Maia twists and meets my gaze.

"I learned to live like a regular person, not a billionaire."

"You've known about your personal wealth for... three months. It isn't long. I'm sure Papa Mencia told you to take the time you need."

"He did, but I don't want to string anyone along."

"You aren't. Jake gave you an extended leave of absence to care for Parker."

"Because of my father," I admit.

"Partially. It was one thing for you to be announced as his son by press release. It was something more when his opponent's supporters stormed his event and I was shot at your first public event."

"I wouldn't change it though. Avoiding you being shot would've been preferable, but reaching out was the right choice. The problem is…."

She slides her hands along my jaw. "No, Jake gave you the time. Use it. Enjoy it. While you're killing your role as his dad and my other half, consider your options. Nothing wrong with being thoughtful and careful with your choice."

"I don't know what I would do without you. I love you, Maia."

"I love you. Now, what's for dinner?"

I laugh. It's an ongoing joke since she can't cook well and I'm home all day, dinner should be at least planned. "We're having chicken lime tacos. Are you training first?"

"Yeah. I need to shift my workout to the end of the day. Mornings are tough with our lack of sleep at the moment."

"Agreed. Get moving. We'll be fine."

She smiles and kisses me. "I have no doubt."

After her workout and a delicious dinner, she feeds Parker and we watch a movie before turning in for the night. Near two in the morning, I drag myself out of bed and feed him again. Today's surprise is going to be long and tiring.

In the morning, I wake to find Maia feeding our son in the cozy chair near the fireplace in our bedroom. I've never seen her look more at peace than she is with Parker.

"Morning," I whisper.

"Morning. Why is there a bag packed for him?"

"We're going out today, just the two of us."

She tilts her head in question.

"Alex is going to watch him while we're gone."

"Okay. Where are we going?"

I smile widely. "When I was able to take you on our first date, I knew it wasn't what you would want."

"What do you mean?"

"Today we're going on your ideal first date."

"Really?"

"Yes."

"I'm game."

"I'm sure you're wondering what other things you inadvertently divulged."

Surprise materializes on her face. "Maybe a little."

"You're going to have to stick with me to see if I've been paying attention."

"Deal. When are we leaving?"

"We're dropping him off at Alex's at eight."

This isn't the first time we've all left the house at once, but it is the first time the SUV is filled with baby gear. Containing my laughter is impossible.

"How could one tiny person need a mountain of stuff to survive the day?" Maia asks once we're on our way.

"No idea. You and I didn't have half of these things." I hear my words in my head and quickly continue, "I mean, they didn't exist."

"I know." Maia doesn't say things she doesn't mean, but the rest of the ride passes in silence.

Luckily, Reese jumps for joy the moment we cross the threshold into her house. "I'm so excited for this!"

"I can tell," I admit while Alex and Maia hug.

"Parker and I are going to have an amazing day. Don't you worry about him at all, Auntie!"

"Not possible, Reese, but I know he'll be safe and happy with you and your mom," Maia replies.

"Makes sense." Reese loops her arm around the carrier and sets Parker onto the tufted leather ottoman.

"Please wait to lift him out, Reese," Alex warns.

"Okay, Mom." Reese offers my son her pinky, and he grabs onto it with his chubby hand.

"We've got this, Maia. Go have a wonderful date," Alex offers.

"Do you know where we're going?"

"Yup, and I'm not sharing. Get going. Then you'll know too. Love you, Maia."

"Love you too."

They hug again, and Alex whispers something I can't make out.

"Ready?" I ask, extending my hand to her.

She threads her fingers in mine, and we leave our son in Alex's capable hands.

"He's going to be fine."

"I know but…."

"Still feels weird leaving him with someone other than me?"

"Exactly."

I kiss the top of her hand after she settles into her seat. "I'm sure Alex won't mind if we check in on him now and then throughout the day." Two hours and a coffee break later, I pull to the rear gate.

"Good morning, Mr. Phillips. Miss Park. If you would pull into the first spot on the right, your guide, Jesse, will escort you inside." Our guide is older, short, and portly. Yet he seems content about his job for the day.

Glee is plastered on Maia's face. We have arrived at an amusement park. "What else do you remember?" she asks and crushes her lips to mine.

"Everything."

"Isn't the park closed for the season though?"

"Yes. I may have used my newfound wealth to facilitate having the park to ourselves today."

"Seriously?"

"Worth it." I kiss the top of her hand. "I'll get your door." She probably doesn't need the reminder, but I give it to her anyway.

Our guide whisks us into the park, and Maia is stunned speechless. With wide eyes, as if she's never been here before, she runs to the first roller coaster she can see.

"Are you sure about this?" I ask.

"Absolutely. We're going on each one, multiple times before we leave today. We also need—"

"One of every ooey, gooey, and delicious but not good for us amusement park food we can handle even the fried Oreos?"

"You truly do remember it all, don't you? You know things fried that normally aren't are a huge weakness for me."

"Yes, I've been memorizing you for four years."

Our guide smiles and nods, acknowledging the fact I planned well today. I couldn't fail with our destination. Fumbling over my words later is a possibility.

Instead of ducking under the dividers, we zigzag through the turnstiles while Jesse readies our seats. This coaster tops out at sixty miles per hour while riding on the top rail.

"I know this isn't your favorite type of ride. Thank you, Nolan."

"I'll do anything for you and Parker."

Giddiness passes over her as we climb the first hill. While Maia throws her arms overhead, I hold on as if my life depends on it. My head is spinning after the second full loop.

"How was the ride, Miss Park?" Jesse asks once it's over.

"It was fantastic! My partner in crime may not think so, but he'll stick it out. We only have thirteen more to go!"

I wrap my arms around her from behind. "I'm with you for this epic first date!"

"First date?" he asks in disbelief.

"Not exactly." Maia explains our relationship history and how, because of her pregnancy, we couldn't ride the coasters.

"Makes sense. On to the next?"

"Yes!" Maia exclaims, and we make our way through the next five before taking a break for food.

Instead of having them open each food vendor, I narrowed it down, and Maia selected her choices about an hour ago. We're eating in one of the gazebos in the center of the park. Jesse left to refill our drinks.

"In case I forget later, our first date has been perfect. Thank you."

"You're welcome, but you wouldn't forget. Ready to tackle the rest of the coasters and then the carousel before we go home?"

"Yes, but…."

I pull out my phone, push the last number called, and Alex's face appears on my screen.

"Hi, Maia. How is your date?"

She wrinkles her nose. "Kind of perfect. No, actually perfect."

Alex offers her a rundown of Parker's morning, including his feedings, diaper changes, and activities. Currently, he's sleeping.

"Thanks, Alex. Please know I trust you completely. Leaving him is new for me."

"It's no problem. I'm surprised this is your first call," she chides.

Maia smiles and laughs softly. "Could you…?"

Alex deciphering what Maia wants is elite bestie telepathy. She walks over to the bassinet and turns the camera toward our son. He's sleeping soundly, swaddled tightly in his softest blanket.

"You're the best, Alex."

"You too. Have a great afternoon. We'll be here when you return," Alex replies.

Maia relaxes, and with our refilled drinks in hand, we walk to the next ride. The roller coaster is completely enclosed, so the ride is pitch-black. I'm more nervous for this ride simply because I won't know when the twists and turns are coming.

"Let's do this!" My bravado is fake and hopefully my gorgeous woman will ignore it.

"We don't have to ride this one if it freaks you out," Maia states.

So much for thinking she isn't on to me. "I'm scared, but I'm doing it… with you." We strap into the seat, and I thread my fingers into hers.

The moment the ride starts, we slip into the tunnel and I lose my ability to see. Maia tightens her hold on me. Before long, the track drops and twists. A scream resonates through me, and I own it.

After three minutes of twists, turns, drops, and yes, screams, the car pulls beside the platform.

"You good?" Maia inquires.

My heart is pounding in my chest, and sweat drips down my temple. "That may have been more terrifying than any awry assignment I've been on."

She buries her face into my shoulder and laughs softly. "You like to be in control. On an assignment you are, even when things go wrong because you have a plan. Here, you have no idea what's coming."

"I agree. What do you say to a break from roller coasters and try a ride more my speed?"

Maia turns her eyes to meet mine. "Sure. What do you have in mind? Kiddie rides?"

"No," I scoff. "Kind of?"

With our fingers laced together, I lead her to the carousel. This one is large and has been recently refurbished. Red, yellow, purple, and bold orange are distinctive and bright.

"What's wrong?" she asks softly.

"Nothing."

She wrinkles her nose. "Try again. I know you inside and out. Your palms are sweaty, and you're shaking."

Without answering, I exhale sharply and lead her to one of the seats on the deck. Once we're sitting, the attendant starts the ride. The normal lively and fast music has been replaced by "1000 Times" by Sara Bareilles, a song that spells out my feelings for Maia, even if I can't say the words.

"Nolan, please tell me what is going on?" A trickle of fear is clear in her voice.

I don't like it one bit. "I want…." I pinch the bridge of my nose and take a deep breath. "I want this to be your last first date. As you know, I'm not adept at expressing my feelings well, so I chose this song in case I couldn't. I'm going to try though."

Maia shifts on the bench and scoots in closer.

"You planted me on my ass without hesitation when we met. I was instantly intrigued. Not only was this tiny woman a skillful fighter but gorgeous as hell."

A faint blush creeps into her cheeks.

"The days that followed turned into years. We were together from morning until night, sometimes working, sometimes not. You became my best friend, confidante, incredible lover, and mother of my child."

"You became mine," she adds, then buries her face in her hands.

I lift her gaze back to mine. "I tried to push you away, but you refused. Not once in my entire life did anyone stand by me fully and completely until you. No one made me feel loved and cared for until you. I love you with my whole heart. I don't want to go a day without you beside me."

I shift onto one knee in front of her and open the ring box. Nestled inside is an elongated cushion-cut emerald with trapezoid side stones. "Maia, will you be my crane?"

A single tear rolls down her cheek. "You planned today for me?" Her question is strangled with emotion.

"Yes."

"What is this song?"

"It's '1000 Times.' I chose it because I wasn't confident I could say the words, which I'll repeat. Maia, will you be my crane?"

"Yes."

Slipping my ring on her finger, I kiss her deeply. After kissing for what feels like an eternity, we break apart panting.

"How did you know I wanted a nontraditional ring? It's perfect."

"You told me a few years ago. For whatever reason, we were watching the *Bachelor* and Neil Lane was presenting the options for the final rose. Without hesitation, you said, 'I wouldn't want a ring like every other girl in the world.'"

She nods. "How long do you want to be engaged?"

"I would marry you today if I could."

A wide smile grows on her face. "Does over Thanksgiving work for you?"

"Absolutely."

The carousel slows to a stop, and the attendant brings two glasses of champagne and some snacks. Once we finish our drinks, the ride slows to a stop.

"Ready to tackle the last few rides?"

My fiancée shakes her head. "No, let's go home."

We thank Jesse for his attention and service today.

"You're most welcome, Maia and Nolan. Congratulations and best wishes!"

With her arm looped through mine, we exit the park and start the drive home.

"Alex knows? Anyone else?"

I kiss the back of her hand. "Probably Jordan, maybe Reese, otherwise no."

She takes a shallow breath.

"Why does that make you sad?"

"I have no one."

"You're wrong. You have me, Parker, and our Blackthorne family and friends. I would be bold enough to add my father and Sera. Our relationship with them is new, but it's coming together well."

She swipes a tear and replies, "You're right."

I chuckle. "Please say that again."

She shakes her head. "You're right, but don't get used to it."

"Never. I love you, Maia."

"I love you, Nolan."

When we arrive at Alex's, Parker is sound asleep. Reese gives me a rundown of his day with excruciating detail while the girls chat about our day. Shortly thereafter, we head home, feed our son, and fall into our bed. You would think exhaustion would take over, but that isn't the case. My fiancée and I are wrapped up in one another until the wee hours of the morning. Luckily, we have nothing planned tomorrow.

EPILOGUE

MAIA

FOUR WEEKS LATER

"Ready to go, babe?"

"Yeah, I think so." Nolan sounds flustered.

I join him in the kitchen, and he's out of breath. "Everything good?"

"Yeah. I had to change myself and Parker again. Then add extra clothes to his bag for the weekend, just in case."

"Okay. My dresses are hanging near the garage door, and this bag is set."

"What else do we need to do?"

"On our way to the rehearsal, we need to pick up our rings from the jeweler, and I need to pick up my clothes from the tailor."

"Right."

With a quick kiss, I scoop up the remaining bags and head toward the car. On my second trip, I grab the garment bags and hang them in the back seat out of Parker's reach.

Nolan locks our son into the car seat base, and we begin our errands for the day. After the necessary stops, we park near the barn at the farm. Jake and Norah graciously offered us the farm as our venue. Not only was the timeline short notice, but the farm provides adequate security for the president-elect to attend his son's wedding under the radar. The three of us are staying at the farm in the guest suite for the next few days. To be honest, the majority of the planning was smooth.

When I worked for Blackthorne, one of my assignments was to secure the Ramirez wedding in York Beach. Kelly Barnett created a dress for me, and it was perfect. The day after our engagement, I called her and asked if she could recreate the dress in ivory, and she agreed. She also sent a cocktail dress for tonight. We're having our rehearsal tonight, holiday dinner tomorrow, and our wedding on Friday afternoon.

I hop out of the SUV and greet Norah and Ben on the porch.

"Hi, almost Mrs. Phillips." She hugs me as close as her bump will allow.

I can't contain the smile hearing my married name a smidge early.

"Hi, Aunt Maia."

I crouch down to Ben's height. "Hey, bud. How are you?"

"Good. Where's Park?" An almost three-year-old asking for a friend to play with.

I laugh softly. "He's here, but he's doesn't walk yet."

Ben shrugs. "We play anyway."

"In a few minutes," I reply.

"What can I carry?" Norah asks.

Jake appears behind her. "Nothing. Nolan and I will handle it."

Norah scowls at her husband. It appears his overprotective husband and father routine has amped up during this pregnancy.

We settle into the guest suite, and Ben is running circles around Parker in his vibrating chair.

"Everything set for tonight?" Jake asks.

"You tell me. Is the plan set for my future father-in-law?"

"Weird to think you're going to be a member of the First Family," Norah offers.

"Yes, completely." Senator Phillips won the election by a decent margin.

Jake answers, "I have been in constant contact with the Secret Service. Christoph will accompany them to and from their home today and the morning of the ceremony."

"It's under control," Nolan states.

"Yes," Jake confirms.

"Good. Feel like a walk, sweetheart?" Nolan asks me.

"Sure. Can you get the stroller?"

"I come? I come too, Auntie?" Ben begs.

I glance at Norah. She lifts her shoulder as if to say it's up to me. "Sure, bud. You need socks, shoes, and a jacket."

"No. Hoodie, instead," he bellows and rushes down the hall.

Jake laughs and follows.

Once the four of us are ready, we exit the rear gate and walk toward the point. Within minutes of traversing the bumpy terrain, Parker is out cold.

"What's on your mind, babe? You only want to come out here when you need to hash out your thoughts or share them."

He shakes his head. "I talked with Jake, my father, and the Secret Service to determine if it was wise or possible for me to continue working with Blackthorne after the inauguration."

"Okay...."

"It would be difficult for Jake to send me on assignments because of the notoriety we've gained since the news broke and his win. We discussed some options, Jake and I, which would keep me at Blackthorne but not take any assignments. We both felt I would be bored out of my mind."

"So?"

"I decided to work at the Mencia Wines."

I plant a kiss on his cheek. "That's amazing! Doing what?"

"I want to start at the bottom and learn every position in the company."

"Wow! Is that possible? How long will it take?"

"Not sure. I'm going to reach out to Papa next week before we go on our honeymoon."

"Yes, a week on a secluded tropical beach, just the two of us will be heavenly."

"It will."

"Uncle Nolan?" Ben stops in front of us with a handful of rocks.

"Yeah, Ben."

"Are you leaving too?"

"Kind of. I got a new job, but we'll still be around for all the fun family stuff, like parties and holidays."

His little shoulders drop. "Okay."

"Why does that make you sad?"

"I'm going to miss Parker."

I smile down at him. "I wouldn't worry about that too much."

He raises his empty hand in question. "Why not, Auntie?"

"Well, Parker is going to be with you and Uncle Connor's kids starting after Christmas."

"Really?" Sheer excitement laces his voice.

"Yup."

He throws his arms around our legs as best he can. Thankfully, we're side by side. "Let's go back. I need to tell Mommy."

Nolan ruffles his hair. "All right, lead the way."

When we arrive back at the house, the property is crawling with caterers and workmen. After a recommendation from Jill, we hired an event planner to take some of the tasks off my plate.

"Mommy, Mommy," Ben shouts, running toward the back porch where she and Jake are kissing. It doesn't faze me in the slightest either. From the moment they met, their affection has been outward and constant.

"Slow down," Norah requests.

Ben spills the details of our talk at the point.

Jake extends his hand to Nolan. "It's official now?"

He tilts his head in my direction. "Yeah. Mrs. Phillips gave the go-ahead."

"Not Mrs. Phillips yet." I twist my stunning and unique ring on my finger.

"Close enough," Nolan retorts.

Jake laughs. "Happy wife, happy life. We're sad to see both of you go, but we're family and always will be."

"Thank you, Jake." They bro hug, and we head inside to dress for the rehearsal dinner.

A few hours later, I'm standing under an arbor in the barn intertwined with leaves and fall foliage.

The officiant had us start at the front and worked our way backward the first time through.

"Who will be giving you away?" he whispers.

"I'm walking alone."

Alex, who has been beside me since the rehearsal began, grips my forearm in support.

"Very well."

We line up to walk out after the ceremony and then start from the top. Once we run through the procession twice, we celebrate with an amazing meal prepared by Jill. As expected, the dinner is exceptional and we're grateful for our found family. The night ends with a toast blessing our marriage.

Two days later, I'm pacing the suite, dressed but barefoot. My dress is ivory with a cowl back and buttons covering the zipper. Alex finished my hair and makeup and left to check on the flowers. The holiday yesterday was lower key than normal given our wedding day is today and the guest list is virtually identical.

After a decent amount of time passes, there's a soft knock on the door.

"Come in, Alex," I state.

"You look stunning," a feminine voice says.

Not Alex. I turn and see Mrs. Phillips, the original, wearing a gorgeous floor-length, navy dress with a sheath silhouette and lace overlay.

"Thank you, Sera." I hug her loosely.

"I asked Alex if I could speak with you for a few moments. Hopefully, I haven't overstepped."

"No, of course not."

"If I may, I would like to share a story." She motions for me to sit beside her.

Odd, but... "Sure."

"My childhood was similar to yours. My father murdered my mother and then took his own life when I was twelve. Luckily, I was not home at the time, or I may not be here."

"I'm sorry."

She nods politely and continues. "I went to live with my aunt and uncle who couldn't bear children. They took me in and treated me as if I were their own, but it wasn't *my* parents. I never knew parents who could be loving, supportive, and walk through fire or bullets for their spouse. However, Edward knows what it means to come from a stable family.

Margaret and Edward Sr. were nothing short of wonderful when I joined their family. We would like to extend the same to you and Nolan. I realize gaining parental figures in your late twenties is markedly different than twelve. All of this is a long way to say we would like to be there for you and Nolan in any capacity you're willing to accept. Whether you want meddling in-laws, middle of the road ones, or nonexistent ones, we're offering it to you. Frankly, we hope you don't choose the latter. We realize it may be difficult after he takes office, but we're willing to carve out the time to be with you and our grandson as frequently as possible."

I exhale and fan my face to avoid ruining Alex's makeup. "We would love that."

"Wonderful. I brought you a gift of sorts. I would be honored if you would wear this as your something borrowed." She extends a velvet box in my direction.

I open the box and pull out a bracelet with pavé diamonds set in an intricate pattern. "It's beautiful."

"It belongs to Margaret, and I wore it when I married Edward."

My hands are shaking to the point where Sera takes the bracelet and fastens it to my wrist. "You don't know how much we appreciate you and Edward." I throw my arms around her.

"I do."

Alex steps into the room with a box of flowers. "Oh, I didn't mean to interrupt. I can come back."

"Please come in," Sera states. "I'm—"

"It's a pleasure to meet you, Mrs. Phillips." Alex offers her hand.

"She's Alex, my best friend."

"Well, the girl best friend," Alex clarifies.

Sera laughs and leaves after a long hug and wiped tears. After a brief conversation, Alex escorts me to the barn.

"Can't believe you're getting hitched so quickly," Alex states to lighten the mood.

"I didn't want to wait or give him the chance to change his mind."

Alex laughs and hugs me. "Never going to happen."

The music changes. "My cue. You've got this. Love you, Maia."

"Love you too."

I watch Alex walk down the runner. Jordan sits on the right with Reese, an infectious smile on his face. The music changes again with my cue to walk toward my future. Yet my feet have grown roots. A rush of fear washes over me. The rows of my family and friends cast their gaze in my direction. As I settle my thoughts, Edward joins me at the end of the aisle.

He sets his hands over mine. "Would you like me to escort you out the door or down this aisle to my son? It's up to you, but I would recommend choosing Nolan. He's utterly and completely in love with you."

I close my eyes and shake my head. "I wasn't doubting Nolan in any way. I was doubting me. Then Sera's words from earlier came back to me. With guidance from our found family, Nolan and I can figure out how to fireproof our relationship."

President-elect Phillips offers me his arm and escorts me down the aisle.

The relief on Nolan's face is palpable. "We don't have to do this to be a family," he murmurs when I stop beside him.

I glance over at Parker sound asleep with Sera in the front row. "No, we don't, but … I want to be Mrs. Nolan Phillips… today."

"Let's get married!" Nolan exclaims. Our friends and family laugh, followed by the officiant beginning our ceremony. We opted for short and simple, like Christoph and Madeleine.

Less than fifteen minutes later, the justice of the peace states, "You may now kiss your bride."

Nolan wastes no time hauling me close and kissing me breathless.

"It is my pleasure to introduce for the first time Mr. and Mrs. Nolan Phillips," our officiant adds, and we hurry down the runner.

After a short time alone in the guest suite, we suffer through pictures before joining our friends and family to celebrate our future together.

Thank you so much for reading *Protecting our Family*!

Did you love *Protecting Our Family?*

Thank you for taking the time to read it. I hope you loved it!

If you liked this book or another one of my books, please consider

posting a review.

A short line or two will be perfect! It helps indie authors like me get

noticed. I appreciate your support and feedback.

COMING SOON

Two new stories are coming soon!

A Matchmakers' Book Club Novel

For Love & Cookies

A Scala Talent and Sports Management Novel

Moonshot

MY BOOKS

Protecting Us

Hers to Protect

MATCHMAKERS' BOOK CLUB

For Love & Coffee

For Love & Basketball

All my books in one place: www.nicolevidal.com/books